Irish Twins

Also By Michele VanOrt Cozzens

NONFICTION

I'm Living Your Dream Life:
The Story of a Northwoods Resort Owner
The Things I Wish I'd Said

FICTION

A Line Between Friends
It's Not Your Mother's Bridge Club

Irish Twins

Michele VanOrt Cozzens

McKenna Publishing Group
San Luis Obispo, California

Irish Twins

McKenna Publishing Group
San Luis Obispo, California, USA

Printed in the United States of America

10 9 8 7 6 5 4 3 2

ISBN: 1-932172-36-2

LCCN: 2010932440

Cover design by Leslie Parker
Cover models: Camille Ellen and Willow Gayle
Interior design by Leslie Parker

Visit us on the Web at: www.mckennapubgrp.com

For Hardrock, Coco and ... Gayle

Nothing worth doing is completed in our lifetime; Therefore, we are saved by hope.

Nothing true or beautiful or good makes complete sense in an immediate context of history; Therefore, we are saved by faith.

Nothing we do, however virtuous, can be accomplished alone; Therefore, we are saved by love.

No virtuous act is quite as virtuous from the standpoint of our friend or foe as from our own; Therefore, we are saved by the final form of love, which is forgiveness.

—Reinhold Niebuhr

PROLOGUE

"Irish Twins" is a slang description of two children born to the same mother within twelve months. Some consider it a highly offensive term.

The origin isn't certain, but its suspected roots date back to the 1800's Potato Famine era, when approximately one million Irish came to North America. They often arrived penniless and were considered uncultured, uneducated and dirty—a pox on good society. Unskilled workers who made as little as eight cents a day back in Ireland could earn a dollar a day in America. This caused resentment from American workers fearful of losing jobs and being undercut by the Irish. In Eastern cities such as New York and Boston, signs reading "Irish Need Not Apply" sprung up in store windows. Several derogatory terms followed. For example, "Irish confetti" for thrown bricks and "Irish kiss" for a slap. Irish Twins fits into this vernacular.

The term Irish Twins mocks the fertility of Irish Catholic families and their disdain for practicing birth control methods, while failing to plan ahead or control themselves sexually. It also may suggest that the Irish didn't understand the true medical definition of twins, or two children conceived and born together.

Like the parents of twins or other multiples, parents who have Irish Twins face the challenges of having two young children at one time. As the children grow up, parents encounter the difficulties of medical and extracurricular activity expenses, and the simultaneous payment of college tuition fees. On the positive side, since the space between Irish twins is so small, it intensifies the sibling bond, and Irish Twins often end up being very close and affectionate with one other.

Or not . . .

Irish Twins Family Tree

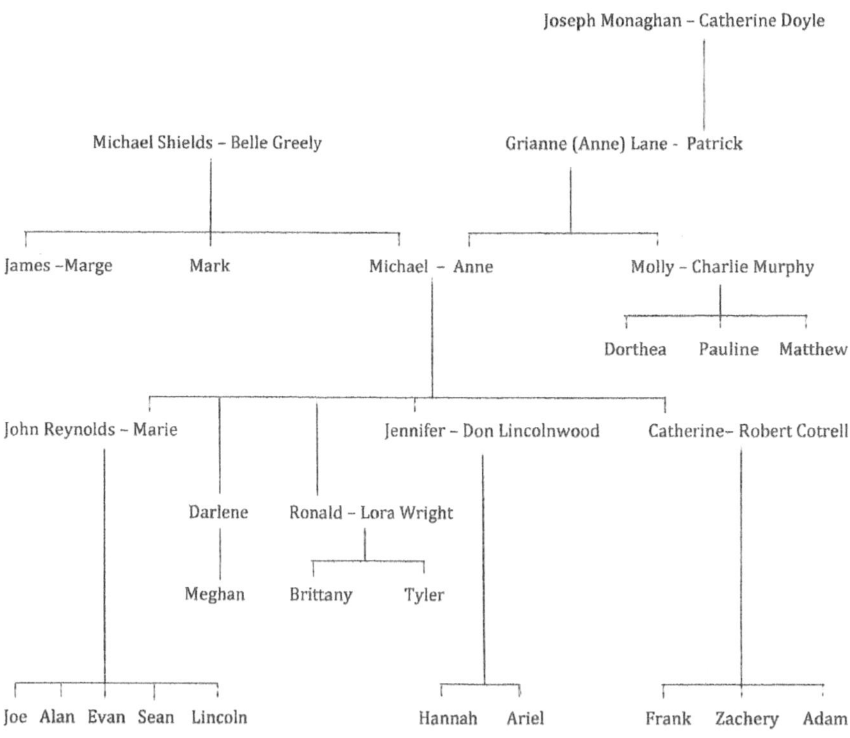

CHAPTER 1

I have a little God in me. It's a power I use to keep watch over my children, who are still on earth. I played many roles during my eighty years of human life, but the one role I couldn't shake in spite of passing on, was the role of mother to my five children.

We say once we're mothers we're always in mother mode—even when our kids are grown and gone and having kids of their own. Now I know it's true even when we're dead. And from my vantage point of three hundred and sixty-degree Light, I see all. I see my five children as babies, as adolescents, teens, college students, newlyweds, young adults, and parents.

I didn't share much about myself with my children when I was still alive, although I gave them everything. I gave them hot breakfasts and bagged lunches. I gave them corned beef and cabbage, boiled potatoes and chicken on the spit. I gave them clean laundry pressed to perfection and thin ankles. I demonstrated what it meant to be a dutiful wife and I taught them faith by example. I gave them all full heads of curly hair, which I inherited from my own mother.

Unfortunately, none of my children knew my mother. She died before they were born.

For everything I gave them, they gave so much more in return. They kept me young. And seeing the world through their eyes gave me the higher education I didn't have as a young woman. I didn't go to college because during the Great Depression all luxuries came to a grinding halt. Higher education was definitely a luxury—especially for girls. I vowed it wouldn't be the same for my children.

My children had all the benefits of the baby boom generation, including the finest educations we could afford on my husband's blue-collar salary. They attended Catholic school. And today, as I watch from my vantage point in a place we don't call "Heaven," but rather, "*Ohr*," which is Hebrew for the word "light," I see that only one of my five children still attends church on a regular basis. But she's no longer a Catholic. Jenny, my fourth child and one of my Irish Twins, is an Episcopalian. The rest of them are just busy.

It really doesn't matter, however. In *Ohr*, there's no such thing as organized religion. Here we do not recognize our differences, because we are all alike.

We are all in the image of God.

Throughout my life I was aware I was going to die. Human beings are supposed to know this; however, it's amazing how many don't. Of course, I didn't know when or how it would happen, and as I grew older it became less important to me compared to when I still had young children. One mistake I made was that I assumed my husband and I would die at the same time. I couldn't bring myself to imagine life without him. And as it turned out, it was he who had to face life on earth without me.

On a July morning, exactly six months past my eightieth birthday, I was doing what I enjoyed doing most. I was waterskiing. My husband of fifty-six years, Michael, was behind the steering wheel of our tri-hull boat, while I held onto a knotted rope sixty feet behind him, maintaining my balance on a wide wooden ski. Don't be impressed by my ability to slalom ski. When Michael first taught me, we only had one ski. I didn't know most people started out on two and then learned to drop one before taking on the challenge of slalom skiing. But I was never a hotshot. I rarely ventured outside of the V-shaped wake or tried to lean back to make a spray—unlike my children, all of whom raced back-and-forth, comparing spray sizes and the angles of their cuts.

On that warm, cloudless day—the day I died—I kept one eye on Michael's broad sunburned back. The rigidity of his spine was like the white line of the highway. I kept the ski tip pointed at him and held on, using the padded handle as my steering wheel to adjust around the turns.

As was their custom, our Mitten Lake neighbors, Freda and Henry Stanton, were outside on their dock taking coffee. They waved each time we zipped by. I only waved on the first pass, but Michael waved every time as though he were the Grand Marshal of the Veteran's Day parade. I knew most of the neighbors considered me an anomaly—mere fodder for country club cocktail parties I didn't attend. "Did you see Anne Shields on the lake today in her little black bathing suit? She goes round and round all morning hanging onto that rope for dear life."

Dear life. Yes.

I had skied around the small bay of the lake a couple times when Michael slowed down and I sunk to my armpits. He said he needed to check the gas tank. I thought he'd filled it the previous day, however, he suspected an air bubble in the gas line because the motor was jumping. It wasn't unusual for our old, forty-horsepower Johnson to sometimes have what my teenaged grandson, Frankie, called a case of the yips.

Fully immersed in the lake, the yellowed, cracked ski belt I'd been using since the 1960s crawled up my torso and supported me like a life ring. It had a permanent aroma of Coppertone and the nostalgic scent filled my nostrils, reminding me of my children. My feet remained in the rubber boots of the ski. Paddling the water in small figure eights, I watched Michael lift the Naugahyde flap covering the gas tank. His weight made the back end of the boat sit low in the water. Looking up, he gave me the OK sign.

He was so handsome—as handsome as the day I first saw him just before our country entered the War.

Leaning back, I dipped my hair into the tepid water and thought of that summer in Virginia Beach. It was 1941. I was down from Boston with my girlfriends, Mary Margaret and Lolly Kerrigan. In spite of the Coast Guard station there, we were surprised to see so many men in uniform strolling the Boardwalk. It added a certain charge to the air, which was already alive with big band music. We were at the Cavalier Beach Club when Michael showed up with a group of fellow sailors, all of whom were dressed in baggy white pants and jaunty sailor caps. Michael, the tallest, wore his cap far back on his head exposing a tuft of yellow hair. He walked quickly and was full of purpose.

"Ooh," cried Lolly. "Here comes Van Johnson!"

Too bashful to look him in the eye when he approached our table, I hid behind the brim of my hat and kept my hands folded on the table. It was the well-trained stance of many a Catholic schoolgirl. Why

Michael ultimately chose me instead of one of the more striking Kerrigan sisters, I wouldn't know; however, many years later he told me it was because my hat was the smallest and he could actually see my face. I'm not sure if he was kidding.

It wasn't truly important why Michael chose me, it was merely important that he did. I never believed I had a right to choose anything. My faith-based education was all about unquestioned acceptance. When I was alive I wouldn't have admitted that I prayed for a loving and handsome husband. But I did. And that my prayers were answered in the form of Michael Shields, it only served to strengthen my faith. Now I know that good luck had something to do with it as well.

Once Michael and I were married, my strongest prayers were for the ability to keep him, particularly after the children arrived.

I knew what it was like to grow up in a fatherless home, and I refused to have that happen to my children. When the last of our five came along, our Irish Twins, the challenge of raising them in the midst of what was essentially a midlife crisis for my husband, made me wonder if he would stick around. But he did, and I continually counted my many blessings.

Holding my hour—that was my mother's way of suggesting patience—while Michael shored up the gas line, I allowed the lake water to cascade across my palms and indulged in the recurring thought I'd had since the age of seven, which was that my life was speeding by very quickly. I wished my children were with me—either in the boat or on the shore—even up at the house throwing around wet towels and waiting to be fed. Who would have thought I'd miss their messes?

Michael restarted the motor and turned the boat toward me—a task he'd performed countless times. "Stay there and I'll bring the rope to you," he called.

I know, I said to myself. My darling, I know. I knew the ritual of getting up to water-ski as well as I knew the sun would rise each morning. It was hard to blame Michael for instructing me. It's what he did. And I always let him.

With that thought, I closed my eyes and listened to the buzz of the motor as the boat drew near. Briefly ingesting the noxious gas fumes, I knew I'd better look for the rope so I wouldn't miss it and cause Michael to make another pass. But when I opened my eyes, I looked directly into the brilliant light of the sun.

And that's when I heard a "pop."

It was brief and sharp, like the sound of a light bulb giving out. Everything—the water, the boat, the pine trees surrounding the lake, my ski, even my skin—turned to black and white. It was like the dreams I'd had before color television. My first thought was that my recently removed cataracts had returned. And then all at once, I felt as though I were sinking. "Mi—chael?" I heard panic in my voice.

"What is it Anne?" He was right next to me, but his figure was a shadow—first solid black, then gray, and then only a pair of concerned blue eyes. I knew the deep vertical line between them as well as I knew his signature.

"I think I'm drowning."

Those were the last words I, Anne Catherine Monaghan Shields, ever spoke.

Michael struggled getting my limp, soaked body, which was still attached to the ski, into the boat. "No, you're not," he said.

I was no help to Michael. Physically, I couldn't feel anything—not even the vibration of the forty-horse as he sped toward Freda and Henry's pier. Emotionally, though, Michael's fear was palpable. And poor Freda. She took one look at me, and her eyes filled with tears. "I'll get a pillow," she whispered.

"Call 9-1-1," directed her husband, Henry. Henry had a deep, authoritative voice. He was a retired police chief and well-respected in the retirement community. "Mike, do you know C.P.R?"

Michael clamped his mouth onto the mouth of this now foreign body and filled it with his breath. I tried to feel my chest inflate. Then Henry laid his hands over the heart—*my* heart—and compressed. Meanwhile, I continued to float upward and away from the scene, as slowly and weightlessly as a helium balloon. "I think she had a stroke," said Henry.

"Come on, Anne," encouraged Michael.

I wanted to cooperate. I wanted the head—*my* head—to lift and make it easier for Freda to slip the pillow underneath it, but I no longer had control over the thin neck and limp arms of the body in the black bathing suit. Each time Michael made a command, "Breathe!" I wanted to obey—to be the dutiful wife. But I couldn't.

The sun grew brighter, blinding me with light. I tried to focus, but the only thing remaining with me were the blue eyes of my husband.

I grew lighter, the sun filled me, and I let myself be carried to it. I traveled to the Light, leaving behind Michael, his eyes, our neighbors, Freda and Henry, the boat that had pulled me around the lake every morning, the wooden ski, the cracked lifebelt, and the body in the black bathing suit.

And then my babies—the core of my strongest love for most of my life on earth—came to me in a vision, one at a time. First my eldest daughter, Marie, lovely and gentle, full of worry and grief, followed by hard-edged, dark-haired Darlene wielding a stethoscope and explaining to everyone what was happening. Next came my lone, quiet son, Ron. First the boy in the middle—like salami on a sandwich—and now married and a part of his wife's family, seldom seen among the Shields. Finally, my Irish Twins, Jennifer and Catherine, whom we always called Jenny and Caylie, came to me together.

Together. That's always how I pictured them, holding hands and mirroring one another the way only sisters can do. Their images filled me with an overwhelming sense of joy. Because Jenny and Caylie had come so late in life, I spent a lot of sleepless nights worrying that I wouldn't live long enough to see them grow up, get married and have children of their own. But that didn't happen. I did witness all those things and they, along with their older siblings, were well on their journeys, far away from the very brief nest I had built for them.

Yes, I always knew that my life on earth would one day come to an end. And this was it. This was peace.

The images of my children faded, and I sensed a powerful and unusual aroma. It was as potent and sweet as Easter lilies, but with a bit of spice. Nutmeg? Using my earthly olfactory sense as a guide, it steered me effortlessly toward what I believed was an outstretched hand. I couldn't make out to whom the hand belonged. Was this my Guardian Angel? Was it God?

As I drew nearer and nearer, the image came into focus. It was a woman. She was fair-skinned, with dark hair. Her eyes were green. She was lovely.

Her hand remained outstretched, and she appeared to be making an offering to me. I drew closer, the Light became a part of me, and I focused on the offering held in this beautiful, welcoming hand. It was a cup of tea. A steaming, hot cup of tea.

"Hello Anne," she said. "I've been waiting for you."

My focus shifted from the cup to this lovely woman's face and I gasped.

"Molly!"

"Yes," she said, and handed me the cup.

It was my sister—my own Irish Twin. I hadn't seen her in . . . years.

Or had it been yesterday?

CHAPTER 2

Being dead has been like a perpetual dream. Random thoughts and visions of people are trapped in a crazy quilt of time and place and emotion. Set in a background of rough-cut edges, they played out like clips from a film editor's floor, and I viewed them through endless cups of tea.

In *Obr*, visions of my children materialized and diminished as quickly as passing thoughts. As they continued to live on earth, I saw them when they wanted me to—when they prayed. And I also connected with them through their dreams, just as my sister had done with me. I had dreamed of her often since her untimely death; however, I didn't realize when she appeared in my dreams that she was actually visiting me.

It was therefore fitting that Molly served as my guide. She saw to it that my teacup remained full.

In *Obr*, Molly looked as she did when we were girls—the way she always appeared in my dreams—with lustrous black curls, high cheekbones and plump lips. She was the spitting image of my youngest daughter, Caylie. Her voice was musical and carried a strong Bostonian accent. I'd heard only the flat, nasal tones of the Midwest for so many years, that it sounded foreign and familiar at the same time.

Molly studied me. "That sensation you feel at the back of your neck, is it a pain?"

I nodded.

"You're in transition. It will pass and not soon be felt again. But for your children it's a different story. The first days are the most difficult for them. You may remember from when Mother passed."

"What about Michael?"

"Oh, don't worry about Michael. He'll probably remarry. Most of them do."

"Molly, that's cruel!"

"Anne, you were always my naïve little Irish Twin. Did my husband waste any time?"

"I don't know what happened to your husband. He never . . ."

"Sip your tea, Anne. It's hot. Just as you like it."

I brought the cup to my lips and blew into the amber liquid. "Nice and hot. You remember?"

"Of course."

Before sipping, I studied the delicate teacup and saucer. They were pale green and trimmed with gold. Turning over the saucer, I read the words, "Hand Painted China. Occupied Japan." That made sense. It was during this period after the War when Molly passed away, only a short time after we'd lost our mother. Mother died from natural causes. As for Molly, we were told she had a severe asthma attack.

I never believed it.

I swallowed my first sip. "And you, Molly? You had an asthma attack? Is that what happened to you?"

"Ah, my dear sister, everything will reveal itself in time. It's not I who is important at this moment."

Steam rose from the tea and through it I saw a vision of all five of my children surrounding a hospital bed. Michael sat in a chair near the door. The body in the bed had my dark, gray-laced hair and olive skin, tanned from the summer sun. A breathing tube protruded from the mouth. Monitors beeped. There was no life in this body, and I sensed, no hope from my children. They had been told the truth and they accepted it.

Holding hands, their father joining them, they prayed.

"Our Father, who art in Heaven . . ."

Darlene and Jenny spoke the loudest and clearest. The others, including my husband, whispered the words—the same way they had always done at Mass. We were not a front pew, gift-carrying kind of family. Our attendance was regular, but we sat toward the back of the cavernous St. Teresa's Cathedral in Grossdale, Illinois, and mostly kept to ourselves. Michael didn't approve of the changes in the Catholic service—first when they went from Latin to English and then when the priests started belting out songs like street corner folk singers during the guitar masses. He especially didn't like shaking everyone's germ-filled hands during the sign of peace.

"Thy will be done, on earth as it is in Heaven . . ."

A woman with a collar, presumably the hospital chaplain, joined them. Clearly, she wasn't a Catholic priest. Michael would not be happy about this.

"And lead us not into temptation, but deliver us from evil . . ." Michael released Caylie and Marie's hands. "Amen," he said. Only Darlene, Jenny, and the lady chaplain continued, *"For thine is the kingdom . . ."*

"WE don't say that," snapped Michael. A vertical line, an exclamation point between his thick, snow-white brows, cut deep, and the room fell silent. Only the heart monitor kept pace.

Jenny looked at her dad. "Yes you do," she said. "You DO say it."

Darlene squeezed her younger sister's hand and Jenny held her tongue. Moments later in a whisper, she defended the closing of the Lord's Prayer, now accustomed to saying it this way each Sunday in her Episcopal church. "Catholics DO say 'for thine is the kingdom, and the power and the glory,' " she insisted, "it's just that the priest interrupts before they get to it. They DO say it!"

"Let it go, Jenny," whispered Darlene. "It's bad enough there's not a Catholic priest on hand to give Mom her last rites. I'm surprised Dad didn't stroke out when that woman walked into Mom's room wearing a Roman collar."

In spite of herself, Jenny laughed. Then after more silent prayers and an overwhelming waft of disbelief in the room, Darlene, Marie and Ronnie each pressed their lips to the forehead of my lifeless body, said goodbye and walked out into the hallway.

"I just can't believe she's gone," uttered Ronnie, his only words that day.

Michael remained at the bedside and his eyes became pools of Caribbean blue. "She's still warm," he said. "She's still breathing."

The chaplain put her hand on his shoulder. "It's the respirator doing all the work right now. They need to keep her in this state to make use of her organs."

He brought his thumb to his mouth and bit on his nail, something I hadn't seen him do since his own mother passed. Her name was Belle and the image of her made my tea go cold. Belle was a terse, unpleasant woman. I turned to Molly. "Can I expect to encounter my dead mother-in-law anytime soon here in *Obr*?"

"Not unless you want to," she said with a sardonic grin. Touching the saucer, Molly moved it enough to stir the tea. The ripples cleared and steam once again rose from the cup. I saw a tear escape and slowly fall from Michael's face to the rail of the hospital bed. It was too much for me. I blew into the tea, erasing the pain of my husband's face.

Caylie and Jenny were still there. They were reluctant to leave. During their time at the hospital they had taken turns tending to my lifeless body. Caylie combed my hair. Jenny filed my nails. She never stopped talking as she conducted a one-sided conversation, believing with all her heart that I heard every word.

And I did.

On the day of my death, my Irish Twins were nearly forty years old and yet to me, the faces I saw were the same faces that beamed up at me from their cribs. By the time they were in high school, Marie was married and gone. She married young, so young she still had braces on her teeth. Darlene was pushing toward graduate school to pursue the endless education, and Ronnie was away at college hoping to find a way to turn his interest in sports into a career. When all five of them were home, I was so busy catering to their needs I didn't notice time pass by. Before I knew it, however, we only had Jenny and Caylie at our Grossdale home.

The girls were happy, healthy, and stayed out of trouble. Unfortunately it was during their high school years when everything fell apart for Michael. Michael's midlife crisis coincided with the OPEC oil embargo and subsequent energy crisis. He turned fifty-five at the same time the national speed limit was reduced to 55. Working as an electrician for a commercial contractor, he was transferred to a site requiring an hour commute, and in Chicago-area traffic, that could turn into two hours on any given day. The reduced speed limit annoyed him no-end and he complained about the speeding ticket he received on the Dan Ryan Expressway until the day I died.

During this period, our last years in Illinois before we permanently moved to our retirement home in northern Michigan, his hair went from blond to gray, and each evening he came home from work red-faced and cross. His kisses, one on each cheek, had no greeting behind them. He deposited his thermos on the kitchen counter and headed straight to the basement. The whiskey awaited.

Jenny and Caylie were busy with after school activities and he didn't allow me to drive the car to pick them up. "When I was their age, I had to walk home from school and I lived five miles away, not two."

I tried to convince him that even two miles in sub-zero temperatures was a tortuous walk for the girls, especially after dark, but he complained of the price of gas—up to sixty cents a gallon—and felt they needed to build their characters.

He didn't know them at all.

It was a shame Michael had lost interest in his youngest daughters. They were such lovely, smart girls—popular in school and excelling academically. He didn't attend their sporting events, didn't ask them about their classes or their friends. Except for slurred harangues at the dinner table, he didn't speak to them. He refused to pay for class rings or senior trips and felt neither deserved to go to college. "College is no place for girls," he said. "If they want to go so badly, they should find a way to pay for it—just like I had to support myself and my family from the time I was fourteen years old."

"But this isn't the Depression, dear," I said. "And you allowed Darlene and Ronnie to go to college. Neither of them had the grades the twins have. You'd know that if you weren't so selfish right now."

There was a long pause and he narrowed his eyes in a disapproving glare. "Don't ever speak to me like that again."

I didn't. Instead I got a job. Some of the neighborhood women had gone back to work, so I thought, why shouldn't I? It was the 1970s and my daughters told me it was in the name of Women's Lib. I, of course, knew that it wasn't about women's rights. Instead it was about what work had always been about for me. It wasn't a choice. It was a need to support my family.

In the 1930s after our father's green grocer business failed and he left us, my sister, mother and I did everything we could to keep food on our table. My mother's family owned our house just north of Boston, so we weren't afraid of losing our home, however, during the Depression we had an underlying fear about making ends meet. I contributed by tutoring young children at St. Mary's, where I was a prefect in the Sodality. After high school, I did office work—typing and filing—and during the War I was a telephone operator. So, in 1975 when Caylie entered high school and Jenny was a sophomore, I tested for a temp agency called Kelly Girl. There were a couple temp agencies looking for help, but to me, Kelly Girl sounded Irish and therefore, it was the place for me.

Michael didn't approve of me working outside the home, but gave me little argument as he sunk deeper and deeper into his midlife depression. I insisted he see a doctor about it, which only resulted in a prescription for Valium because of his high blood pressure. Mixing that with the whiskey didn't make for a pretty picture during evening meals. Both girls found reasons to miss dinner so they didn't have to sit through their dad's rambling lectures on the lack of morals in modern society and their need to contribute more to the family.

Having no experience living with a middle-aged man, I didn't realize at the time that Michael's behavior was merely a phase. I kept my faith, believing everything would be okay and praying that my sweet Michael would shed this anger and resentment toward his children. I took jobs when they were offered and stashed enough money to pay Jenny's tuition for her first year of school. And I bought her a class ring too.

When Jenny left for school, her father hardly noticed. He focused only on early retirement. And then, on the day of Caylie's high school graduation, he abandoned them all together, and he took me with him to Mitten Lake.

"*He* abandoned them?" asked Molly.

"Wait, you're reading my thoughts?"

"Are you kidding? I've read your thoughts since we were three years old. Anyway, I told you not to worry about Michael. He will do things as he's always done—in his own way. Just as you led your life in your own way."

"Are you saying I abandoned them too?"

"Anne, you led your life quietly and with dignity. And it's how you died—very quietly. Not even a death rattle. Mother always said, 'speak little but speak wise,' and you lived by that rule. Do you believe you abandoned your children?"

"I wasn't referring to my death."

"I know, dear," she said, once again filling my cup. "Drink your tea."

The steam rose from the tea and I took in the aroma. The sweetness had evaporated leaving a more potent, spicy scent. At first I had thought the spice was nutmeg. This was stronger. Like cloves. Lifting the cup I noticed it had changed as well. It was no longer the delicate China cup initially handed to me by my sister. It was now a heavier, ceramic cup—avocado green. It was from the set of dishes we received when we took out the loan to build our retirement home at Mitten Lake. I remember having the choice between avocado green and harvest gold, the two popular kitchen appliance colors of the era. They called it Stoneware, and unlike the China of our youth, it was indestructible. How many times had I banged those dishes against the faucet or the sink? Or dropped them on the floor? There was nary a chip.

Through the steam emanating from the cup I now saw my family assembled in the quaint St. Joseph's Catholic church where Michael and I had spent the last quarter century as members—just another pair of gray retirees who filled Catholic churches across the country. At St. Joseph's, as at St. Teresa's, we were still not front row, gift-carrying members. Michael was never an usher, and I was never a member of the altar guild. We didn't read the lessons from the podium or even sing the hymns from the pew—neither of us could carry a tune. We drove to town from our house on Mitten Lake some twenty miles away every Sunday out of habit, and out of faith that our Sunday attendance would keep us on the proper path.

The steam grew into a thin, wispy cloud, camouflaging an odd scene. All five of my children had never been together in that church. In the last years of my life, they didn't visit us from their various corners of the country together. They'd all separated and created their own families.

"Make three wishes," Darlene whispered to her teenage daughter, Meghan. Meghan screwed up her face as though taking in a bad scent. It was a familiar teenage expression—one I'd seen on all four of my daughters.

"Why?" she asked.

"Your Nana always told us that when you enter a church for the first time, you get to make three wishes."

"Does it work?"

Darlene didn't answer.

"Of course it works," answered Molly from behind me.

"You see what I'm seeing too." It was not a question.

"For now," said Molly. "It's lovely your daughter is passing on that anecdote. Of course, it was Mother who told us about making three wishes in a new church. She said it was the reason Catholics sought out new churches in every place they visited."

"Where is Mother? Is she here?"

"Yes," said Molly. "Keep watching."

Molly wrapped her hands around the teacup and pulled it toward her so that we shared the view of my funeral service. Together we watched Jenny and Caylie standing at the lectern, Jenny still a good five inches taller than her younger sister. Behind them, a statue of the Virgin Mary looked down upon them as they held hands.

"I don't know if I can bear to listen to their eulogy." I blew into the steam and the vision disappeared. Only the tea remained. I raised the cup to my lips and sipped. "I've waited too long. The tea has gone cold."

Molly smiled. "You like it hot."

"Some do."

"At first most of us can't listen to the eulogies. It's a summation of your life—a judgment fitting for those who remain. But it's not *your* judgment." She filled my cup. "The task before you is to examine everything carefully and hold fast to that which is good."

"You mean, judge myself?"

"Precisely, dearest. The road has risen to meet you. You have the gift of God."

Of course I didn't understand what she meant right away. I had so many questions. I wanted to know what happened to Molly. I was never clear about how she had died. And where was our mother? Was our father here?

Molly assured me. "Everything will reveal itself in time."

It's hard to put my finger on how much time has passed since my death. I have spent much of it watching my children. Molly suggested even before the life support system was removed from my body that I look after and listen to the prayers of my second child, Darlene.

Darlene, the doctor, had done a good job with her siblings and her father explaining what had happened to me, and I admired her bedside manner. "Over the past few years Mom has experienced what are known as Transient Ischemic Attacks—or TIAs," she said. "They are like mini strokes, or tremors, that affected her brain so that she couldn't always find the right word. But this was no tremor. This stroke was more like an earthquake registering ten on the Richter scale." Darlene was straightforward but compassionate and kept busy in public, grieving silently when she was alone. She may have appeared to be the most scientific of the lot, but I soon learned she prayed the hardest. I stood by her and listened, and found she had, perhaps, the greatest understanding of life and death. She moved forward with life after just a short period. Darlene and her daughter, Meghan, returned to their home in Atlanta immediately after the funeral.

Marie needed me too. I recalled the Irish Blessing I had heard and recited during all the days of my youth, and held my eldest child in the palm of my hand, just as I did the constant cups of tea provided by my sister.

The only one to remain in her hometown of Grossdale, Marie was never the typical eldest child in terms of behavior traits and trying to live up to expectations. After I died, she didn't immediately step into the role of replacement mother to her younger sisters. Having spent her last thirty years mothering her own brood of five—all boys—she didn't have much left to give beyond the walls of her worried mother mind. Of all my children, losing me had the greatest impact on her. I could see through her dreams that she was filled with fear. This same fear of my absence was apparent when she was a child. Marie was never one I could leave with a neighbor or a baby-sitter without her issuing an incredible bout of irritability. By visiting her through her dreams, I helped ease her into accepting the permanence of my departure.

My son, who had lived in Phoenix, Arizona for thirty years, had been off the radar of my concern for quite some time. "A daughter is a daughter for the rest of her life," sang Molly, "but a son is only a son until he takes a wife." I found no need to visit Ronnie at first, but believe he'll need me as his years progress.

It was my Irish Twins, Jenny and Caylie, who appeared to need me the most. Even though I always pictured them together—the way they were as children—and I saw them come together at my deathbed and during my funeral, I knew that they had grown apart. I had come to believe they were on the verge of abandoning one another, similar to the way I once abandoned them.

It was not the legacy I had imagined.

CHAPTER 3

"You need a new cup," said Molly. She took the steaming teacup from my hands and held up a tall white travel mug.

I read the label. "Starbucks?"

"It's not tea. It's coffee."

"But Molly, you know I'm a tea drinker. Coffee's too bitter for me."

"Yes, but we're looking in on Jenny. And I promise you, coffee is more appropriate."

She twisted the black plastic lid, unscrewing it and removing it from the elongated cup. She directed me to look through the steam, and the first thing I saw was Jenny's husband, Don Lincolnwood.

I smiled.

Don was tall with sandy hair and turquoise eyes. Jenny always said he had the physique of a Greek god, and that he constantly worked out to maintain it. In spite of this, he wasn't vain. And he was a man who always made me smile.

Don Lincolnwood was definitely a coffee drinker and he had a vast collection of travel mugs. I discovered the collection one morning when visiting them in San Diego shortly after the birth of their second child, my granddaughter Ariel. One morning when looking for a teacup, I opened the doors of a cabinet next to the stove. To my surprise there were no teacups. Instead, all three shelves of the cabinet were filled with tall containers made of plastic, stainless steel and newfangled products I'd never before seen.

"Jenny," I had called. "Can you come here for a moment?"

"What is it Mom?"

I pulled open both doors of the cabinet and pointed to the contents as if I were Vanna White. Looking up into the pale blue eyes of my daughter I said, "Explain."

Jenny threw back her head and her red ringlets bounced as she laughed. "I can explain that in one word." Holding up her index finger, she paused for effect. "Don."

Jenny opened another cabinet where I found my teacup, but in the meantime, I was happy to finally know what to buy my son-in-law for his next birthday. After my discovery of his stash, I added to his travel mug collection every year until I died.

Taking the Starbuck's traveler from Molly's hands, I breathed in the aroma of the coffee and heard music. It was an electronic version of Pachelbel's "Canon in D", which was the song of Don and Jenny's ringing telephone. The tone pierced through their otherwise quiet bedroom.

It was Don's forty-fourth birthday. Jenny knew the call would be for him, and yet Don sat on their unmade bed and didn't reach for the receiver. Jenny leaned over him and grabbed the phone on his nightstand. Holding the receiver at arm's length and squinting her eyes to make out the caller ID, she recognized the San Francisco area code and saw her sister's name. Don had three siblings who usually forgot his birthday, however Caylie always remembered to call and send a funny card.

Without answering it, she tossed the phone to him. A down comforter and bright, burnt orange bedspread were clumped at his side. He was about to put on his running shoes. "It's for *you* birthday boy."

"Who is it?" he asked, slipping his foot into a black Nike. "Can't be anyone in my family."

"Caylie."

Don smiled, crow's feet accenting his eyes. "Hello?"

Jenny watched Don's smile grow and light his face. He cradled the phone between his ear and shoulder, bent over and tied his shoes.

"Happy birthday toooo yoooou!" sang Caylie and her boys. *"And many more ... on channel four ..."*

Don stood up and laughed. "Thanks guys. It's so cool that you always remember my birthday."

After the song he was immediately caught up in conversation with Caylie.

Jenny left the room and he didn't watch her leave. Fine, she thought. Caylie would rather talk to him. Whatever. She hadn't had a real conversation with her sister in nearly a month. And at first it was a relief not being involved with her sister's daily drama, but as she turned into the laundry room and her eyes fell upon the waiting piles of her family's soiled clothing, she felt a twinge of resentment.

Lately Caylie only called her when she needed something.

Jenny sighed, weary of the endless cycle of home maintenance. Picking up a pair of jeans and placing them in the hamper, she shook her head, thankful for only having two children. She often wondered how I, her mother, managed five.

Next she gathered two pastel-colored shirts, a white blouse, and several stray socks, and put them in a separate hamper. "White on the right," she said mechanically, while reaching back and tightening her ponytail. She opened the lid to the Maytag and then located the scooper inside the Costco-sized box of Tide. There really ought to be a warning, she thought, to any woman thinking about having children: YOUR LIFE WILL BE FULL OF SORTING AND FOLDING CLOTHES. Pulling out the knob, the machine kicked into action, and the small room was filled with the sound of running water. She peeked her head out the door and looked down the hall. Don was still on the phone.

What on earth were they were they chatting about?

As Jenny finished separating the last of the darks into two piles, she placed jeans and shirts in the washer, and quickly realized that only two pieces in the load belonged to her. She closed the lid and then her hand froze.

"Oh my God," she said. "I've turned into my mother."

When Jenny was a child she often wondered why I wore the same outfit two and even three days in a row. Looking at her own shorts and tank top, she realized it was a second go-around for each and she knew exactly why. They had passed the sniff test, and were perfectly capable of getting her through another day around the house.

Jenny realized that she had witnessed and now emulated a housewife's sense of monotony. "It's the feminine fucking mystique," she said and bent over to pick up yet another stray sock. A stabbing pain of grief hit her as she added the dirty sock to the machine.

She missed me.

What a shame, she thought, that I didn't make it to the twenty-first century to witness the experiences and revelations of her own middle age. Surely it was one of life's most poignant cruelties. What Jenny didn't know, of course, was that I did witness them. I just couldn't comment.

The night of her husband's birthday was long and sleepless for Jenny. She blamed the second glass of chardonnay she'd had during Don's birthday dinner. But her restlessness wasn't because of the wine. It was because of Caylie.

Apparently, Caylie was getting married again.

It had been a nice dinner with their two daughters at a Japanese restaurant, however, between bites of sushi, Jenny stewed about Caylie telling Don instead of her that she was engaged.

Caylie had been divorced from her first husband, Robert Cotrell, for six lonely years. Since their separation, there had been a series of boyfriends—most of them bad boyfriends—but none, in anyone's opinion, were potential husband material. Obviously, at least according to her conversation with Don, that had changed. Caylie said she was planning to marry a man named Albert Powell.

It was a mistake.

Jenny had met Albert once when visiting her sister in San Francisco and she couldn't stand him. He was one of those guys who always looked around the room for a better conversation. He was overweight, drank too much, and had what Jenny called "that macho schmuck" characteristic she abhorred. From what Caylie had said, Albert never wanted to do anything with her kids. Why would she want to marry a man like that?

It could only be because he was wealthy. Caylie said he was an investor. He was the kind of guy who never got his hands dirty, and made money off of other people's work. He wasn't the dad-type—probably didn't even own a tool belt. Or if he did, the extent of his knowledge of tools would be limited to knowing the difference between a flathead and Phillips head screwdriver.

Caylie's three boys were the best part of her life and without a doubt, her top priority. They were all active in football, baseball, lacrosse and a host of school activities. But Albert never went to their games. He didn't take them camping or involve himself with raising them. Divorced as well, he had two kids of his own. But they were older, and from what they could garner, the responsibility of his ex-wife.

Why couldn't Caylie see the warning signs? Hadn't one failed marriage been enough? Jenny had tried to warn her sister about the first man she married, Robert, but Caylie wouldn't listen. Three kids, massive debt and twenty pounds later, Caylie was divorced and miserable enough to believe that Albert Powell was the answer to her ultimate happily ever after.

Watching our sisters marry the wrong man was something Jenny and I had in common. The difference between Jenny and me; however, is that I never voiced my opinion to Molly.

So often I wished I had.

When Jenny finally managed to fall asleep on the night of her husband's birthday, I went into her dreams. I had been visiting my older daughters, Darlene and Marie, in this manner for months and had yet to reveal myself to Jenny in a dream. I wasn't sure why, but I suppose it was because she didn't seem to need me. I had felt the poignancy of how much she missed me and I often came to her mind during her seemingly endless household chores. I also knew that Jenny, more than any of my daughters, often made the mistake when wanting to share something with me, of picking up the phone and punching in the first one or two digits of my phone number before realizing I wouldn't answer.

In her dream she saw me as I looked in the 1970s when she was a teenager. My hair was rich brunette, smooth on top but curled under just above my shoulders. I had never worn tidy, beauty parlor up-dos like the rest of the women in our Grossdale neighborhood. Most of these women were at least ten years younger than I, and they strode through the grocery store aisles with single-colored helmets of tresses so lacquered they'd stay put in a tornado. The only makeup I wore was a smudge of pink lipstick whenever I left the house. Jenny used to be horrified—or grossed-out, as she would put it—at the sight of my blotted tissues in the bathroom wastebasket, and would have preferred it if I wore nothing at all on my face. Jenny was the only one of my four daughters who didn't wear makeup. Lately, though, I noticed she added color to her lips. But she never pressed them into a tissue.

I hadn't been aware of my clothing during my time in *Obr*, but I did notice my attire in Jenny's dream. In her dream I wore a sleeveless, white eyelet blouse and seersucker white shorts. My skin had an olive tan like the one I usually sported after a summer filled with hanging clothes on the line and riding my bicycle around the neighborhood.

Jenny always envied my ability to tan. Black Irish in complexion, I had dark hair and green eyes, while Jenny was more of the red-hair-milky-white-and-freckled skin variety Irish. Caylie, her Irish twin, and the oldest, Marie, both had richer, even coloring. Jenny believed *they* were the lucky ones—the ones the boys always called.

In her dream it was just Jenny and I. We were in a room with an olive green sofa and my white attire looked especially bright against the drab upholstery. I had pulled my outfit off a clothesline, and it may have even been frozen since I always hung all our clothes on the line during winter. Freezing clothes was part of my Hints from Heloise wisdom, and it made the whites whiter than any bleach could make them. Caylie and Jenny were often mortified bringing over friends after school during winter days in Grossdale, only to find a week's worth of frozen brassieres hanging next to the kitchen door. If Jenny had remained in the Chicago-area instead of raising her daughters in the temperate San Diego climate, she too, would have frozen her family's clothes in the winter. She emulated my household routines more than she realized.

But I wasn't dressed for winter, and, of course, there was my luminous tan. I appeared the way I knew Jenny pictured me whenever she thought of me.

In her dream, Jenny was obviously happy to see me, as happy as the times Michael and I visited her when she lived in Chicago after college and before she got married and moved to San Diego. That was during a very brief period when she was adult enough to appreciate her dad and I as people—and before we became old.

I greeted her, using one of my pet names for her. "Hey there pussy foot."

Jenny rolled her eyes, full of teenaged emotion. "Mom, why do you always call me pussy foot?"

"It's because you're so soft, just like a little pussy foot."

"Well, *pussy* really isn't a great word to use around your daughter."

"Oh that's nonsense. Come here."

Jenny shuffled toward me and fell into the sofa. "You're so weird, Mom."

I couldn't help but laugh, and then mimicked her Chicago accent. *"You're so weird, Mom."*

In her next breath Jenny was an adult again, and she realized I was dead and this was a dream. "I miss you, Mom," she said with an overwhelming sense of yearning—the all-too familiar feeling of something being just out of reach.

She didn't say these things, but I knew what she was feeling. She wanted to tell me that she hadn't gotten enough time with me to appreciate me from the perspective of a grown-up. She wanted to ask why I hadn't come to her sooner—why Darlene and Marie were dreaming about her regularly and she wasn't. She wanted to tell me about how more than once she had picked up the phone and stopped short of punching my number.There were so many things she wanted, it was like a fantasy Christmas list, where you write down everything you think you want, knowing fully well the list would not be fulfilled.

More than anything she wanted to tell me that her relationship with Caylie was falling apart and she didn't know what to do about it. But I already knew this.And I knew Jenny wasn't sure she even wanted to work it out. She was sick of her Irish Twin. It had been incredibly insulting to her that Caylie told Don instead of her that she was getting married again—especially after everything Jenny felt she had done for her sister.

"I'm right here, my darling Jenny," I said."And I know how you feel. Say, I was wondering . . ." My fingers gently massaged her scalp. ". . . I was wondering about Caylie."

Jenny snapped. "What about her?" It was the petulant teenager again—hardly a woman who wished to discuss her sister's behavior with their mother. "You finally visit me and you want to talk about Caylie? Why don't you just go to *her*?"

"Oh, my dear, you are indeed the salt of the earth." My fingers stopped moving.

"Mom?"

"I was wondering about *you* and Caylie. I want you to think about—"

Jenny forcefully pulled away and turned her head, looking at me as though I were a stranger. In her eyes I saw that I had become much smaller, with my gray hair cropped short. It was my eighty-year-old self.

"What is it, Mom?" she asked.

Jenny's eyes didn't pop open in a dramatic wake-up, like a falling-from-a-roof-and-gasping-yourself-into-consciousness-before-you-hit-the-ground kind of wake-up. Slowly, she opened her eyes, and for a moment she expected me to be in the room. Hovering between consciousness states—disoriented and drunken with the dream—she had the exact fleeting feeling of picking up the phone and starting to punch in my number, before the sweet delusion ended in a flash.

Reality took over, righting her to time and place and bringing back the disappointment of my death. Miniature green stick figures across the room on the VCR read 5:13. Jenny wondered if she closed her eyes and rolled into her soft pillow, would she feel my fingers in her hair again? Could she fall back asleep and pick up where she had left off?

No. Dreams didn't work that way. At least not for the living.

Jenny shook her head, feeling ridiculous. *It was only a dream.* And what about Caylie? *Oh God,* Caylie. Up until a month ago she had called Jenny everyday with all of her bad news—all of her problems. She finally had what was supposed to be good, happy news and she didn't think her own sister was worthy of hearing it? How could she even think about marrying that drunken loser, Albert Powell? Of course she didn't want to tell Jenny. She knew her sister would tell her it was a mistake—the same way she had warned her about marrying her now ex-husband, Robert.

Don lay in the fetal position, motionless and silent on his side of their king-sized bed. Sighing, she rolled onto her stomach. She realized what Caylie was doing. She was making Jenny pay the price for not being happy about her first engagement.

Yeah, and look how that turned out.

Jenny bitterly believed if Caylie would have listened to her about Robert, she and Don could have saved the ten grand they gave her to pay for the divorce.

"I was wondering about you and Caylie." She silently repeated her mother's words from the dream. *"I want you to think about ..."*

"Don, are you awake?" She poked him in the back and he reluctantly opened one eye.

"Hmmm?"

"I had a dream about my mother. She asked me to think about Caylie."

"When are you *not* thinking about Caylie?" he asked, rolling onto his back.

"Really. I think about her as much as I think about our kids. I have this annoying need to take care of her. It used to be a blessing. But ever since Mom died, it feels like a curse."

* * *

Jenny's earliest memories of Caylie were about taking care of her. In 1964, I was a stay-at-home mom in a blue collar Chicago suburb, and my Irish Twins were the last of my stay-at-home kids. Marie, Darlene and Ronnie were dressed in parochial school uniforms and walked to school daily with sack lunches and a kiss on each cheek. But one day, when I was well into my forties, I had a pregnancy scare. The very idea of having to tell Michael we were expecting another child frightened the daylights out of me. Jenny and Caylie were three and four years old, and the day I went to the doctor, I took them to a nearby childcare service called Miss Martha's Daycare. The girls had never been to day care and they were excited. To them it felt like going to a birthday party.

Miss Martha lived on 26th Street. It was the road against the forest preserve on the edge of Grossdale, about five blocks from our house. Jenny remembered that day in snapshots. There was mowed green grass and a dirt path instead of a sectioned concrete sidewalk separating manicured property from the untamed wilds of the forest surrounding Cinnamon Creek. Big shady elms and oaks heavy with late-summer growth kept the air damp and chilly. The songs of red-breasted robins and fire engine red cardinals filled the air with distant and distinct whistles. Jenny's shoes were out-of-season white, scuffed Mary Janes, and she wore folded white anklets. Each bony knee sported a pepperoni-sized scab.

Before I said goodbye there was some discussion about Caylie being too young to be there; however, my neighbor, who often brought her kids there, said Miss Martha's only requirement was that the children be out of diapers. Caylie had been out of diapers for a year. But she was very small and noticeably quiet compared to her sister. Jenny often did the talking for both of them. And it was Jenny who spoke up and promised she would keep tabs her sister. "Look Caylie," she said excitedly. "They have bubbles!"

"Bubbles!" babbled Caylie. She let go of my hand and grabbed Jenny's as Jenny led her to a table filled with plastic bottles.

Bubbles were a delicious treat—better than cookies because they couldn't get them at home. At least not real ones. At home our bubble solution was homemade and flawed: tap water and dish soap. We didn't know about the need for glycerin or even Karo Syrup. Before I finally discovered the secret to successful homemade bubbles in

Family Circle magazine, we were lucky to create anything round that would hold its shape and drift away effortlessly, full of aurora borealis color and the fantasies of a child. Mostly, my kids created suds and spit.

Miss Martha's Daycare provided four-ounce bottles from the Five and Dime store. The hard plastic bottles were purple, hot pink or robin's egg blue. Inside was liquid magic—a thick, syrupy solution containing a ridged wand, which the children fished out with their tiny index fingers. Filling the wand with a glassy surface, their eager baby's breath held the power to create spherical, colorful perfection. And unlike watching an errant helium balloon float into space, which always triggered a sense of loss, a bubble floating off was triumphant. Releasing it from the wand—the bigger the better—filled them with joy and satisfaction.

After Jenny and Caylie selected their plastic bottles, Jenny wandered away from her sister and kept busy creating and chasing bubbles at one end of the grassy yard. Soon, she heard a commotion. Looking toward the noise she spied her three-year-old sister standing still with her arm outstretched. Caylie had short, thin blonde hair. At the time it was stick straight—a notable contrast to Jenny's riot of strawberry curls. She looked at Jenny and smiled a tight-lipped smile, hiding her teeth. Sensing trouble, Jenny clutched her purple bubble bottle tightly and walked toward her sister. She mimicked Caylie's smile and watched as her sister took her other hand and rubbed her forearm. Back-and-forth, she frothed up the bubbles coating her skin. She looked as happy as a kid frosting cup cakes. Jenny didn't know if Caylie had spilled the bubbles or simply poured them on her arm. Meanwhile, the children around her were laughing and pointing.

"We told you not to spill the bubbles," came a scolding voice far above their heads.

"I knew she was *too* young," said another voice.

Stymied by the angry voices, Jenny stopped in place and watched as the blue bubble bottle was snatched from her sister's glistening hand. Caylie's eyes popped open in shock while long, polished fingers grabbed her under the arm. She was pulled away. Jenny threw her bubble bottle to the grass and ran after them. "Wait!" she cried.

Caylie turned her head. They locked eyes and Jenny saw her sister's forehead crush into a thousand wrinkles.

Caylie called out her sister's name. "Jen-ny?'

Jenny would never forget the sound of her name uttered in panic. It sounded more like: *"Jeeeeennn-nnnneeeeeey?"*

Jenny didn't know what to do while watching her helpless sister dragged away. She was sure Caylie expected her to jump in and save her, but Jenny didn't know how. Instead of standing up for her, she froze.

Meanwhile, I learned from the doctor that I was not carrying another child, and returned to Miss Martha's with a lightened load. When I arrived two hours after leaving them there, both girls were crying. Apparently, spilling bubbles was a capital offense, and all the ammunition the Miss Martha administrators needed to justify expulsion. Of course, the girls didn't understand that. They only understood unfair punishment.

Their tears broke my heart. I lost track of the number of times my heart broke on account of my children's tears. Again I was thankful that day that my pregnancy test was negative. In raising five children, I didn't know how much heart I had left.

After loading Jenny and Caylie into the car, I drove to the Five and Dime and bought them each a twenty-five-cent bottle of bubbles. They created and chased them for the rest of the afternoon, all earlier sorrows, fears and humiliations forgotten.

Jenny was still fascinated by bubbles. She especially liked watching them meet, whether on the wand or in the air. When two bubbles meet they merge to share a common wall. If the bubbles are the same size the wall is flat, equal. If one bubble is smaller than the other, it has a higher internal pressure and will bulge into the larger bubble. Regardless of size, when bubble meets bubble the result is a union of total sharing and compromise.

Caylie and Jenny were like two bubbles. Jenny was the larger of the two. On the day of the bubble-spilling incident at Miss Martha's, she experienced the feeling of indignity on behalf of her sister for the first time. And just like the smaller bubble meeting the larger, that day her sister bulged into her life and shared her wall—her very core, her strength. That day, even though she didn't realize it, Jenny made a vow to take care of Caylie. She swore she would never freeze up again and would always be there to save her sister.

CHAPTER 4

Molly handed me the pale green cup and saucer, the same set she offered when I first arrived in *Obr*. "Just like Jenny, you didn't approve of my choice in husbands either," she said.

"It wasn't my place to judge you. Or Charlie Murphy."

"I wish you had told me what you were feeling."

"So do I. But would you have listened?"

Molly smiled. "Probably not."

"Molly, did Charlie...?"

"Don't ask me about how I died. Not yet."

"But Molly—"

"Anne, it's not important now. It's your youngest, Caylie, who's praying for your attention. You didn't offer your opinion the first time she got married—when she impulsively married her childhood sweetheart just as I did."

"I didn't believe in interfering with my children's choices either. They only would have resented me for it."

Molly turned and whispered over her shoulder. "Did it ever occur to you that your children may have held more resentment toward you for *not* voicing your opinions?"

As she walked away from me, the cup I held in my hands changed from pale green to bright orange. Containing only a small puddle of tea with green leaves at the bottom, reminiscent of Mitten Lake seaweed, I saw an image form of my beautiful Caylie, her blonde hair haphazardly piled on top of her head like a weathered bird's nest. The aroma of the tea wafted through my senses and smelled toxic, a bit like alcohol. I studied my daughter. She looked tired and confused. Her thoughts drifted to me, as if she were speaking:

I'm lost. Goddamnit. I have no clue why I said 'yes' to Albert's proposal. I'm not sure I like him, let alone love him. But he got down on one knee. He had a ring. He's got money! He can get me out of this mess—out of this horrible house with the leaky roof and moldy walls. Oh God! What am I supposed to do?

Why hasn't Jenny called me? I can't believe my sister knows I'm engaged and she hasn't called to congratulate me. It's been three weeks. Does she think it's a bad idea? Or is it that she just doesn't want me to have what she has. Like she owns the rights to a happy marriage.

Now that Mom's dead, she's all I have. Marie and Darlene don't give two shits about my life. But where is she when I need her?

"Yo!" called a voice from behind the paneled, white door of Caylie's office. She wasn't sure which of her boys was calling her. All three sounded alike.

"I'm in here."

Caylie shoved a stemmed glass half full of pinot grigio behind her computer so whichever kid it was entering her office wouldn't see it. It was only two in the afternoon. There would be judgment.

"Hey Mom!"

"I said I'm in my office. What is it?"

She hit the escape button on her keyboard and turned toward the door. A hand covered with ink marks grabbed the doorframe. It was Frankie, her eldest, who had been drawing on himself for weeks, auditioning tattoos. He stepped into the room, smiling a mouth full of braces. He was the spitting image of Caylie's ex-husband at the age of thirteen.

"Can I go over to Jason's house? He wants to play basketball."

"Only if your room is clean and you're packed for Michigan. And you have to be back by six. Your dad is picking you up."

He slumped into a bright orange beanbag chair. "Do I have to go?"

Caylie rose from her desk chair, crossed the room, and wedged into the beanbag beside him. Frankie had his father's hair. She couldn't stop her fingers from combing the unruly bangs away from his brow. He shrugged her off.

"Oh come on, babe.You love Michigan," she said.

"I love Mitten Lake, Mom. Not Dad's lake. I don't want to go there knowing I can't see Nana."

Caylie put her hand to her heart, and it felt like someone had just pinched her nose. "Yes, my darling, I understand," she said, knowing she was using my words, my voice. She buried her aching nose in his hair, hiding her emotions. Her tone grew dulcet. "I miss Mitten Lake too."

And I miss Nana far more than you'll ever know.

I wanted to tell my sweet child that I was with her; but all I could do was blow into the tea.

Caylie's image faded and the cup was empty. I hadn't taken a sip. "Molly?"

There had been no sign of my sister since she posed the question of whether or not my children resented me for not voicing my opinions. Was that her way of saying I should have told her not to marry Charlie Murphy? I was confused and I didn't know how to look for her. There were no walls in *Ohr*—no boundaries. It was so different from my life on earth.

But this wasn't life. This was death.

If I'd been asked to diagram my days on earth spent as Anne Catherine Monaghan Shields, the shape would have been a pyramid. At my birth, seemingly all things were possible. There were endless directions my life could have taken. I was happy, secure. But our father leaving and the onset of the Great Depression narrowed the scope of my vision of the future. There would be no college education and no high standing in social circles. Molly married the first boy who asked her, the flamboyant Charlie "Red" Murphy. I, on the other hand grew more reserved. Rather than making rash decisions, mostly I allowed fate and the choices of others to direct my life. Meeting Michael and agreeing to be his wife took me away from my mother and my sister. A year later, my mother was gone. In my grief I told myself I should have never moved away—that if I had stayed home she would have lived. I learned to narrow my focus to my life with Michael, believing life was for the living. Then Molly died suddenly, and I accepted her death as God's will, blocking out all reasoning.

"She had an asthma attack," reported Charlie.

When had my sister developed asthma?

I took care of Molly's children until the birth of my own children, which narrowed my options even further. My days and nights became dedicated to them and the schedule of running our Grossdale home. Then as Marie, Darlene, Ronnie, Jenny and Caylie grew up and away from me, I once again set my future only upon Michael—with an aim of pleasing him and keeping him with me—until he was the last living being to hear me speak and see me cross over.

In *Obr*, at the tip of the pyramid that has been my ultimate existence, I looked down and saw every aspect of my life—how it was and how it is—and the scenes around me changed as often as the teacups I periodically found in my hands.

Aside from Molly I hadn't encountered any people from my life. I had always thought that when I died and went to Heaven, I would be reunited with my mother and friends who had gone before me. So far, this was not the case. Molly served as my guide and allowed me to set my own pace, to discover the course of my judgment. She assured me all my desires would be fulfilled, my questions would be answered, and I would be reunited with anyone who served a purpose.

But for now, my focus continued upon Jenny and Caylie.

I had come to believe that in 1979, when I followed my husband to his early retirement at Mitten Lake, I not only abandoned my youngest children, I also gave up the right to counsel them. What difference would my opinion have made on their decisions?

"Molly?"

I spotted a small table, a replica of one we first had in the kitchen of our Grossdale home, and the one piece of furniture I insisted we move to Mitten Lake. There was a teakettle atop it, which was covered with a white linen tea cozy. It, too, was something I recognized. Printed on the linen was an illustration of the Michigan state bird, the robin. The red of its breast had faded to pink. The idea of tea and robins amused me. I had often associated the two. When I was alive, I learned during solitary mornings while drinking tea before either the sun or my husband arose, that the robin was always the first to sing before daybreak. And after sundown, it, too, was the last to sing before the whir of the crickets and the croaks of bullfrogs took over the night air. In spite of the robin's prominence and before we made Mitten Lake our year-round home, I had always associated the blue jay with Michigan. Bright, cocky blue jays dominated the forested lands around Mitten

Lake with their screechy whistles and musical melodies. Caylie called them "Michigan birds." So, we all called them Michigan birds.

I removed the tea cozy to reveal a bright orange kettle with an iron black handle. It was the kettle from the cottage we rented on Mitten Lake when Caylie and Jenny were still very young. Those were the early days of Mitten Lake—before we tried to turn our vacation destination into our home. The tea was piping hot—just as I liked it. I filled the orange cup I'd been holding in my hand.

* * *

It was February of 1966 when Caylie first started drawing pictures of our Mitten Lake cottage. She drew on anything she could get her hands on—napkins, paper plates, grocery lists, the older kids' discarded homework. The wooden cottage was a quaint, two bedroom unit, owned by an old woman named Mrs. Bowers. Mrs. Bowers wore a hairnet over her tidy French twist and had the same build and same voice as Aunt Bee of Mayberry. We all called her "Aunt Bee" behind her back. She was one of our Mitten Lake characters, and her cottage was our first Mitten Lake home—even though we only rented it for two weeks each July. With white horizontal siding and multi-paned windows trimmed in forest green paint, Aunt Bee's cottage had a screened-in front porch with a slanted wooden floor. The whole place reeked of mildew and septic, but the breeze off the lake filled the front porch with the smell of a never-ending summer.

Caylie knew every inch of Aunt Bee's cottage. It was her Eden. And each night in the months leading to our four-hour journey—an eternity to a five-year-old—she begged her sister, Jenny, to "talk about the lake." Jenny never let her down. Jenny told Caylie stories based on their summer vacations at the lake and included rich details of the colors and the voices and the characters. Sometimes they talked long into the night and I had to journey up two flights of stairs from my bedroom to tell them to go to sleep.

Caylie and Jenny began sharing their attic bedroom in our tri-level home in Grossdale earlier that year. It essentially qualified as the fourth floor. Their twin beds, nestled under the slanted ceiling, had matching pink quilts and were only three feet apart. When they were babies, they had shared a bedroom on the second floor and Ronnie called the attic annex his own. By the time our Irish Twins were four and five years old, however, their teenaged sisters, Marie and Darlene, no longer wanted their brother passing through their room to climb the steps to the attic. So, bedroom rearrangement was in order. Ronnie moved to the second floor bedroom adjacent to our room, and all four girls were on the top floors.

In June, Marie completed her sophomore year of high school, Darlene graduated from eighth grade, Ronnie finished fifth grade and Jenny, after a few run-ins with the nuns at St. Teresa's, escaped first grade with a reputation as a fiery redhead. In the meantime, Caylie excelled in kindergarten. Her teacher, Miss Simmons, who always had a soft spot for little blonde Caylie, commended her advanced drawing skills. On Caylie's final report card there was a note reading, "I think you may have a future architect on your hands."

By July Caylie's cottage drawings continued to multiply, and they went well beyond pencil renderings on scraps of paper. The night before our trip to Mitten Lake, after packing her duffel bag with swimsuits, tennis shoes and sweatshirts, she made a full color crayon drawing on the wall next to her bed. No one saw her sweet secret. Not even Jenny.

In the morning, all seven of us piled into our fire engine red, four door Dodge 330 sedan. With a wooden Milocraft speedboat containing all our gear hitched to the back, Michael—Dad—took the wheel. Jenny sat in front, and Marie and Darlene were in the backseat with a stash of *Seventeen* magazines and penny candy. Ronnie and Caylie took turns lying prone on the ledge between the seat and the window. They shared endless bags of Cheetos and *Richie Rich* comic books. Caylie couldn't yet read the comic bubbles, but she loved looking at the drawings.

Managing only one stop along the Indiana Toll Road for a truck stop lunch, the anticipation among all my children built as we crossed the Michigan border. The road shrank to two lanes and they shouted, "DO NOT PASS" and "PASS WITH CARE" as we whizzed past the alternating street signs. Their excitement came to a peak when our red Dodge turned north on Coon Hollow Road, the undulating final leg to Mitten Lake.

Jenny lifted her head from my lap, her coppertop curls in wild disarray. "I want to be the first one to see the lake."

"No! Me!" cried Caylie.

"We just got on Coon Hollow," Michael said. "It'll be a wee bit before we see Mitten Lake."

"Coon Hollow Road.What a name," scoffed Darlene."I think Stokely Carmichael might have something to say about such a blatantly derogatory name."

"What's she talking about?" asked Ronnie."Who?"

I cringed because the subject of race relations was not a good topic to bring up near my husband. One of the first things I had learned about the Shields family was that they were very narrow-minded. Bigotry was a trait I didn't understand, but to keep peace, I learned to tolerate it by holding my breath. I watched as Michael tightened his grip on the steering wheel and called over his shoulder."He's that uppity so-and-so who raised his fist last month and proclaimed black power."

Marie flipped a magazine page in disgust."The road is named after raccoons, not black people. For God's sake, Darlene, lighten up!"

"Marie!" I scolded."Mind your tongue."

Jenny got on her knees and hung over the front seat facing her siblings."Are there more Cheetos? I didn't get any."

Darlene held a lipstick tube in her hand and blindly applied a coat of white to her lower lip."Yeah, but you *did* get the front seat the entire time, ya little squirt."

"I'm not a squirt!" Jenny turned around and whispered to me."It smells back there."

"There it is!" cried Caylie."There's Mitten Lake. I saw it first! I saw it first!"

Mitten Lake was outside the town of Running Rivers, Michigan. It was one of the Great Lake State's prime vacation destinations for those escaping the concrete suburbs of Chicago. There were seven lakes between two rivers—actually a river and a creek—in Running Rivers. Mitten Lake, *our* lake, was the biggest and, according to the Shields family, the best. There was also Harland Lake, Driftwood Lake, Potawatomi Lake, Long Lake, Lake Rita and the lake that was the butt of all our jokes, Mud Lake. Even though a silk-screen map of all the lakes was on the Running Rivers souvenir sweatshirts we all possessed, no one truly knew the exact location of Mud Lake.

Around the next forested bend, when Mitten Lake momentarily went out of view, Ronnie spotted a swamp. "Oh look!" he said. "There's Mud Lake!"

We all laughed and Ronnie beamed, showing off his chipped front teeth. He was delighted to be the first one to utter the annual family joke.

When we arrived at the cottage,Aunt Bee was there to greet us. She stood at the end of the dirt road with her arms outstretched and her long flour sack cotton print dress hanging unevenly below her knees. As she did every year she embraced Michael and me, and commented on how much the children had grown.

"I'll be across the bay at my sister Hilda's house," she said, handing Michael a red and white bobber-turned keychain with a solitary key. "Just come over in the boat if you need anything."

Michael took the key and put his hand on Aunt Bee's shoulder. He looked like a giant standing next to her. "We'll be just fine."

"I get the top bunk!" cried Caylie. She raced passed her siblings and went inside the cottage.The door slammed shut behind her and a puff of pine pollen emanated from the rusted screen door, forming a momentary pale green cloud.

Ronnie sneezed.

"I'm looking forward to watching you all water-ski," said Aunt Bee. "I imagine the little ones will be on the Flexiboard this year?"

"I was off the trainer last year," said Jenny. "I'm gonna try dropping one."

"Yeah, right," said Ronnie with a scoff. "It'll be fun watching you fall on your face, squirt!"

"I'm NOT a squirt," cried Jenny. "And how much you wanna make a hundred dollar bet I'll do it?"

"Okay hotshot," I said. "Why don't you grab your sister's things and go help her unpack? The rest of you know what to do.Thank you Aunt—er, Mrs. Bowers."

"You are quite welcome. Enjoy yourselves," she said, turning and waddling toward her pickup truck.

"That's a Chevy Cameo," said Ronnie.

Michael gave his son a quick pat on the back. "That's right, son. She bought it new in '58 and it looks like she only drives it to church on Sundays."

Darlene rolled her eyes. "Are we going to have to go to church while we're here?"

"Of course," said Michael. "Catholics always go to church on Sunday no matter where they are. Right Mommy?"

I nodded while grabbing my white toiletry case from the trunk. "Maybe we'll find a new church and you'll all get to make three wishes."

"I'd only wish that I didn't have to be in stupid church instead of in the lake," moaned Darlene.

"Mind your tongue young lady."

I followed Darlene and Marie as they shuffled inside the cottage dragging their luggage. They moved it into a shoebox-sized room next to the screened-in front porch, where for the duration of our vacation they shared a double bed and small closet. There was only one small open piece of floor space and they used it to store their record player, a luxury they refused to leave in Grossdale.

We all knew our places in the cottage and within minutes, it was like we had never left. After Ronnie helped his dad unpack the boat, he laid claim to the cot on the porch. Jenny and Caylie used the bunk beds in the bigger of the two bedrooms, which were on the opposite end of the room from our bed.

The next morning Jenny awoke first. Eager to become the youngest Shields' child to learn to ski on one, her eyes popped open to what she thought was the sound of a motor on the water. To her disappointment, it was only the sound of her father's snoring.

Caylie was still asleep and Jenny wasted no time rousing her. She pressed her feet to the springs of the bunk above her and pushed her sleeping sister into the air.

"Hey!" called Caylie. "Cut it out."

"Come on Caylie. Let's get up."

Caylie scurried to the ladder as quickly as she could. Meeting her sister at the bottom, they clutched one another's hands and ran to the front porch. They were met with a stiff, cool breeze.

"Oh no! It's cold!" cried Caylie. "Look at the waves on the lake. Daddy's not going to take us on the boat today."

Jenny sighed. "Poop."

"Hey you two," said Ronnie groggily. He was buried under blankets on the corner cot. "Go tell mom to make pancakes."

They had run right past the kitchen and failed to see me, clad in Aunt Bee's yellow flowered apron, already ladling the first round of pancake batter onto the skillet. They both breathed in, savoring the aroma of butter and syrup.

"Pancakes!" they shouted.

"Shhhhh! Don't wake your father on his first day of vacation."

The girls sat down at a picnic table, which served as the cottage's only dining table. It was covered with a red-checked, plastic tablecloth and set with of a rainbow of Fiestaware dishes. At once they picked up their forks and knives and rhythmically banged them on the table in a tom-tom beat. "**More**, *more, more, more!* **More**, *more, more, more* . . . **PANCAKES!"**

Ronnie ambled to the table, scratching his backside. "You're not supposed to say that until you've already had some."

Weather schizophrenia was not unique to Michigan summers. One day it would be hot and humid and the next, we'd have to pull out the Running Rivers sweatshirts and look for knit caps. Since it was too cold to ski or swim, the girls were restless.

Ronnie had taken off to his friend's house, a boy named Joe who lived five cottages over, while Michael and I went to town to get groceries. We left Marie and Darlene in charge of the younger girls. But Marie and Darlene never came out of their room. They spent the morning listening to records.

"If I hear that stupid 'Johnny Angel,' song one more time I'm gonna puke," said Jenny. "Come on Caylie. Let's go outside."

"Are we allowed?"

"Ye-es? C'mon. Let's go over to the Dunlap's place."

With the screen door slamming behind them, Jenny led Caylie across the backyard, which backed up to a thick forest. There were hiking trails leading in myriad directions, one of which led to the Dunlap's small farm just behind the cottage.

Mr. Dunlap was another one of our Mitten Lake regular-characters. Mr. Dunlap had a farm. He always wore overalls and a stained white shirt. He had slicked-back, shoe polish black hair, and the rumor was he had a glass eye because he lost one setting off fireworks when he was a kid.

The bigger attraction at Dunlap's farm was Suzie Dunlap's miniature horse, Sugar. The girls loved Sugar, especially because she had straight blonde bangs just like Caylie's, and because she was so small, they weren't afraid to pet her.

When they reached the white wooden fence surrounding the corral, neither Mr. Dunlap nor Sugar was there. Caylie stooped down and picked white daisies at the base of the fence post and formed a bouquet while Jenny roamed to the opposite end of the corral fence and collected rocks. No one had a bigger rock collection than Jenny Shields.

Holding one rock in each hand she threw one toward Caylie that landed at her feet. "Nice catch," she said.

"I wasn't ready."

Jenny folded up her sweatshirt, making a pocket, and filled it with rocks. But within minutes she let them spill to the ground. "This is boring."

"I'm making this bouquet for Mommy." Caylie stretched out her arm, showing off her collection of daisies. "Like it?"

"No."

"You're mean."

"Hey," Jenny said, "let's go spy on the kids who swing from the trees."

Caylie dropped her daisies. "Jenny! We're not supposed to do that."

"So what? I know where they are."

"You do?"

The kids who swung from the trees were the bad kids. They were Ronnie's age, maybe a bit older. Marie called them "motherless monkeys." Darlene called them "greasers" and "hoodlums." The kids who swung from the trees claimed the thick grapevines draped around the old growth trees belonged to them, and only they were allowed to swing like Tarzan. "Go back to Illinois!" they had shouted at all five of my kids last July during our vacation. "Flatlanders! Get the fuck outta here!"

Jenny returned to Aunt Bee's cottage that day and asked me what the word *fuck* meant. After getting over my shock at hearing my five-year-old utter that repulsive word, I told all of them in very plain terms to stay away from those kids.

To Jenny, last year was old news. This was the year she was going to learn to ski on one *and* she was going to swing on the vines. Surely at the age of six she was old enough. "C'mon," she called to her Irish Twin. "Follow me."

Not waiting for Caylie's answer, Jenny took off into the forest. Her sister stumbled behind her, trying fervently to keep up. Monstrous trees—white and red oaks, hickories, maples, beech trees, and quaking aspens—surrounded them. Sumac shrubs, wildflowers and silver dollars lined the path. The distinct whistles of blue jays punctuated the air.

"Listen," said Caylie. "Michigan birds."

Jenny stopped and listened. "Yeah. Michigan birds. C'mon."

The girls hiked deeper and deeper into the forest along a shadowless path and far away from Aunt Bee's cottage. The sun stayed hidden behind thick gray clouds and they grew cold. Caylie's teeth chattered, and she reached for her sister's hand. Jenny continued to lead them on the unfamiliar path, and she didn't have a clue where she was going. Yet she'd never admit it.

They walked and walked until they heard a loud swooshing sound ahead of them. Jenny stopped abruptly. "What was that?" she asked.

"I'm scared," said Caylie in a tiny voice.

"Don't be a baby. C'mon. This way." She yanked her sister's hand and led her up an embankment. Everything looked brighter at the top and Jenny thought it would help her to get her bearings. But when they got to the top, another car zoomed by—making the same swooshing sound—and they both fell back.

"I think it's Coon Hollow Road!" said Jenny.

"Which way's the cottage?" whined Caylie. "I wanna go back! I don't want to see those stupid kids. Mommy said we weren't supposed to Jenny."

Jenny bit her finger. "I'm not sure." Absently, she led her sister along the solid white line of the narrow, two-lane road. Behind her she heard Caylie sniffling, and within moments her own eyes filled with tears.

The two little girls realized they were lost. Jenny knew she was going to be in big trouble. Then they heard a shout. "Hey you! Hey you kids!"

Turning in unison, their eyes cast downward into the forest, again they heard someone call to them. "Hey! Little girls!" A teenaged girl with long, blonde braids emerged. She was with a boy who looked a little like Ronnie.

"It's the kids who swing from the trees!" screamed Caylie.

Jenny stepped in front of her sister. "Leave us alone!" she cried.

"We're not gonna hurt you," said the girl with the braids. She didn't look like a mean girl. She looked nice. And she smiled. "Your mom's down there looking for you."

"No she's not!" said Jenny.

"How does she know our mom?" Caylie asked.

"Be quiet." Jenny saw the bushes behind the kids rustle almost violently. How many more were there? She squeezed Caylie's hand and watched as a gray head of hair encased in a hairnet emerged from the shrubs.

"Jenny! Caylie! There you are you little rug rats," the woman attached to the hairnet said with an exhausted puff of air. It was Aunt Bee, of course, and Jenny and Caylie had never been more relieved to see anyone in their lives. The old woman dropped to her knees after climbing the embankment and the girls ran into her waiting arms.

"I stopped by to give your mother a kettle I bought for the cottage since I know how much she likes to drink tea," she said. "Your sisters had no idea where you two had gotten to."

"Jenny wanted to see the kids who swing from the trees."

"Shut up Caylie!"

"The vine trees are way back over there," said the girl with blonde braids. "We can take you there."

"No, no. Not today," said Aunt Bee. "I best be getting these youngins' back to my cottage before their folks return from town."

"Okay," said Braids. "But anytime you want to swing, we can come by and get you."

"Now, now. I don't think they're old enough for that," said Aunt Bee.

"We're never old enough for anything," said Caylie.

Jenny headed back down the embankment toward the forest and called over her shoulder. "Speak for yourself, squirt."

"I'm not a squirt," cried Caylie.

When they returned to the cottage, Aunt Bee reported to Marie and Darlene that she found the Irish Twins at the Dunlap farm, which was still within their boundaries. And with a furtive wink, she told Jenny and Caylie that their secret was safe with her. Caylie spent the rest of the two-week vacation creating detailed drawings of the cottage on the fronts and backs of paper plates, the only drawing paper she could find. Each had a label reading, "From Caylie Shields." They were gifts for her new best friend, Aunt Bee.

Later that year when we were back in Grossdale where we looked out our windows onto a gray, curbed street rather than the waves of Mitten Lake, and with the songs of the robins and the noisy whistles of the blue jays a distant memory, we'd gotten word that Aunt Bee had died peacefully in her sleep.

No one cried harder than my Caylie.

Pained by the memory of my daughter's genuine hurt over losing

Aunt Bee, once again I saw grown-up Caylie through the steam of the orange cup. She was nestled in the beanbag chair, asleep, and dreaming of Mitten Lake.

A trio of voices shouted for her. "Mom!"

Startled, Caylie swore. "Jesus Christ! Can I get just five minutes?" She forced open her heavy lids and the first thing she saw was the suede corduroy orange of the beanbag chair. She ran her hand across her throbbing forehead, and it landed with a thud into the chair. "How long have I been here?"

"Mom, wake up! Dad's here. We're leaving for Michigan. Don't you even want to say goodbye?"

"I really don't want to go, Mom," said Frankie. "This is so freaking unfair."

I closed my eyes. Oh, how I knew what it was like to feel the pain of a broken marriage. When our father left us, Molly and I never knew why, and we didn't talk about it. But I know we shared the feeling that it was because of us.

Caylie's children felt the same way.

I wondered if Caylie had done everything she could to make it work with Robert. Was it really the right decision to leave him and have the children shuffle back-and-forth?

When things had grown a little rocky in my marriage—when Michael grew impatient with the children or when he verbalized his prejudices in front of them—I made every effort to honor my vows. I stuck by my husband, for better or for worse, even when it ultimately meant leaving my youngest children.

Caylie didn't ask for my opinions about if she should marry or divorce Robert Cotrell and I didn't offer them. I will therefore never know whether or not I would have advised her not to take vows with him. I knew people on the verge of either decision don't want to hear anyone disagree with them.

A tingle at the base of my neck arose and a medicinal smell enveloped me. "Molly?"

Turning to my right, I saw a figure approach. It was a woman, but it wasn't Molly. She was older and bigger. I watched as she removed the linen tea cozy with the faded robin, picked up the orange teakettle and brought it toward me. Her skin was luminous, yet it had the quality of leather. I scanned her face from bottom to top, where I saw the familiar hairnet. She smiled and filled my cup.

"Hello Mrs. Shields," she said. "It's nice to see you again."

"Hello Mrs. Bowers."

"May I call you Anne?"

"Of course," I said, returning her smile. "But only if I can call you Aunt Bee."

CHAPTER 5

Aunt Bee filled another orange cup using her old kettle, and then took the cup from my hand. She set it upon a picnic table with a red and white checked tablecloth, and then extended her arm, inviting me to sit down. "I've been waiting for you, Anne."

"But I—"

"You haven't thought of me in years?" Aunt Bee laughed and maneuvered her robust frame between the table and the bench.

"Actually, I was just thinking of you."

"I know," she said. "It's why I'm here. I was always terribly fond of you and your family. I thought you were the perfect family." She took a moment to look me up-and-down, from head to toe, and she grinned. "My, my. You always did wear the most stylish bathing suits. You look like a Miss America contestant."

"Excuse me?" I looked down. I was dressed in a navy blue, one-piece Catalina swimsuit. It had a rounded neckline and a full skirt. "How did I—?"

"You died while water-skiing."

"But I wasn't wearing *this* suit." I remembered this navy blue swimsuit, however. Bringing my hands to my shoulders, I felt buttons at the shoulder straps, knowing they'd be there.

"No, it was from the early days—as you called them—at Mitten Lake," said Aunt Bee as she filled my cup. "My last days at Mitten Lake."

I sat. "Well, I didn't die while skiing. I was in the water attached to a ski. I haven't worn this suit since—"

"Since the last summer I saw you." Aunt Bee sipped her tea. "I used to love watching you and your family ski round and round Mitten Lake. Your husband's shoulders grew redder than a boiled lobster with each passing day for how much time he spent in the sun. We didn't really know about that so-called melanoma cancer back then did we?"

"No. A lot has changed in the world."

"And the world will go on changing without us."

"Yes, I suppose you're right." I sighed. "You were always very kind to us, Mrs. Bowers."

"Well, I admired you! Every year I looked forward to the two weeks your family came to Mitten Lake. With all those kids, it put life into the little cottage. And they were all so cute—especially that little Caylie."

"Yes, Caylie. I'm afraid she's feeling lost right now."

"She is. And she's behaving the way she's behaved since the day she was lost with her sister on Coon Hollow Road. She's waiting for a rescue."

"How do you know?"

"Dear, the reason I'm here is because you remembered how sad she was when I passed over. Your grief at the time was for her—not for me. But look, she moved ahead and has led a productive and fascinating life." She placed her hand atop of mine. "Listen to me, you're going to learn more about your children now than you knew when you were alive."

"And this is all a part of my judgment?"

"Precisely."

I looked into the tea and recalled Caylie's dream of the early days at Mitten Lake. Because her life was currently in turmoil, she called to mind a happier, more innocent time. A time when she was lost, yet found. This time, however, she wasn't relying on her sister, Jenny, to guide her. Deep down she knew marrying Albert wasn't the answer, but just as I couldn't tell her not to marry her childhood sweetheart, I couldn't—nor could Jenny—advise her on whether or not to marry Albert Powell.

"Your children will continue making decisions on their own," said Aunt Bee. "You taught both Caylie and Jenny how do that at a young age."

It's understandable why Caylie continually returned to Mitten Lake in her dreams. There was no question we all loved being there. But the experience changed the year after Aunt Bee died and we could no longer rent her cottage. Her sister, Hilda, sold the property and the new owners immediately tore down our beloved cottage and built a stylish A-frame. Michael found a new place to rent, a larger guesthouse on the hill behind one of the lake's historical homes, the Hudson estate. It was certainly more accommodating for our large family, but it didn't hold the same degree of magic as Aunt Bee's cottage. Caylie, for example, never drew pictures of it. With each passing year, Mitten Lake became less and less magical for all my children.

As teenagers, Marie and Darlene were blasé about family vacations, preferring to spend the afternoons covering their bodies with baby oil and soaking up the sun. Every night they ran off with their friends to the town of Running Rivers and hung out at the drive-in. Thankfully they stayed out of trouble. Ronnie soon began working at the Mitten Lake YMCA camp in any job he could get—a lifeguard, a counselor, even the kitchen staff. Only Jenny and Caylie kept the magic alive. Even when they were teenagers, they were content skiing and swimming all day, and catching fireflies at night. They fed off one another's energy and I truly felt they kept me young.

Aunt Bee reminded me how Jenny and Caylie were always together, laughing and singing—collecting wildflowers and rocks, and calling one another "Sissy." I felt so lucky to witness what would become their lovely childhood memories, especially because, aside from my close relationship with Molly, my own childhood memories held little joy.

"Their childhood was quite different than the one you shared with your sister Molly," said Aunt Bee. "And it was you who made it that way for them."

I looked into my tea, and an image of my father formed. His name was Patrick Monaghan. He was first generation American, the fourth son of Catherine and Joseph Monaghan, both refugees of Ireland's great Potato Famine. I never knew my grandparents; however, my grandmother was known in their town of Lynn, Massachusetts for her extensive garden. My grandfather, Joseph, was the son of a fisherman, and he worked any job he could get at Lynn Harbor.

Father attended school through fifth grade, the longest of any of his brothers. He dropped out after finding a job as an apprentice, or a "seamster" as it was called, at a shoe crafting shop. He was one of three boys who sewed shoes for the master shoemaker in a ten-foot by ten-foot space. Soon, with the invention of the shoe lasting machine, the town of Lynn boasted the first mass production of shoes. It became known as "the shoe capital of the world."

I still have no idea how my parents met. And I have few, if any, memories of them together. Neither has come to me since my arrival in *Ohr*; however, first Molly and now Aunt Bee, continually assured me with every cup of tea more would be revealed.

My sister, Molly, was born in 1918 and then I came along in 1919. At that time our father had worked his way to leather cutter. Unfortunately, he lost his job during the economic downturn of the early 1920s, and so he turned to the gardening skills he had learned from his mother. We had an enormous yard in the town of Melrose, where we lived in a house owned by our mother's family. I remember Father spending all his time tending his vegetables and managing a green grocer business.

I was nine when the business failed and that's when he left us.

My mother gave piano lessons to keep food on our table and Molly and I took whatever jobs we could find to help out. We had never even heard the term "family vacation."

I'm not sure my children realized how lucky they were. I chose not to tell them about my difficult childhood and therefore, their body of knowledge about the world was based on their own education and experience, not mine. And this was one big difference between Michael and me.

I didn't begrudge my children their privileges.

In 1972 Mr. Hudson, owner of the notorious Mitten Lake Hudson estate, reportedly had run into some tax issues. Parceling off his acreage, he offered Michael a piece of lakefront property. Ten thousand dollars seemed an enormous sum, but for lakefront property, my husband assured me it was a bargain. Mind you, he didn't consult me about the purchase. He merely informed me of the decision.

That's how our marriage worked.

Two years later he obtained a loan from the Running Rivers First National Bank and met with a builder to formulate plans for his dream house. This was the same bank that gave us the set of avocado Stoneware dishes when we signed the loan papers. Choosing avocado green over harvest orange was the only decision I was allowed to make.

The new house, "Our Dream House," as Michael called it, had only two bedrooms, an enormous one for us with a one hundred, eighty-degree view of the lake, and a tiny one "for when the kids came to visit." Because Jenny and Caylie still had high school in front of them, we referred to this second bedroom as "the twins' room;" yet I knew Michael had no intention of having any of his children living there. We all used it for family vacations, but he couldn't wait for our Irish Twins to grow up so he could get out of Grossdale and live at the lake full time.

He couldn't wait, and he didn't.

* * *

It rained all morning, threatening the likelihood of an outdoor ceremony. By three o'clock, however, the West Grossdale High School principal decided the football field was dry enough to set up even rows of folding chairs for the 424 graduates making up the class of 1979.

Caylie's three-inch heels sank into the soft grass making her wobble as she tried to maintain an expression of dignity required of the prom queen. Parents and family members filling the concrete stadium fanned the thick June air with their stapled-paper programs. Michael and I, our son, Ronnie, and eldest daughter, Marie, were the only family members present for Caylie. When her name was announced over the loud speaker, however, there was an outburst of applause and whistles.

She certainly was the most popular of my five children.

Marie elbowed me—a bad habit. "Hey Ma. How does it feel to have the last of your brood make it through high school?"

I didn't respond. I understood my children were meant to grow up and leave me. But I didn't understand why shortly after the ceremony it would be the other way around.

"C'mon," said Ronnie. "Let's go find her before she runs off with her friends. I've got somewhere I need to be."

"I see her," said Marie. "She's looking for her mortar cap."

Michael was edgy. "When did they start throwing their caps? Are they trying to start off their adult lives with a bunch of head injuries?"

Their adult lives.

Yes, that's what my husband believed. High school graduation was his definition of parental emancipation. He had a red circle around the June 7 graduation date of his fifth and final child on his basement calendar for months. His plan was to finish packing and leave for Michigan that night.

"One photo, Anne. And that's it. We've already said our goodbyes."

Marie and I locked eyes. She mouthed a single word. "Unbelievable."

Along with her husband, John Reynolds, and their sons, Marie lived only two miles from our Grossdale home. Having her so close was the justification I used for leaving my seventeen-year-old daughter alone. That and Jenny, who was eighteen, would be back from college in less than two weeks. In a letter she had informed me she that she landed a high paying position in the production department of the university newspaper between the spring and summer terms. Jenny claimed she couldn't pass up the job because she needed to earn money to pay for her second year. She added that she'd be sharing a house with three young men after the dorms closed, but assured me they were "like brothers." She offered the information breezily; however, I was horrified about her living in a co-ed situation. I kept this from Michael even though he never asked when or if she'd be home. He was busy making his own plans.

We made our way down the concrete steps of the stadium and milled around with the other parents all trying to locate their graduates. Caylie's boyfriend, Robert, found us first. "She's right over there," he said, eyeing the camera hanging around Michael's neck. "Follow me. I'll get a picture of all of you."

Robert had been Caylie's steady boyfriend since middle school. An amiable kid, he was a little cheap for my tastes, always managing to "forget his wallet" whenever we were out. I believed she could have done much better than the likes of Robert Cottrell. "Caylie!" he shouted, far too close to my ear.

She turned and her long blonde hair swung around to one shoulder. The blue graduation gown brought out the color of her eyes. Without a doubt our fifth child, the perfect combination of Michael as a young sailor at Virginia Beach and my lovely sister, Molly, was our masterpiece. Occasionally I remembered how miserable I'd been while pregnant with her so late in life; however, since the moment I first laid eyes upon her I never regretted her birth. My beautiful girl flashed us a high-beam smile and waved.

Robert awkwardly positioned Marie and Ronnie on either side of Caylie and suggested her father and I bookend the group. "That's perfect." He stepped back and then raised the camera to his face. "Now say 'cheese!' "A flash bulb exploded, momentarily filling our eyes with blue light.

Caylie broke free and reached for the camera. "Hey Dad, will you get one of Robert and me?"

"One more and then we've got to take off. I want to get out of town before dark."

Caylie forced a smile for the camera, and her father failed to notice the beams of light fade from her eyes. We kissed her goodbye and went in four different directions. Caylie ran off hand-in-hand with Robert. Ronnie went to a meeting to finalize his plans for a summer job. Marie headed home to her husband and children, and I followed Michael back to our home of twenty-three years. It would be the last time the word "home" would apply to this house.

Michael's final act before leaving Grossdale for good was to hammer a FOR SALE sign in the front yard. I swear there was more ceremony displayed in this action than there was from him at Caylie's graduation. As he closed the car door and turned our packed car to the north, he felt as though his life were beginning again.

To me, however, it was an end to everything.

Oh, how I wanted to wait those two weeks for Jenny to return home. But Michael wouldn't hear of it. And so I quietly followed him—the same way I followed him from Melrose to Grossdale and now from Grossdale to Mitten Lake.

Again, it was how our marriage worked.

Ten days later I was still trying to wrap my mind around the idea of the Mitten Lake house as my home and Running Rivers instead of Grossdale as my town. It was that day, a Sunday, when Jenny returned from her first year of college.

One of her temporary roommates, a mop-headed boy named Steve, provided the ride. He was from the nearby suburb of Hillside and planned to be home for a week before going back south.

"I know this neighborhood," he said after turning off Grossdale Road. "I went out with a girl who lived near here."

"What's her name?"

"Patricia Something," he said. "Riley maybe?"

"Patricia Riley? You actually went out with that skank? She's like five years older than us."

"What can I say? She put out."

"That's pathetic." Jenny reached down to collect her purse and backpack. "Third house on the right. Red bricks." Jenny wondered if anyone would be home. She had spent the last four weeks in a house without a phone and had had no communication with anyone in the family.

"I see it." Steve pulled in the driveway, maneuvered the gearshift and turned the key. The tired, rusty Datsun hiccoughed before turning off completely.

She straightened and looked out the window, seeing the FOR SALE sign in the middle of the lawn. It took away her breath. "What the *fuck* is that?"

"What the fuck is what?"

Jenny threw out her arm, pointing across Steve's chest. "That. *THAT!* I don't believe it. My parents didn't think it was necessary to tell me they were selling the house?"

"They didn't tell you?"

"No! I mean I knew they were eventually going to move to Mitten Lake but I didn't know it would be this soon." She slammed the car door and followed the ribbon of driveway to the backyard. Steve trailed behind her carrying her duffel bags.

The backdoor was open and they both walked into the kitchen. "Hello?" called Jenny. "Anybody home?"

The kitchen table was the only thing in the room. The hutch was gone, and the small desk that had normally been full of mail and important papers wasn't there either. Cookie jars, recipe boxes and utensil containers, the antique tea caddy, had all been removed from the counters. She poked her head into the dining room. Empty. The living room held only two canvas director's chairs. The room seemed large for the first time in her life. In fact, to her it was cavernous and it smelled like the disinfectant used in public bathrooms.

Steve lifted her bags. "Where shall I put these?"

"Drop them anywhere. Obviously there's plenty of space. Man, I don't even know if I have a bed here."

A voice came from behind them. "Jenny! I didn't know you were coming back today."

Jenny and Steve both turned to see Caylie at the top of the basement stairs. "Caylie! You're here!" Jenny walked toward her and gave her a quick hug. "What's going on? Are Mom and Dad gone?"

"Surprise! Welcome to the bachelorette pad."

"The bachelorette pad? You're here . . . alone?"

"Yeah, and I get the basement. It's too hot up in the attic and Dad's not paying for air conditioning. You can sleep in Ronnie's old room. But you have to keep everything clean. The scumbag realtor they hired pops in at all hours with prospective buyers. But he only brings in the Mexicans after dark. So be prepared."

Jenny threw back her head. "What does *that* mean?"

Steve dropped her bags to the bare wooden floor. His face had taken on a glazed-over expression—an expression most young men exhibited when first laying eyes on Caylie. "I'm Steve, by the way" he said. "Jenny's friend." He reached out his hand for a shake but Caylie kept both hands firmly planted on her hips.

"Hi," she said absently. "And I'm having people over tonight so you might want to make yourself scarce. No offense, Stan."

"Caylie! What the fuck? I'm meeting someone in the city tomorrow morning about a job. I've got to get up at six to get to the train, and I'll probably have to ride my bike. Wait, are there any bikes left in the garage?"

"Not my problem." Caylie turned and closed the basement door behind her. They heard her footsteps descend the stairs.

"Nice girl," said Steve. "Did she just call me Stan?"

Jenny shook her head. "I have no idea what's happening here. Sorry Steve."

"Whatever. Listen, you've got another bag in the Datsun. I'll get it and then I better 'make myself scarce.' I'm around for a week before I go back. Call me if you wanna do something."

"Thanks but I doubt I'll have time. If everything works out like I've planned, I'll have three jobs by the end of the week."

"You're kidding, right? Summer's supposed to be for relaxing. You should spend some time recovering from freshman year. Don't ya think?"

"Yeah, well, my parents aren't paying for college from here on out. They gave me the first year. That's it. So, I don't have a choice."

"Bummer," he said, and walked out the kitchen door.

Jenny opened the basement door. Greeting her was the familiar, faint smell of springtime flooding, an annual neighborhood occurrence. It was a half-finished room with plywood paneling and speckled tile floors. The setting for all of their adolescent slumber parties, a six-foot pyramid of RC cola cans still stood in the corner next to an old Westinghouse refrigerator. She noticed her dad's two-door cabinet that housed his 78-vinyl collection, record player, and hi-fi on one side, and his liquor on the other, was as gone as almost all the other furniture in the house.

A folding screen sectioned off the back half of the room. Jenny peeked beyond it to see Caylie lounging on a twin bed and looking through a magazine. The dresser and vanity from their attic bedroom as well as a television made the bedroom complete.

"Looks good down here," Jenny said. "Where'd you get the TV?"

"It's mine. Robert's dad gave it to me. And you can't use it. Like I said, you get the upstairs. This is my apartment now."

"Your apartment? Give me a break."

"You can go back upstairs now."

"Caylie! Aren't you the least bit happy to see me?"

"Happy? You didn't even come to my graduation, Jenny! How do you think that made me feel?"

"I *couldn't* make it back. I was over 300 miles away. You know that. And besides, I had to work."

"Yeah, right. Whatever. Get out of here. I told you I've got friends coming over."

"And I told you I have a job to go to early in the morning."

"Boo-hoo."

"Gee Caylie, did you forget to take your nice pills today?"

"Ha-ha, very funny. See ya!"

Jenny put her hands on her hips and shook her head. "So this is your life now? Your own bachelorette pad with parties every night? Did you even look for a summer job?"

Caylie tossed her magazine aside. "I'm not *you* Jenny. I don't feel the need to work every waking minute of the day."

"You think I want to work three jobs? I do it because I have to! And so do you."

"Are you my mother now?"

"Who's going to buy your food? And what are you planning to use for spending money at school next year?"

"Don't worry about it. I'll be fine."

"You're an idiot, Caylie. And it smells like sewer down here." Jenny pushed the tri-fold room divider and it crashed to the tile floor with an ear-piercing slap.

"You bitch!" screamed Caylie.

Jenny ran up the stairs, closed the basement door and saw Steve enter the kitchen with her last bag."What was that noise?" he asked.

"It was the sound of my sister's life crashing before her eyes."

"I thought you two were close," he said.

"So did I."

* * *

By watching the reunion of my daughters after their first year apart, I learned how the rift had developed between them. During that year, Jenny had grown up quickly. In school she not only fulfilled her general studies requirements, but she also learned the meaning of responsibility. She learned to get herself to class, to find work to support her lifestyle, and even to do her own laundry. At eighteen, just as her father had planned, she was a bona fide adult.

Caylie, on the other hand, was still a child—an abandoned child.

The big difference between their reactions to our leaving was that Jenny openly resented Michael and me from the moment she first saw the FOR SALE sign. Caylie didn't recognize the anger and resentment inside her. She thought it was "cool" having the house to herself. And then Jenny came home and spoiled that. Jenny was and had always been a looking glass into her future. And it was a future Caylie wasn't ready to see. She blamed Jenny for abandoning her at her graduation ceremony instead of blaming her father and me for ending her childhood so abruptly.

I closed my eyes. "I should have never left them alone," I said to Aunt Bee.

But it wasn't Aunt Bee who stood at my side. It was Molly. "We give birth to them," she said. "We raise them, we love them. But we all leave them to live their own lives. You knew from the day you married Michael that you would always put his needs first."

"But I never anticipated my children would suffer because of it."

"They didn't suffer, Anne. They grew up."

CHAPTER 6

When I was still alive, my favorite cup—they call them *mugs*—was blue. It was from the University of Michigan and it was a gift from our daughter Darlene. I was so proud of her for putting herself through medical school. In my wildest dreams, I never believed that one of my children would become a doctor. I thought only doctors spawned doctors. My second-born child, however, managed to not only acquire a white collar, but also a white jacket.

In *Ohr*, where the concept of time eluded me, I held a blue mug with a golden "M." With Molly at my side, I sipped my tea and through the steam I saw Michael—the man who I believed defined me.

During a marriage—especially one that lasts for over fifty years—we spend so much time thinking about our partner. "What God has joined, let no man separate." These were the words by which I had lived. By definition, we—man and woman—became one. When I married Michael, I truly understood the meaning of the word "we," and from that day forward, I was no longer Anne or Annie Monaghan. I was Mrs. Michael Shields.

After the births of my children, I was renamed once again. First I was Marie's mom. Then, Darlene and Marie's mom. Soon I was the mother of three, "two girls and a boy." Ultimately I became the mother of Irish Twins and we were known as "The Shields Family—the one with all the kids."

From the time I was married, I don't remember ever being just plain Anne.

Since my death, Michael tried to keep my essence alive by sleeping next to my Michigan ball cap, the cap I always wore when riding in our boat. It was the same color as the mug I held, and it had the same solitary "M." On his first night alone in our bed, he placed the cap on my pillow, and each subsequent night before turning out the lights, he kissed the brim. "Goodnight Mommy," he said.

Michael had called me Mommy from the day our first child, Marie, was born. He only called me "Anne" when he was angry—or very serious about something. Whether he kept the cap in place to capture or reminisce about the essence of Anne the woman, Anne the wife or Anne the mother, I cannot know, nor is it for me to judge.

After I died he moved around in a fog. He didn't clean out the drawers or rearrange the items hanging in any of the closets. He didn't move a single shoe. He believed if he left my possessions in place, I was somehow still in the house.

I *was* there, but not because he didn't move my things.

When that first summer ended and the leaves fell from the trees, our children insisted he leave the lake and spend time with them. It was the first time in his life that he let his children tell him what to do.

While packing, he purposefully left the blue cap on my pillow.

Michael left Mitten Lake shortly before Thanksgiving, and first stayed with Marie in Grossdale, then Darlene in Atlanta. From there he worked his way through the progeny line and went to Phoenix to be with Ronnie. By June, he was with Jenny in San Diego. When Molly topped off my Michigan mug, this is where I saw him as I looked through the steam of the tea.

* * *

"Still sleeping," said Jenny. She looked tired, even haggard. Her face was drawn, her hair pulled into a high ponytail, with uncombed tendrils spilling like a waterfall atop her head. Stepping back from the picture window of her guesthouse bedroom, she folded her arms, sighed, and glanced at her wristwatch. Both hands straight up. Twelve noon.

"He's worse than a teenager," she said with a sigh.

Her father's sleeping body took up most of the double bed. The mound of pastel blankets covering everything but a crop of silver hair, showed little sign of life. These days he was always cold. Even on sunny, Southern California days, his grief had left him exposed and shivering.

The anniversary of my death was looming, and during the past year, he had grown increasingly frail. Jenny furrowed her brow and prayed silently, and I heard her.

Please don't let him die in that bed.

She focused on the handprint she'd left on the glass. It could have been from the previous day. Or even the day before. He'd been staying with her for just over a week, and after the first two days, she developed the habit of checking whether or not her father was awake before bringing him a powdered doughnut, orange juice and the morning newspaper.

I sipped my tea and realized that Jenny never dreamed I would die before her father.

Sunlight bounced around the yard, reflecting off the azure water of the swimming pool. The coastal breeze had been escalating all morning, causing the fans of tall palm trees to fill the air with whispers. Jenny took a moment to admire the warm weather growth of her landscaping, a scene she had tried to recreate from a photo in *Sunset* magazine and without the help of her sister, Caylie, the landscape architect. She breathed in the sweet scent of jasmine from a mature vine clinging to the bamboo trellis against the guesthouse.

"What is that lovely, intoxicating smell?" I used to ask every time I inhaled it.

"It's jasmine, Mom. See the pinkish, white flowers over there?"

During the last three years of my life, I asked this same question of my daughter at least four or five times during our San Diego visits. That and, "what time does *Jeopardy* come on at your house?" At first this drove Jenny crazy; however, her sister-the-doctor informed all her siblings that the repeated questions were only symptoms of the mini strokes I had experienced. "It's more funny than tragic," Darlene had said. She encouraged Jenny and the others to try to find the humor in what was essentially a form of dementia. "When it comes to the human condition, if you can, it's better to laugh than to cry."

In my last years on earth, I knew I was losing my mind a tad. I'd had an uncle who suffered from Alzheimer's, and it was why, as Molly pointed out, I desperately copied and recopied my recipe books after the first two stroke episodes. I tried whatever *Good*

Housekeeping tip offered to me to keep my mind sharp.

As a military plane cut through the clear sky above her, Jenny approached the trellis and pressed her nose to the sticky, tubular flowers. Listening to what she thought was Darlene's voice in her head, oh, how she wanted to laugh. Instead, however, her eyes filled with tears. I heard her prayers. They were more like regrets. What she wouldn't give to hear me ask about this lovely, intoxicating smell just one more time.

One.

More.

Time.

Tightening her ponytail and then smoothing the wiry, flyaway grays sprouting among her once lustrous red curls, she couldn't help but notice a hummingbird suddenly throbbing above her head. The tiny bird startled her, and she jumped back from the trellis. Mesmerized by its stunning, metallic colors glistening in the sunlight, she watched as it poked its long, narrow bill into a jasmine flower. The bird moved from flower to flower. Its movements were jerky and somehow, desperate. Jenny marveled at the wing-speed capable of making such a powerful noise. She pursed her lips and rolled her tongue, mimicking the sound.

Instantly, as though hearing her communication, the hummingbird pulled away from the vine and faced her. Jenny would have sworn it looked right into her eyes.

And it most certainly did.

With her father sleeping away the day in the guesthouse, the kids at day camp and Don at work, Jenny only had the previous night's dishes to keep her busy. Filling every available space in the dishwasher, she turned to the pots and pans. I taught her to never put them in the dishwasher. "Dishes with which you eat in the dishwasher," I instructed. "Dishes with which you cook in the sink." On a daily basis, my words of household wisdom—delivered with flawless, Catholic school grammar—came to my daughter like a bulleted list. It's what I left behind, and Jenny was the living legacy of my career as a housewife.

Jenny sometimes wondered if that would have made me proud, or it would have made me cringe. She was actually thinking about herself. There was never any question for her that she'd go to college and become something other than a mere housewife—other than her mother. That she ended up a lot like me may have made her cringe, but it made me proud.

I was proud of all my children; however, Jenny believed I was only truly proud of Darlene the doctor. She thought nothing could compare to the golden stethoscope Darlene wore around her neck. In Jenny's eyes, that she worked her way from an entry-level proofreader to an editor at *Chicago* magazine before she got married was of little import to me. She was wrong, of course, but I do know I was relieved when Jenny quit her job to plan her wedding.

"Are you making your bed everyday, dear?" I asked her regularly. I suppose the role of wife was the only one in which I was qualified to mentor any of my daughters. And I was definitely proud of Jenny for having such a good marriage; however, I realized she was not and could never be the kind of wife I was to Michael. For one thing, as much as I knew Jenny loved Don, she would *never* abandon her daughters to follow him to his retirement from fatherhood. Or would she? Her daughters were still young. Still sweet.

Jenny turned on the water and tested the temperature by holding her hand in the stream. That's when the phone rang. Why, she wondered, did it always ring when her hands were wet? I used to wonder the same thing. She reached for the receiver and waited for caller ID to activate. Two rings. Nothing. Caller ID had been failing all week. She took a chance and answered it.

"Hello?"

"Jen-ny?"

Relieved it wasn't a fourth grade room-mother asking her to volunteer for something, she knew at once it was her sister Caylie. And even though she hadn't heard it in two months, she knew by the sound of her sister's voice that something was wrong. "What's the matter?"

"I didn't get the job."

She had no idea what Caylie was talking about. Jenny held up her right hand, palm down, and examined her chipped, unpolished nails. "What job would that be, Caylie? A landscaping job you bid on, or what?"

"Didn't Don tell you? I gave him the whole story when I called on his birthday."

"His birthday? That was, like, over a month ago."

"I know."

"Wait a minute. Are you referring to your new status as Albert Powell's fiancé as a job?"

"What?"

"The only thing Don told me was that you were getting married to Albert."

"Oh, that." Caylie was completely nonchalant. "No, not that. Business is really slow so I applied for a job in the City Planner's office. I was on the short list and thought I had it nailed."

Jenny threw back her head. *What was she talking about?* "Caylie, I haven't spoken with you in ages. You can't expect me to know all the details of your business life. So, the city of San Francisco had an opening for a landscape architect?"

"It was Moraga, actually. A town in the East Bay with good schools. I was definitely willing to become a resident."

She wondered if it were possible that Don *did* mention this back on his birthday, and she didn't hear anything beyond Caylie's impending marriage to Albert. "Oh. Well. Sorry."

"I really didn't figure on being out of work this long. I was outbid on my last three proposals. And Robert's being a champion prick about the money. He won't even buy the boys new shoes. He cares more about refugees in Africa than he does his own kids."

"Sounds like Robert's just being Robert."

"Yeah, well, Mom always said he was cheap."

"Too bad she waited to offer her opinion until after you divorced him."

There. Right. I shook my head, mimicking my daughter as she shook her own head. She believed I was notorious for not speaking up about the things that were truly on my mind. Of course, she was correct, and Jenny further believed this was a trait I passed on to Caylie.

The last time her sister actually came right out and asked Jenny for money was to pay her divorce lawyer's retainer. Then again, maybe it was the money she needed to start her own landscaping business. Jenny actually couldn't remember. She'd written so many checks over the years, both before and after her sister's divorce, she'd clearly lost count.

Normally during their conversations, this would be the point where the Irish Twins commiserated over Caylie's unreasonable ex-husband, Jenny felt sorry for her, and then offered to send money. But instead of reaching for her checkbook, Jenny pulled open a drawer and fished for a nail file. "So, how does Albert feel about moving out of the city for any potential job you might get?"

"I don't know. I didn't really discuss it with him."

Jenny let out an exasperated sigh, closed the elongated junk drawer of the kitchen bar counter and opened the one next to it. Was Caylie ever going to tell her about her plans to get married again? "What do you mean you didn't discuss it with Albert?"

"That's not why I called you, Jenny."

"Caylie! Are you actually planning to marry this guy? I mean, you didn't even bother to call me and tell me about it. Instead you tell Don?"

"Well, you could have called me once you heard the news."

"I'm pretty sure you don't want my opinion on the matter. And I'm definitely sure you remember what I said when you told me you were marrying Robert."

"Don't start," she said. "Okay?"

"I don't believe for one second you're going to go through with this."

"How's Dad doing? He's there, right?"

An image of Michael appeared before me. He was stirring out in the guesthouse. Finally awake.

"Aha!" cried Jenny, pulling my attention back into her kitchen. At last she found an emery board. She used her hip to close the drawer. Fine, she thought. Change the subject. She didn't really want to talk about Albert either. The loser. She tucked the phone between her ear and shoulder and went after the chipped pinkie nail on her left hand. "How's Dad, you ask? He's sleeping. It's practically all he does."

"At two in the afternoon?"

Jenny glanced up at the kitchen clock. Caylie was right. Where had the day gone? "He's depressed Cay. I hate to tell you, but he's withering away. I have to force him to eat."

There was no response. She moved the emery board to her ring finger. "Hello?"

"How long's he staying with you?" asked Cayle.

"I don't know. I think we should wait until after the one-year anniversary of Mom's death to take him back to the lake. Maybe I'll wait till the end of the month and then the girls and I will go with him and spend a week or two. San Diego's getting far too touristy. All the desert dwellers are here."

"He's not coming to *my* place?"

"Where would he stay? You barely have enough room for your kids."

"Right. That. Well, not all of us can afford a guesthouse."

"Please Caylie, don't make me apologize for my lifestyle."

This was where my daughters' paths truly diverged. When it came to marriage, Jenny got lucky. Caylie, on the other hand, got Robert. And now she wanted to add Albert? It was amazing how one choice, a choice you think you believe you made for all the right reasons, could entirely alter your life.

Jenny caught a glimpse of herself in the oven door, and focused on the deep, vertical line between her eyebrows. She was horrified. It was just like her dad's.

"Hey, how about we go to Mitten Lake at the same time," Caylie suggested. "The kids could all bunk together in the living room."

"Hmmm, yeah." Jenny was not interested. She moved away from the disappointing oven reflection and brought the nail file to her middle finger. She didn't want to share our Mitten Lake house with Caylie and her boys. And, she wondered, would Caylie be married by then? Would Albert be with them? Would he be blowing his boozy breath and off-color jokes all over the place while always looking for someone more interesting to talk to? "Dad told me the boys were already in Michigan with Robert over Memorial Day weekend."

"Yeah, they stayed over on Mud Lake."

"Ha!" In spite of her annoyance with Caylie, Jenny couldn't help but laugh. Robert's family had a summer cottage not on Mud Lake, of course, but on Harland Lake, about five miles from our Mitten Lake home. Michigan was the connection between Caylie and Robert. They had been classmates since kindergarten, but first spoke to one another in seventh grade when Caylie was only thirteen. That's when they realized they had Michigan in common. The next time they were both at their family cottages, this coincidence led to late night kissing next to the campfire under a velvet black sky filled with glittering stars.

Caylie then made the mistake of trying to turn her summer romance into a marriage. Five minutes after earning her bachelors degree, she fulfilled her white lace dreams by wearing a vintage wedding gown she found at a local Thrift Store. She had wanted to wear mine; however, I didn't own my gown. I had borrowed it. This was very disappointing for Caylie because she believed if she could wear my gown, she, too, could have a marriage that would have the long-term duration of ours.

She was too naive to know it took a lot more than a wedding gown.

Eight years, four of them living together in East Africa, and three children later, the marriage between Caylie and Robert was over.

"They didn't even go to Mitten Lake," said Caylie. "With Dad away there was no reason."

"I'm not sure there's a good reason to take Dad back there now," said Jenny. "I don't like the idea of leaving him alone, Cay. I think we should look into some kind of in-home care or assisted living. All five of us can split the cost."

"I can't afford to support Dad, Jenny. I can't even afford to support myself. I told you business was slow. And why can't he just move into your guesthouse?"

"He doesn't want to. He wants to go back to the lake."

Caylie sighed. "Wouldn't we all?"

With her nails in satisfactory condition and not wanting to talk about money with Caylie, Jenny thought about what might be in the refrigerator for dinner that night. Approaching the sub-zero to formulate a healthy meal that would please not only Don and the girls but also her father, she heard the back door slam.

"Shit."

"What's the matter?" asked Caylie.

"Cay," Jenny said, "I gotta run. Dad's finally up and just came through the backdoor, and I'm wondering if he even took the time to get dressed."

"What about Michigan?"

Jenny heard her father's footsteps shuffle through the solarium. "We'll talk later. Okay Cay?"

"Will we?"

There was no mistaking Caylie's tone. Her accusation. Jenny knew she wasn't being a very good sister. She wasn't being Caylie's Jenny. She was just so sick of taking care of her and she resented how Caylie always found a way to push her buttons. "Sorry, Cay. I really have to go."

She pushed the OFF button of her phone and returned it to the wall mount.

The pace of Michael's step was very slow. Jenny swore again under her breath. She didn't want him to come to the main house before dinnertime. She wanted him to have his breakfast in the guesthouse, read the paper and then relax by the pool. If he were in the house when the girls got home from camp, they'd freak. They just didn't get the whole "grandpa" vibe from Michael. He never hugged them, kissed them, or asked about school or day camp. He showed as little interest in them as he did in Caylie and Jenny when they were adolescents.

"Mommy!" he called, his voice full of gravel. "Are you in here?"

Did he just call her Mommy?

His footsteps drew nearer and Jenny realized he was wearing his slippers. "Dad?"

She walked from the kitchen to the solarium, the room with a door leading to the guesthouse, and there he was, dressed in yesterday's clothes. "Good morning—I mean afternoon—Dad. I came out there a little while ago, but—"

"Where's my coffee?" he bellowed. "And do you have any more of those doughnuts?"

"Uh, sure Dad." She turned her back to him and returned to the kitchen. With a dash of guilt, she knew she should have given him a hand. But she didn't.

Jenny firmly believed that there was one thing her father was going to learn by the end of his stay: She wasn't his *Mommy*. And she certainly wasn't his wife.

No, that was *my* job. But unfortunately, I didn't get to finish it.

CHAPTER 7

I didn't need to raise the cup to my lips to know my tea had gone cold. It was a foreign cup, evocative of no one, and heavy—too heavy for tea. Obviously hand-made, it had smile faces, hearts and four-leaf clovers drawn into the ceramic glaze. It must have been a gift from one of my children. But which one? Mother's Day and birthday gifts from my progeny filled our Mitten Lake home. I had left behind nothing of this nature when we moved away from Grossdale, and yet en route to *Ohr*, behind me it all stayed.

When we first left Grossdale and I attempted to unpack, everything Jenny and Caylie had given me over the years blended together. I couldn't tell one trinket from the next and had far less space in which to display the items. So, much of it stayed in packing crates. Soon, our Mitten Lake decor became even more cluttered with art projects from our grandchildren, along with endless school photos and snapshots from sports teams, school plays and dance recitals.

Our parental collection of baby pictures had slowed dramatically after Ronnie's baby portraits. We had albums filled with black and white photos of Marie, Darlene and our son, but the camera wasn't as handy when Jenny and Caylie were infants. There were a few group photos of the five children, and even fewer of all seven of us together. But our Irish Twins' pictorial memories of their childhoods are tangible primarily in their memories.

That's what happens at the tail end of a large brood. First-words aren't remembered and first-steps are unremarkable. Lost teeth go unrecorded, and sometimes the tooth fairy fails to visit. It didn't mean I loved my youngest children less; however, I have come to realize that the true labors of motherhood kick in long after the children are born. I may have been stretched too thin when Jenny and Caylie were babies, but I was there for them during their adolescence. And, well, they didn't seem to need me much when they were teenagers. They weaned themselves from holding my hand and grasping my skirt far quicker than my first three children. And they had their older sisters to explain things. Marie and Darlene were more qualified to talk to them about things like boys and feminine products.

Times had changed. Personal subjects were more openly discussed; however, I had no intention of changing with the times.

Motherhood and the job of mothering were for me—and I suspect, most women—a learn-as-you-go process. Not everyone is qualified for the job. My mother died shortly after I was married, and my sister, Molly, who had three children and died before I gave birth to Marie, had only one piece of advice about raising children: "When you have them, and you will, just love them."

Meanwhile, I didn't learn how to be a good mother in school. There weren't books called *What to Expect While You're Expecting* and *What to Expect the First Year* and the myriad collection of how-to books that fill bookshelves and nightstands across America. These days, there were books about everything from how to deal with incessant thumb sucking to confronting the first-grade bully. The home-economics classes I took in high school during the 1930s taught me to cook and to sew. They taught nothing of motherhood. The mother we worshipped at St. Mary's was the Virgin Mother—Mary, Holy Mother of our Lord Jesus.

Hail Mary full of grace, the Lord is with Thee ...

It was our daily recitation, always following the Lord's Prayer. The father came first, the mother second. In my school, being cast as the Mother of God in the annual Christmas Pageant held more honor than earning the title of Valedictorian. I was neither; however, I *was* Salutatorian and I played the wife of the Innkeeper who showed Mary and Joseph to the stable. I knew I was second fiddle. I was the second child, the quiet and well-behaved girl in the shadow of an older sister, Molly. I wasn't taught my place. By birth order, I instinctually knew it.

* * *

In 1949, six years into my marriage, my face had grown as round and pale as a full moon. It wasn't fat. No one would ever describe anything about me as fat. I was just over five-foot-three in height, and until my seventh month of pregnancy, had never cracked a hundred pounds. The truth is, I didn't actually know my weight before I became pregnant. I hadn't set foot in a doctor's office until my bossy, Southside Chicago sister-in-law, Marge, insisted I go. My doctor back in Melrose was my neighbor, Dr. Kerrigan, and he always made house calls.

Until the spring of 1949, I hadn't experienced or shown any signs of pregnancy—not that I would have recognized them. But Marge sure did. She'd had two children, which in her mind, made her an expert on everything.

Marge was married to Michael's oldest brother, James, and she was as tall as Michael, but still a good six inches shorter than her husband. The Shields men, three brothers, joked they were half Irish, half skyscraper. Later I learned the family was also of German descent, but they had learned to disguise this during World War I and the first wave of expanded anti-German sentiment in the United States. This was a time when frankfurters became "hot dogs" and German shepherds, "liberty dogs." As for the Shields family? They just became Irish. From the time the soon-to-be skyscraping boys were born, the next generation of the Shields family embraced only their Irish heritage, and did so for the remainder of the century.

When we moved to Chicago after the War ended and Michael's Coast Guard duties brought him to the Great Lakes Naval Station, the first thing I discovered was that my husband was not only the baby of his family, at six-foot-one, he was also the runt of the litter. Where I came from, six-one was TALL. That wasn't the case in Chicago—the City of Big Shoulders—and apparently big feet AND big mouths. Everything about my new sister-in-law, Margaret "Marge" Shields, was B-I-G. Behind her back, her brothers-in-law called her "Large Marge." She had taken her place in the Shields family as the eldest sister-in-law, and I fell in line as I had done all my life, as the younger, quieter sister.

Molly remained in Boston with her husband, Charlie Murphy, a Melrose boy we all knew as "Red." Like our father, he never finished school and ended up working in the Golden Rule Shoe Factory in Lynn, Massachusetts. Charlie's father, also a shoe worker, bought stock in the company, which secured them jobs. In 1936 having a job—even one that paid fifty-five cents an hour—made him a catch.

Molly married him right out of high school.

Since she quickly produced three children and couldn't work outside the home, Molly starting taking in sewing jobs to supplement their paltry income and make ends meet. She was determined to keep out of the bread lines. Soon, the War began, but Red was deemed 4-F, not qualified for service due to flat-feet, or some-such thing. Socially, it made him a pariah. Rumors about "four-effers" were heartless. They included unspeakable afflictions—everything from mental retardation to venereal disease. Red's social status didn't help their marriage; however, Molly never talked about her marriage. When she referred to him, she didn't call him by name. Not Red, not Charlie. It was always just "he" or "him." During the War, he did manage to find work at the new General Electric plant in Lynn, where they specialized in making aircraft engines. The pay was better but that didn't keep Molly from taking every sewing job she could find.

Molly was always busy. My mother and I helped to look after her children whenever she asked. We often brought them with us to Sunday Mass at St. Mary's. I missed having my sister next to me in church, and missed her strong singing voice covering for me when I only mouthed the words. And I especially missed her when things grew serious between Michael and me. Even though she didn't share much with me about her first intimate experiences and ensuing childbirths, I still hoped she could provide some counsel. As young, Catholic girls we were taught, primarily by omission, that these things were private—not to be discussed. Anything having to do with s-e-x—I could barely utter the word for most of my life—was shrouded in a veil of mystery. This is one reason why I remained a virgin, even on my wedding night. Molly, as my maid of honor, provided the exquisite nightgown for my first night as Mrs. Michael Shields, but unfortunately, she didn't provide the information I needed to successfully consummate the marriage.

I think God may have also had a hand in it.

Quartermaster Michael Shields, U.S. Coast Guard, proposed to me eight weeks prior to our wedding day. There was no ring—only a gardenia wristband and a promise. "Next time I'm in port, we'll get married," he said. He didn't really ask me. And he wasn't on his knee. He was simply matter-of-fact about the whole thing. And I was nothing if not obedient. I was accustomed to following orders and accepting my fate as it presented itself to me. Growing up in the Catholic Church meant my future held two choices: Number one, I'd become a nun; or number two, I'd become a wife and a mother. Molly knew the convent was no place for her, which I believed was the reason why at the age of eighteen she married the first boy to ask her. And if boys were looking in my direction, I never knew it. After high school I worked to support my mother, and if it hadn't been for the fateful day in Virginia Beach when my Van Johnson-lookalike sauntered by, I may have spent the rest of my life known as Sister Anne rather than Mrs. Michael Shields.

My fate was a blessing. I was crazy about Michael and lived for the days when his cutter ship sailed into Boston harbor. War was for me, romantic and mysterious. It meant a handsome sailor and big band music. It meant romance and flowers—giant lily and gardenia corsages. It was all about dressing up, garter belts and prized silk stockings, my dark, curly hair in a barrel-rolled updo. And dancing—dancing until my high-heeled feet ached with blisters. Glenn Miller had us "In the Mood," and we could go all night as the band continued to tease and play, tease and play.

My mother, however, wasn't sure Michael's intentions were pure. "He's a sailor," she said with disdain. "And he's from Chicago. He can't be trusted." I think the same way Chicagoans thought of Bostonians as tea-party rebels, Bostonians thought of Chicagoans as Al Capone gangsters. I knew the first time she voiced objections to my choice that I would never offer my opinions about the man my daughter—if I were lucky enough to have a daughter—might choose for a husband. Once my Mother got to know Michael, however, she too was taken in by his charm. And yet she never understood why Michael and his shipmates spent all their liberty pay on flowers, cocktails and shows, as if money were no object. Michael told us he and his shipmates spent like there was no tomorrow because of their experiences taking fire while convoying across the Atlantic Ocean.

His military service illustrated a new definition of "tomorrow."

For Michael, the War was a far darker era, filled with deep swells of a heaving ocean and the unpredictability of German U-boats. "Tomorrow" wasn't in his vocabulary. Except, of course, for the day he used it in a ten-word Western Union telegram on the last day of August, 1943.

"In port tomorrow. [STOP] Plan wedding. [STOP] We have three days. [STOP] Love. [FULL STOP]"

We were to be married on a Thursday morning. I was twenty-four years old and I was ready. In spite of my mother's initial skepticism I knew Michael was the right man for me, and she liked that I'd remain living with her while he continued his service with the Coast Guard. Molly, also, was fully supportive of the union.

And so, with my sister's assistance I, Little Annie Monaghan, went into action.

We enlisted the help of the well-connected and popular Kerrigan sisters, the girls with me the day I first met Michael at Virginia Beach, and together we planned this whirlwind event. We went to Father Barry at St. Mary's who agreed to forgo the traditional posting of the banns because of my status with the Sodality and, of course, the War. Mr. Callahan, who owned the corner bakery, provided the cake. His wife agreed to be the soloist at the ceremony. I borrowed my neighbor's dress. It was white satin with old lace. The fingertip veil was held in place by a coronet of seeded pearls, and I carried a bouquet of roses with an orchid in the center. Molly wore turquoise blue silk with a velvet bodice and matching hat, and she carried yellow roses. The Kerrigan sisters also wore blue, the twin dresses they had worn as bridesmaids for another friend. Michael's shipmate, Joe, served as his best man. In addition, he asked four shipmates to serve as ushers at the early morning nuptial Mass. Two handsome sailors escorted the Kerrigans and the other two escorted our mothers. My father, of course, was not present. We never heard from him after he left and didn't know whether or not he were alive or dead. In his stead, I asked my cousin, Lieutenant Theodore Lane, U.S. Navy, to give me away.

Michael's brothers were both overseas serving in the military, and his father died an early death of arthritis and alcoholism. So, his mother was his only family member to attend our wedding. Her name was Belle. She was a tall, angular woman of very few words. And she was cranky. Michael defended her, saying she was tired from the flight from Chicago on such short notice; however, I found it hard to forgive her for only speaking two words to me on our wedding day: "Hello Anne," she said when Michael introduced us.

That was it. Not another word.

I returned her greeting by calling her "Mrs. Shields," hoping she'd ask me to call her Mother. She never did. I called her Mrs. Shields until Marie was born, and then after that, it was "Grandma" until the day she died.

Quickly, I erased all thoughts of Belle. The last time I thought of an old woman so intensely, Aunt Bee from Mitten Lake appeared with my next cup of tea. I didn't want that to happen with my mother-in-law. I still wasn't exactly sure how things worked in *Ohr.*

I focused back upon my wedding day.

My cousin, Teddy, as stand-in for my father, had arranged a room for our wedding night at the Boston Park Plaza Hotel. It was a luxurious property, and our room—a suite—was adorned with white lilies, chocolate-covered strawberries and champagne. We took a taxi from Melrose, south to the city, and our wedding night began at four o'clock in the afternoon.

Michael was eager. I was frightened.

Not only had I no idea how to perform what I knew was expected of me, I was also petrified to tell Michael that I was experiencing my monthly menses. I'd been petrified all day of staining the white satin of my neighbor's gown; however, that was nothing compared to my fear of breaking the news to my new husband that we wouldn't be able to consummate the marriage until the next time he was in port. Whenever that would be.

Old Testament law strictly forbade intercourse during the menstrual cycle, and I believed this was why brides carried the responsibility of setting the wedding date. But the War changed that—and Michael, too, changed that with his telegram. I realized Father Barry had set aside the laws of the church to perform our ceremony, but could I set aside Biblical law?

There was no one with whom I felt comfortable talking about this problem.

At five o'clock, I stood in the bathroom, a room quite cramped compared to the suite attached to it, and brushed through my long, dark curls. Standing before a full-length, gilded-gold mirror, I studied the curves I didn't know I possessed. The silken nightgown clung to my hips, my breasts, and my stomach. I felt like a movie star—like Rita Hayworth about to meet Van Johnson.

"Anne!"

Hearing my name barked, my body stiffened to rigid attention. I went from being a bride to being a sailor, dressed in whites, at attention and waiting for orders. Only my heartbeat responded. It visibly beat through the silky folds of the fabric barely covering my breasts.

Again, my husband barked his impatience. "What's keeping you?" Clearly, he had never learned to 'hold his hour,' the expression my mother always used when she wanted us to be patient.

"I'm coming," I said. I took a deep breath, smoothed my hair, and emerged from the room. My eyes remained lowered as I focused on the subtle gold pattern on the red carpet beneath my bare feet.

"I thought you drowned in there," he said. "The Shields family will never accept a poor swimmer. We're all experts in the water. It's why I'm a sailor for crying out loud."

Slowly, I raised my eyes and saw a look of approval softening Michael's face as his ocean blue eyes scanned me repeatedly from head to toe. He was shirtless, wearing only pale green pajama bottoms. I had never seen his smile look so large—his teeth so white.

My children were going to have lovely teeth.

His hands were at once around my waist and he maneuvered me toward the bed. It was the biggest bed I'd ever seen. Was it a double bed? A queen? I didn't know. My heart raced, and I couldn't catch my breath. I had to tell him. And I tried. I tried to formulate the words. But only one thing fell from my lips:

"Michael."

"Anne," he said. He placed his large hands on my shoulders, epaulettes, and lowered me to the tapestry spread still covering the bed.

I froze with fear.

"It's okay, Sweetheart," he whispered. "You need to relax."

"I . . . I can't."

"You *can*." He took my left hand into his. "Do you see this gold band on your finger? It means you can."

"But no. No. I'm afraid it doesn't. I'm sorry. I'm so sorry. But I can't. I have my—I mean I'm . . . um, it's my time of the. . . ."

His expression hardened. A deep vertical line formed between his eyes. "Are you trying to tell me you have your period?"

What did he call it? My period? I had never heard it called that. It sounded like punctuation. How crass!

Michael's expression grew stormy. He appeared as angry as the punctuation—the exclamation point—that had formed between his eyes. It made his thick eyebrows, far darker than his blond tresses, knit together in a villainous V. His hands became as stiff as skeletons and first clutched, then abruptly left my shoulders. He sat up and turned his smooth, naked back to me and sighed.

I felt crushed into a thousand shards of Rita Hayworth and Van Johnson fantasies. "Michael?"

"You don't understand what this means, Anne."

I placed my hand on his back, my gold ring reflecting the light. "You're right. I don't. Please help me."

He turned and looked at me with an expression I had never seen him use. There was a darkness about him, an angry cloud. He raised his hand and I cowered, thinking he might slap me. But he didn't. He put his hand behind his head and clutched his neck. Sighing and relaxing his brow, he reached toward my eye and gently wiped away a tear I didn't realize had formed. "What you don't understand, my naïve little Irish lass, my virgin Anne, is that I have a hard-on. I've had one since the moment you finally stepped out of that bathroom and I saw you in this gown. Why would you wear this if you knew you couldn't give yourself to me?"

My eyes stung with tears and I believed my nose, tight with emotion, would drip at any minute. I felt a gushing between my legs and was filled with the horrible knowledge that I'd probably stain both the nightgown and the Park Plaza tapestry with my fateful, ill-timed menstrual blood.

I'd planned such a beautiful wedding in a remarkably short period of time. I'd endured my mother's skepticism and the complete dismissal of my mother-in-law. I was an impetuous war bride, marrying for love and for the promise of a life I believed Michael would offer. And yet, I couldn't fulfill the first thing required of me as an obedient wife. How would I ever hope to keep him?

"Did you hear what I said?" he asked. "I said I have a hard-on."

"Yes, Michael," I uttered with a small sniffle. "I heard you. But . . . I don't know—I'm sorry. What's a hard-on?"

Because Michael had to return to his ship, it was six months before we consummated our marriage and six years before I finally became pregnant. By this time, we lived in Chicago, and I had received word that my mother had died. My grief over losing her was profound. It shrouded me in a blanket of numbness. I moved through a foggy existence, crying and disappointed that my unborn child would never know his or her grandmother.

Michael had been discharged from the Coast Guard and while he looked for work, we lived with his mother, his brother James, and his wife and their two children. My sister-in-law, Marge, took me to see her doctor, and when the news of my pregnancy was confirmed, it was she, not I, who announced it to the family.

"This little Irish gal from Boston is finally expecting," she said.

"It's about time," said James. He punched Michael's shoulder. "I was beginning to think you didn't have it in you."

Michael beamed, those pearly white teeth of his exuding light rays around the room. "It's because I started taking Vitamin E and Zinc supplements," he said.

Marge immediately pulled me aside. "The Shields men will always take credit for everything," she said. "Come on little Mother. Off your feet. I'm making supper tonight. You'll need all your strength when you break the news to Belle. She's not exactly the warm-fuzzy grandmother type, if you catch my meaning."

During the weeks that followed, Michael found a job as an electrical apprentice and started looking at houses for us in the suburb of West Grossdale. I would be happy to be away from my cold mother-in-law and bossy sister-in-law, and wanted to raise my child without their interference.

By seven months I'd broken a hundred pounds and sported a full-moon face. Most importantly, I learned to stop being embarrassed during my visits to Marge's doctor.

And then, at thirty-eight weeks and seemingly overnight, all movement of my baby ceased. Marge's doctor assured me this was normal. He told me it was simply because the baby had run out of room. But two weeks later when I went into labor and experienced pains that made me believe my uterus would burst, I found it impossible to believe childbirth would be so difficult. Was it because I was so small?

Good heavens, I worried, would I have babies as large as the Shields men?

Marge drove me to the hospital in the family's one and only car, a 1946 Chevy Fleetmaster. It was an enormous, bulbous black car with lots of sparkling chrome and white-walled tires. The Shields brothers took care of it daily, the same way they took care of their mother—with great attention. More attention than they paid to their wives.

I sat in the back and pressed my face to the cold glass window. Every time we hit a pothole on those rough Chicago-area roads, I moaned in pain. "It'll be all right," Marge called over her shoulder. "I'm a good driver. My dad taught me how to drive before the War. Frankly, I'm better at it than any of the Shields brothers. You're lucky I was home and they weren't. See? Here's the hospital." She drove to the emergency room entrance and hit the brake a wee bit too hard. It threw me against the front seat and coincided with another labor pain.

"I don't think I can do this," I cried.

Marge got out of the car and opened my door. She reached in and grabbed me under the arm. "Women have babies everyday, Boston. You can do this."

She practically carried me through the glass doors and then squared off with the equally-bossy admittance nurse. "Bring this woman a wheelchair, for Christ's sakes. She's having a baby! Her name is Anne Shields and she and I are both patients of Dr. Robert Van Proozen."

"Just a minute," said the nurse. "Let me look up her paperwork."

"Good God, woman!" cried Marge. "Her paperwork? What are you talking about?"

My memory is spotty from this point forward, but I do recall the ill-tempered nurse wheeling me past the maternity ward. She brought me to a small, dark room without a window. "I'll be back shortly," she said. "Try to relax."

Relax?

She closed the door and all the air went out of the room. Immediately, a low, stabbing pain made me want to cry out. I grabbed my bulging stomach with one hand and clamped the other over my mouth. I couldn't help but yell. And yet, no one came. Why had everyone left me alone? Why did they put me in such tight, dreary quarters?

I don't know how long I was there. The labor pains made me drift in and out of consciousness. Surely, enough time had passed. The baby was ready. I wanted to push.

Finally, a hundred labor pains later, a different nurse, this one gray-faced against her starch-white uniform and pointed cap, came in the small room and closed the door behind her. She didn't look me in the face.

"Oh!" I groaned. "It's so painful I can't stand it. The baby is coming."

"Quiet down," she said. "We can hear you all the way at the nurse's station."

"But the baby is coming. I'm ready. I need to push. I have to—"

"No!" she screeched. "Whatever you do, DON'T PUSH!"

"But . . . but—"

I don't remember anything more. And the five children to whom I subsequently gave birth never knew the first child I delivered was dead.

After the stillbirth of our son, a baby we named "Barry," namesake to the priest who married us, we baptized and buried him in the Shields family plot. And as I stood and watched the tiny casket lowered into the dark Chicago soil, I swore I would never have another child.

As if it weren't difficult enough losing my mother and my child in just over a year's time, six weeks after I lost my son, I lost my Irish Twin.

CHAPTER 8

Molly Monaghan Murphy died when she was thirty-one years old. It happened during the three-week period when each year we shared the same age—a stretch of time in which I always felt close to her, in spite of our geographical separation. Still raw with grief over the death of our mother and my son, I felt I'd turned the other cheek already. There was no cheek left to slap. Losing my sister broke my heart.

The only thing for which I could be grateful were the five days I'd had with her after my baby died.

Molly had boarded an airplane for the first time in her life, and flew from Boston to Chicago to be with me. It was a tremendous expense—a burden on Charlie's blue-collar salary—and he griped about having to look after their three kids while she was away. "But Red isn't completely heartless," she said. "He knew you needed me. And his parents look after the kids most of the time anyway."

She stayed for five days. Michael and I were still living on the top floor of my mother-in-law's home. Molly slept on a cot in our sitting room, avoiding Belle and my sister-in-law, Marge. They looked at her as if she were an exotic animal, and constantly asked her to repeat herself because they couldn't understand her accent. For my sister, being in Chicago was like being in a foreign country. And so she spent nearly every waking hour sitting with me, stroking my hair and trying to comfort me.

It had been years since we were together, but from the moment she entered my room, it was like we'd never been apart. I hadn't felt that comfortable with anyone since I left home. Not even Michael. It was amazing how safe Molly made me feel. She talked non-stop, telling me of the sewing business she'd developed, and what she knew about everyone from St. Mary's High School. There were a couple of war widows, a couple of nuns, and a couple of spinsters, including both the Kerrigan sisters. Almost everyone else, however, was married with children, she said, and most were living at the homes of their parents or in-laws. This news made me feel far less contrite about living with my husband's mother.

Our cousin, Teddy, the well-respected Lieutenant Theodore Lane, had taken over the family house in Melrose after our mother passed, and Molly and Charlie continued renting a three-bedroom home in the town of Lynn. Charlie returned to the shoe factory after he lost his job with General Electric. "He drinks a bit," said Molly. I assumed it was why he lost his job. Molly passed the days at my bedside talking about more pleasant things than her husband. She made sure my teacup, a delicate, pale green cup trimmed with gold, was always full. She talked about her kids and how well they were doing in school, and how much they enjoyed spending time with their grandparents.

Listening to Molly, I lost myself in her lovely green eyes and oh, how I wished I were her. Molly had no idea how difficult it was to be her younger sister. She did everything with such ease.

"I will never have a child," I said to her.

"Nonsense. As soon as you're recovered, you and Michael will try again. This particular child just wasn't meant to be. God has a plan. You need to trust this."

"But I carried him for nine months. I delivered him. He had a name!"

Her eyes filled with tears. "I know, Sweetheart. More than you can understand, I know. But you will have— "

"Don't say it! Please don't tell me I will have other children. Like this baby didn't count. This was my son, Molly. Honestly! That Marge, my so-called sister-in-law, and that incredibly cold mother of his have made me feel like a failure. They won't even look at me. They think I'm too old to have babies. I'm already thirty and will be thirty-one next month."

Molly brushed my cheek. "No one knows your age better than I, my sweet Irish Twin." She used a handkerchief to wipe my tears. "Think of St. Anne, the saint for whom you were named."

"The mother of the Holy Virgin?"

"Do you remember the nuns telling us how old she was when she gave birth to Mary?"

"No, Molly. I don't. I remember she and her husband were barren. And then an angel came to her and said she would conceive." My eyes burned with tears and my stomach ached with cramps. "Are you my angel, Molly?"

She shook her head. "Sip your tea, dear," she said.

Molly never had the chance to meet the five children Michael and I eventually brought into the world.

Just then, in *Obr*, I saw a glimmer of white in the distance and heard a rustling sound. I looked up from my teacup and saw my sister. She moved toward me as though gliding, and wore a white satin wedding gown. She indeed, appeared to be an angel.

"I never met your children," she said. "But I have watched each of them grow through your eyes, Anne."

"My wedding gown. You're wearing my— "

"Yes, hardly the two-piece dress I wore when I eloped with Red Murphy."

"I know the dress to which you're referring. It was beautiful."

"Made from a fifteen-cent pattern with three dollars worth of sapphire crepe."

"You were always a remarkable seamstress. I could barely sew on a button."

Molly smiled. "Annie, you wasted time envying me. If you remember, that blue dress was the same one I made for my high school graduation. Dresses did double duty during the Depression." She laughed and grasped the sides of the elegant wedding gown and turned a graceful pirouette. "I always envied you this dress. You had a real wedding dress and a real marriage. Obviously you never knew how jealous I was of you."

Molly took the steaming cup of tea from my hands and her expression turned grave. "Your daughter, Caylie, cannot marry this man—this Albert Powell."

"Molly, I don't understand. Are you telling me I have some kind of power to stop her?"

"No. You don't. Not exactly. There is, however, such a thing as Divine Intervention, if you'd like to call it that. What I mean is *you* don't have the power directly, but both Jenny and Caylie do."

"How am I supposed to—"

"Just listen to their prayers, dear. Listen to their prayers."

* * *

Jenny felt like she was sitting in a dentist's chair. Her feet were up, her head was back, and she was nervous. The room was small and bright, sterile. There were a few framed diplomas and certificates on the eggshell walls. In the corner was a placard with a distasteful BEFORE shot of a fat, puckering thigh full of cottage cheese cellulite, and an AFTER version that looked, well, a little better. Frankly, I didn't see much difference.

Was she in some kind of doctor's office? A plastic surgeon? *My* Jennifer?

Like me, Jenny was low-maintenance when it came to her appearance. She wore no makeup, and had a remarkable head full of red hair. No one was happier than I when discovering those ginger follicles for the first time. Jennifer was my fifth child, the fourth to have stayed alive, and the first delivery for which I was awake. It was 1960 and I had a female obstetrician—they were rare in those days. Her name was Dr. Joanna Counter, and she actually asked me if I wanted to be awake for the delivery. None of my previous physicians—all male—had given me that option. Well, you bet I wanted to be awake. I wanted to see what was going on. This was before fathers were present in the delivery room. They still had the reputation for pacing in the waiting room with a pocket full of cigars. Michael never did that, however. On the day I labored with Jenny, Michael was on an electrical pole down in Lockport, Illinois.

I thought Jenny was a flawlessly beautiful baby. As the 1960s became the 1970s, however, and most adolescent girls craved the Marsha Brady Bunch look, Jenny's milky complexion and coarse, red hair didn't fit it. She felt her sister, Caylie, with her straight blonde hair, was the lucky one—the pretty one. And I have to admit, of all my daughters, Caylie was by far, the most lovely. I always thought Caylie, with her buttercup complexion and big doe eyes, had a look that would stop traffic.

Jenny once heard me say these exact words about her Irish Twin, "Caylie stops traffic," while talking to their Aunt Marge. She often repeated it. Unfortunately, Jenny was still too immature to realize that my comment about Caylie had nothing to do with whether or not I thought Jenny was pretty. I, of course, thought she was beautiful. But Jenny never believed it. She believed she wasn't, nor could she ever be pretty. She, instead, was both athletic and artistic. And she was smart. Jenny put everything she had into her sports and her studies. She sometimes wondered what she could have become if we had afforded her an Ivy League education. Jenny would have made a fine lawyer. Maybe even a judge. She attained a bachelor's degree in rhetoric and speech, but didn't go on to law school. She couldn't afford it. Instead, she took a job first as a proofreader, and then a researcher with a magazine in Chicago. In fact, I believe it was called *Chicago* magazine. We didn't discuss her work. And before too long, instead of going back to school, like she sometimes talked about doing, she gave it all up to be a thirty year-old bride.

Jenny said she was tired of fighting her way to the top through every stage of life. Once there were no longer volleyball and softball teams on which to compete, and earning 'A's' on projects became rewards of the past, Don Lincolnwood offered her not only his devotion and his love, but also the possibility of a comfortable future. He was a successful businessman, a partner in an electronics-manufacturing firm. She believed their children wouldn't have to worry about how they'd pay for college tuition, and this became the most important aspect of her future. Jenny not only would never let her children be on their own at the age of seventeen, but she also never expected them to pay for the privileges of their upbringing.

With the exception of his classic good looks, Don was nothing like Jenny's father, Michael. He was only her second real boyfriend, so no one could say Jenny had a "type;" but winning the attention of Don Lincolnwood was like a winning lottery ticket. The initial thought Jenny had upon seeing him for the first time—even before her college roommate introduced them—was that he was *too* good looking. What she meant was that he was too good looking for *her*. Jenny was genuinely surprised when he asked her to dinner. She wondered if he were doing someone a favor. But that wasn't the case.

My daughter clearly didn't understand how attractive she'd become.

Don was generous, always putting the needs of his loved ones before his own. They say most girls marry men like their fathers. Not Jenny. Don, because he was quiet and kind, reminded Jenny more of her mother.

Yes. He reminded her of me.

Back in *Obr,* Molly handed me a tall glass of iced tea. "Would you say that Jenny was more like me? The older sister? Or was she more like you?"

I didn't answer. I looked at the wedge of lemon perched upon the rim of the glass. The coldness in my hand was refreshing; however, I preferred my tea hot.

The room in which my daughter sat—the white room with framed photos of before and after cellulite reduction—reflected in the glass.

Jenny felt trapped. Judging by her inability to sit still, it was clear she was uncomfortable. Of course, she didn't realize how connected we were at the moment, and there was nothing I could do to control her mood. I watched helplessly as I felt my daughter lapse into grief.

When Jenny grieved, she prayed. She asked for guidance and support and she always pictured me "in a better place." She assured herself that I had lived a long and good life and she hoped for the opportunity to do the same. Usually her moments of missing me were brief. Her grief was brought on by one of her daughters doing something that reminded her of me. Or she'd think about giving me a call and stop herself from picking up the telephone. The reality of her living world pulled her back in quickly, and she moved on. She didn't wallow.

But for some reason, today was different.

As I concentrated on the crescent-shaped cubes inside the tea glass Molly had given to me, I felt Jenny's throat thicken and the sting of tears filling her blue eyes. She wondered when the pain of losing me would end.

I'm right here, Jenny darling.

She wiped away a tear just as a woman with a white coat and a perfect face, as round and smooth as a balloon, burst into the room. The woman had dark hair and green eyes just like—

Jenny noticed the woman's resemblance to me at once. I watched as my daughter blinked a few times to be sure her imagination and her grief hadn't gotten the best of her.

"Hi there, Jenny. I'm Susan, your aesthetician."

"Hello," she said and sniffled.

Susan lowered her eyes to her clipboard, and then sat on a roller stool next to Jenny's lounge chair. "So what's up? What are we doing for you today?"

Jenny pointed to the vertical line between her eyebrows. "I've got a problem right here. I've just spent too much time with my octogenarian father and I'm starting to look like him."

"Mmm," Susan hummed, and raised her copper, rectangular glasses on her nose. She leaned in for a closer look. "Are you okay? You look like you've been crying."

Jenny wiped at her right eye. "I'm fine. It's just that my mother died—"

Susan gasped. "Oh! I'm so sorry."

"No, no. It's been over a year, but I was thinking of her when you came in, and, well, you look a little like her." Jenny waved her hand in front of her face. "Don't mind me. It's silly."

"It's not silly. My mother passed away five years ago and I still grieve for her. You never know when it's going to flare up, right?"

"Exactly."

"Now let's get those worry lines off your face." Susan rolled her chair toward Jenny and leaned close, her green eyes intent. "Raise your eyebrows for me."

She did.

"Now smile." The aesthetician made notations on her chart and then flipped through the file, momentarily studying a series of Jenny's BEFORE photos from a previous procedure. "Mmm. Well, your skin is looking good after the microdermabrasion." She closed the file. "You're certainly not the freckle-faced strawberry I see in these photos."

Jenny's eyebrows shot up toward the ceiling. "You did NOT just call me a freckle-face strawberry."

"Sorry?"

"You should be. I haven't heard that since my sister and her friends teased me in junior high. I'm pretty sure it scarred me for life."

"Oh, nonsense," said Susan. "You're a beautiful woman. I'd kill to have a head of hair like yours."

It always came back to the hair. It was no surprise to me; however, Jenny wondered why every middle-aged woman wanted to be a redhead, when every naturally redheaded teenager loathed the color and the ridicule that accompanied it. She believed I was the only one who truly loved her red hair. "Now you even sound like my mother," she said.

"Squint for me," said Susan. "Good. What do you mean I sound like your mother?"

"Oh, she always went on about my hair. She was a brunette and my dad was a blond. It took her four tries to get the hybrid redheaded offspring, and for her, that was probably the only thing good about giving birth at the advanced age of forty-one. But I'll never know. Our mother didn't talk about how it felt to be pregnant. She, in fact, gave no instruction whatsoever on what it meant to be a woman. If it weren't for my older sisters, Marie and Darlene, I wouldn't have learned a thing about feminine hygiene."

"My mother was the same way. It was a generational thing. You really can't blame her for that. Squint again for me, will you hon?"

Jenny closed her eyes and wrinkled her nose. "Oh, but every once in a while I do. To this day, I'm not exactly sure what a douche is, even though commercials for them were all over the television. Any time one came on while Mom was in the room, she'd race to the set and push the OFF button."

"Ha! I haven't seen a douche commercial in ages. I don't know if it's because I rarely watch anything other than cable TV or if it's because they're no longer advertised. Do women still use them?"

Jenny replied absently. "I can't say."

Susan rolled back in her chair and made a series of notations on Jenny's chart, which was the outline of a woman's face. "Looks like you'll be forty-one on your next birthday. Planning any more pregnancies like your mother?"

"Bite your tongue," said Jenny with a bit of a hiss. "And I highly doubt my mother's last two pregnancies were planned. I'm an Irish Twin, by the way. I have a younger sister."

"An Irish Twin?"

"Two kids born to the same mother in less than a year's time. Parents of Irish Twins must be insane. It's no wonder our mom and dad gave up and left us when we were still teenagers. They were tired!"

Susan stood and placed her clipboard on the counter. "This is your first experience with Botox, right?"

Jenny nodded and caught sight of the cellulite reduction ad. She quickly lowered her eyes. This place, she thought, was like a big, fat drug dealer. Microdermabrasion, a procedure to lessen the freckling of her skin, had been her gateway drug—her marijuana. Botox next. Then what? Liposuction?

Her shudder went unnoticed by Susan. "I think we should start with thirty units," said the perky aesthetician.

My daughter brushed the hair from her forehead. "Well, if it makes me look better— "

"You're gorgeous." Susan moved toward the door. "Let me go get the fresh vials and I'll be right back. Would you like some water? Some iced tea?"

"Sure," Jenny said. "Tea would be nice."

Nice indeed, I thought, as I looked at my own glass of iced tea with diminishing cubes floating atop the amber liquid.

Molly remained at my side. She was silent.

"I prefer my tea hot," I said.

"Yes, dear," Molly said. "I know."

Jenny focused on the crisp white shoulders of Susan's professional jacket as she left the room. She thought she could use a nice, straightforward glass of tea to swallow the bullshit Susan had just fed her. *Gorgeous? Please.* Under no circumstances would Jenny believe the word "gorgeous" applied to her. That word had always been applied to her sister, Caylie.

She leaned back in the chair and closed her eyes. The only time she felt she looked pretty next to her Irish Twin was on Caylie's wedding day, when they were twenty-two and twenty-three years old.

* * *

Caylie graduated from the University of Illinois and returned to Chicago with a plan. A friend in her Landscape Architecture program had hooked her up with an available apartment in the suburb of Oak Park. A spacious Victorian duplex, the top floor had two bedrooms and a rent she couldn't afford, especially because she didn't have a job. That's when she called Jenny.

Jenny had spent her first year out of college sharing a north side apartment with two other women, friends from school. When Caylie called and asked Jenny to share the Oak Park Victorian with her, she jumped at the chance. Jenny's roommates still partied like college students and she was ready to leave what still felt like dorm life behind. The north side apartment was close to her job, which she liked, but she had a car, a 1963 Dodge Dart, and spent most of her free time combing the one-way streets of the city neighborhood looking for a place to park it. She hadn't spent any time with her sister since moving from our Grossdale home and wanted the opportunity to get their relationship back to what she thought it should be.

Jenny wrote a check for the first and last month's rent at the Oak Park Victorian, another for the security deposit, and they made that Victorian their own. For the Irish Twins, moving to Oak Park, just west of Grossdale, was like moving home.

Jenny took the El downtown to work each day, leaving her car for Caylie to use for job interviews. Caylie applied to nearly every suburban nursery, looking for an entry-level position. Within a month, she was on the crew of the west side's largest commercial landscaping operation. From that point forward, they split the rent and household expenses. They decorated with their sister Marie's castoff furniture and a host of Boston ferns, in honor they said, of me. They loved their jobs and in the evening, ate dinner together and then shared tea and Milano cookies before bed.

Jenny didn't have or even covet an active social life during this time. It was all work for her during the week, and relaxation on the weekends. Caylie, on the other hand, had maintained her relationship with Robert during college. Shortly after they graduated, however, he returned to his family's Michigan cottage and worked at a YMCA camp on the lake.

Eight weeks after the girls moved in together Robert showed up. Caylie said it was the anniversary of their first date—the night they kissed next to the campfire—and the couple went to dinner to celebrate.

It was a Thursday night. It was late, and Jenny was fast asleep when Caylie burst into her room. "Jenny! Wake up!"

Jenny rolled out of the fetal position and slowly opened her eyes. "What is it?"

Caylie sat on her sister's bed. "Guess what?"

"What time is it?" As Caylie came into focus, the light coming from the door behind her lit her blonde tresses like a halo. "You look so pretty."

"Robert proposed," she said.

The door closed behind them, causing all the light to escape from the room. Jenny couldn't help but open her eyes wider. Her sister's face was no longer visible. "You're kidding."

"No, I'm not kidding. Wasn't it perfect to do it on our anniversary?

He took me to a really nice dinner downtown and asked me to marry him. When he goes back to Michigan on Sunday he's going to ask Dad for my hand. Can you believe it?"

Jenny sat up and switched on the table lamp next to the bed. "So, you said 'yes?' "

"Of course. And we're going to do it soon because Robert wants us to join the Peace Corps. Married couples have to be married for a year before they can go overseas together."

"Caylie! What the hell are you talking about? Why would you marry Robert Cottrell?"

"Jenny!"

"What? Did you really believe I'd think this was good news? He's more like your brother, for God's sake. Who marries their junior high boyfriend?"

"I'm going to. And he's more than that. You should be happy for me. You're my sister!"

"It's because I'm your sister! Cay, we're so young. We're just getting started."

"Jenny, this wasn't the reaction I expected."

"And I expected this? I just moved in with you! I mean, I suppose I could afford the rent here on my own, but—"

"No, Jen. You'd be moving out. Robert's going to live here with me."

It felt like a punch in the stomach. Jenny couldn't speak.

Caylie stood up. "He needs to earn more money than he makes at the camp and after the summer, he's got a sales job lined up with a big paper company downtown."

Jenny swallowed a heavy, bitter lump and clutched her stomach. She was certain that Caylie had no clue as to the impact of her news. Not only was the elder Irish Twin sure that Robert Cottrell was not the right life partner for her sister, but also, she knew Caylie had so much potential to become an extraordinary woman. She was beautiful. She was educated. She was funny. She had her whole life ahead of her, and to get married at such a young age was. . . .

Jenny couldn't help herself. "It's a mistake, Caylie."

Caylie grabbed the crystal doorknob. "Thanks a lot, Jen." She pulled open the bedroom door with tremendous force. "I come in here to share the happiest night of my life with you, and you shit all over it. And to think, I was going to ask you to be my maid of honor."

The door slammed behind her, an emphatic exclamation point.

Stick figures on the clock across the room read 11:11. Somehow it felt later. Jenny knew if she fell back to sleep immediately, she could still manage a decent night's sleep before the morning alarm. But her heart pounded as though she'd just run a race. Her ears rang with an echo of the slamming door.

She felt so used—so utterly discarded. It was a familiar feeling of abandonment.

Caylie eventually forgave Jenny for her reaction and asked Jenny to be her maid of honor. Supporting her, standing up as her bride's maid, was difficult for Jenny; however, once she found an Oak Park coach house to rent and moved in, Jenny forgave Caylie too. She hoped she was wrong about Robert and that he possessed qualities that could make Caylie happy.

Jenny soon realized she couldn't tell her sister whom she could or couldn't marry.

On Caylie's wedding day, their sisters, Marie and Darlene, also stood up for her. They wore emerald green gowns and with Jenny's long, Lady Godiva hair, for once, even next to Caylie, she felt pretty. After they posed for photos and before the Catholic ceremony at our family church, St. Teresa's Cathedral in Grossdale, I pulled Jenny aside.

"Honey," I said, gently touching my tall daughter's elbow. "I have something for you. Will you come with me?"

"Sure, Mom. What is it?"

"Just follow me."

Still holding Jenny's elbow, I led her from the church vestibule to the bride's room and found my small pink clutch, purchased to match my dress. Opening it, I pulled out a plain, white box. I handed it to Jenny. "Here. I want you to have this today."

"Mom?"

"Just open it, Sweetie. It belonged to my mother and my grandmother before her. Now it belongs to you."

Jenny opened the box and immediately recognized the gold pocket watch, which I had worn around my neck on a gold chain only on very special occasions. "Really? You're giving this to me?" she asked. "Of all four of your daughters, I get to have this?"

I smiled and took the watch from the box. Reaching up I put it around my daughter's neck. "I know how you must feel today, Jennifer, with your younger sister getting married and having to move out of the apartment. I know you don't approve of this marriage, and yet you're doing what you can to support your sister. I didn't approve of my sister's choice either."

"You mean Molly?"

"Yes, Molly. It's a shame you never knew her. Her death came far too soon."

"Asthma, right?"

I nodded, although I felt the burn of the lie. I never believed it was an asthma attack that caused my sister's death. But it was neither the time nor the place to discuss my suspicions about Molly and her husband, Red.

"You just need to be reminded of how special you are, Jenny. And one day, you're going to find someone too, and you're going to have a wonderful life."

"Oh Mom, thank you. I'm really touched." She put her arms around me and pulled me to her chest. The watch hung between us. Jenny knew it was the most valuable gift I had ever given her, and still, she didn't know whether to laugh or cry.

Sharing this memory with my daughter as I stared into my glass of tea, I realized Jenny's conflict. She thought of my old fashioned values—of recognizing the stigma of becoming an "old maid," and making the dramatic gesture of giving her the necklace. And yet, she felt I had failed to recognize the significance or consequences of leaving her and Caylie alone as teenagers to fend for themselves.

For Caylie the result was to find someone to take care of her, hence her early marriage. For Jenny, it meant abandonment, and it tarnished her self-worth.

I lived with that knowledge, however, it took my death to truly understand.

* * *

Back in the aesthetician's room, Jenny waited for Susan to return. She wondered whether or not there was going to be another wedding day for Caylie. And if so, would she even be invited to witness her sister marry the unremarkable Albert Powell? Jenny doubted she'd be asked to wear the dress of a bride's maid; however, if the day did come and she were invited, she knew she would wear the gold pocket watch her mother had given her on the day of Caylie's first wedding.

The aesthetician returned, quietly tiptoeing into the room. Jenny opened her eyes and saw a tall glass of iced tea in front of her. "Here you go," said Susan.

"Thanks." Jenny wrapped her hand around the cold drink. It smelled overwhelmingly of lemon. Raising the glass to her lips, she took too big a sip and felt a sinus freeze.

"Whoops!" Susan cocked her head and there may have been a frown somewhere under her taut skin. "That looks like it hurt. Relax your puss, girl."

Jenny chuckled. "Puss" was the word we all used for "face." I had learned it from the Kerrigan sisters. Jenny looked into her tea. Three crescent ice cubes rested in the top of the glass, and were shaped like a clover. An Irish clover. It made her want to make a wish.

I wish I could forgive my mother for leaving me.

Jenny swung her legs to the side of the chair and stood up. She was nearly a head taller than Susan.

"Jenny? What are you doing?"

"I'm sorry, Susan, but I changed my mind."

"You mean you're not ready for Botox? Honestly, it's not painful at all. And it's perfectly safe."

Jenny took another swallow of the tea and smacked her lips at the sour, lemon flavor. Like her mother, she preferred her tea hot. "That's not it. I didn't mean to waste your time, but I was just thinking about my mom. Do you know she never once dyed her hair or even wore mascara? Granted, she was a naturally beautiful woman."

"I'm sure she was. But so are you."

"No, not really. It's okay, though. My sister is the beautiful one. But all that beauty didn't do a thing to make her life turn out any better than mine."

She set the tea on the counter next to her file of freckle-faced strawberry BEFORE photos. "I think I've got the face I've earned."

CHAPTER 9

Caylie sat on the deck of a large houseboat, which was moored to a docking station at a quiet harbor. She and her boys didn't go to Mitten Lake with Jenny to bring their dad back home. Four roundtrip plane tickets would have cost her two mortgage payments. And she knew she couldn't ask Jenny and Don to pay. They'd already given her so much. Albert didn't offer, and it felt too weird for her to ask him for the money. He did ask them to join him on a rented houseboat for a week, however, and that would have to suffice for a summer vacation.

Taking in the luxury of the sixty-eight foot, four-bedroom boat, Caylie laughed to herself that it was far bigger than Mrs. Bower's old cottage at Mitten Lake—the dwelling she always associated with her Mitten Lake memories.

To Caylie, Mitten Lake seemed so far away and so long ago.

But that's the way she felt about almost every place she had tried to call home. The Grossdale house was sold from under her when she was seventeen, and she wasn't invited to move into our retirement home. Instead, when the house sold to a family with four young children, Caylie spent the last three weeks before her first year of college living with her sister, Marie. She tried to earn her keep by babysitting for her nephews, but spent most of the time fighting with Marie's four-year-old over the television. The *Sesame Street* counting jingles drove her crazy.

Caylie had cursed Jenny for saying it, but it turned out that her sister was right. She should have gotten a job.

And now, years later, there she was, a middle-aged woman with a failing business, an ex-husband who spent most of his time overseas, and three kids to support. Her landscaping business, once very successful, had tanked along with the dot-com industry. Landscape architects working in the designer backyards of the newly rich had taken as big a hit as the personal trainers helping them to achieve their designer bodies. It was the curse of being born at the tail end of the baby boom, she thought. Not only was she the baby of her family, but also she was the baby of a generation.

Caylie believed she'd always been too late for everything.

They docked at Barryessa Harbor early in the morning. Albert offered to take her boys to town to meet his kids, and Caylie was delighted he'd finally invited them to do something. His kids were older, eighteen and twenty, and they planned to join Caylie, Albert and her boys on the boat for the rest of the week. This gave Caylie a couple hours to relax on the front deck. Unfortunately, instead of breathing in the fresh air of the open water, she ingested gasoline fumes. It didn't go at all well with her morning tea and croissant.

Bringing the cup to her nose, she breathed in the earthy aroma and thought of me, and how every morning in Grossdale I sat quietly in the kitchen with my cup and saucer waiting for my children to come to breakfast. Jenny usually ate the same thing: oatmeal and a glass of orange juice. Caylie mixed it up. Cold cereal some days or a brown sugar cinnamon Pop Tart on other days. When cantaloupe was in season, quarter moon slivers were a guarantee.

I always kept my teacup full and I only drank when it was piping hot. I don't believe either of my Irish Twins ever shared a cup of tea with me. Caylie didn't start drinking tea religiously until she lived in Kenya, East Africa.

A year into her marriage to Robert, they were accepted into the Peace Corps and stationed in the Western Provence of Kenya. They didn't have jobs lined up when they got there. They were simply dropped off and told to find work. Caylie always said she and Robert survived off one another's strength. Trying to make use of her degree in Landscape Architecture, she gravitated toward a tree farm and worked there during her two years as a volunteer. Robert managed a lumber mill. They lived in a modest dwelling, a concrete building with a thatched roof, which was adjacent to a tea plantation. Hired help was easy to find in this densely populated area, and for a nominal fee, they had both a cook and a houseboy.

Each morning shortly after the roosters began their morning chorus, their boy "Bob" brought them a tray with tea. Tea came first, and then with a breakfast of sweet rolls and fresh mangoes, they had orange juice and coffee.

When their Peace Corps service was complete, neither Robert nor Caylie wanted to leave Kenya. There was a magical quality about the land, and she felt the people—and their acceptance of her—inspired and shaped her. Caylie believed those were the best two years of her marriage. Robert was amazing, she said. He had an ear for languages and he not only became fluent in Swahili—the intertribal language used between Kenyans—but he also learned the tribal tongues spoken by the Luo, Maragoli and Nandi peoples of Western Provence. Swahili was an easy language for Caylie to learn, but she also learned something far more important. In Kenya, Caylie learned she was an extraordinary woman. And for the first time in her life, she was no one's little sister.

Caylie and Robert moved to the capital city of Nairobi and took up residence at the Boulevard Hotel, an affordable accommodation just down the road from the more famous Norfolk Hotel. It didn't take long for Robert to find a position with the United Nations. Working for the High Commissioner for Refugees, within weeks he was stationed at a refugee camp near the border of Somalia. Spouses weren't allowed. Robert said there wouldn't be enough room on the evacuation planes in case of an uprising.

Caylie applied with CARE and waited to hear whether or not she had gotten a refugee camp position, but it would be as long as three months before her contract began. And during this lonely period, the walls of the Boulevard Hotel closed in on her quickly. She hated being alone.

Years later in California, looking out at the tawny waters of Lake Barryessa and the surrounding hills, she cherished her quiet moments of solitude. On the luxurious houseboat, she sipped her tea and imagined herself not at Lake Barryessa in Northern California, but back in Kenya—back during a time when it still felt like she had her whole life ahead of her.

"Excuse me!" a voice called. "Excuse me, Ma'am?"

Was someone calling her? Calling her "Ma'am"? When, exactly, had she become a ma'am rather than a miss? Caylie set down her teacup and turned to see a redheaded woman waving at her from the dock. The sight of her took away Caylie's breath. "Jenny?"

The young woman brushed back her unruly hair and smiled.

Aah, silly me, thought Caylie. Of course, it wasn't her sister. "Hello?"

"Hi there!" said the redhead. "Are you going to be here long? My friends and I are just going to run into town for some groceries, and I was wondering if you could keep an eye on our boat? We've got skis and life vests in there."

Caylie returned her smile, thinking the woman's resemblance to her sister Jenny was uncanny. "Sure. Happy to. I'll be here for at least an hour."

"Thanks! There'll be a bottle of Napa Valley's finest in it for you."

"I'll take it!"

She watched as the young woman and two girlfriends dressed in flip-flops and terrycloth cover-ups giggled their way down the white-plank dock. Envying their youth and the carefree nature they exuded, she looked past their boat and sighed. On the horizon, the hills were the color of wheat and the elongated, red clay shoreline indicated the low lake level from yet another year of California drought. The view reminded her of Lake Baringo, a lake in the Great Rift Valley, where she and Jenny once stayed together when Jenny visited her in Kenya.

Caylie missed Jenny. She sipped her tea and sighed. All she ever seemed to do was disappoint her sister. What was it about Jenny that made her have such high expectations of everything?

Staring at the tea, she saw the reflection of the dried hillsides. Caylie wished she and her sister could get their relationship back to the way it was when they had been together in Africa. It had been a five-week period when all their childish, teenage fights had fallen away, and they were as close as two sisters could be.

* * *

Leaning against the wall of the arrival area for international passengers, Caylie's heart nearly beat out of her chest anticipating Jenny's arrival. Her sister's flight to Nairobi out of Frankfurt had been delayed by nearly eight hours due to some kind of national strike in Germany. She'd heard about it on the BBC and then somehow, Jenny managed to have a telex sent through the Lufthansa computers to the Boulevard

Hotel, letting Caylie know the long-haul flights would be the first ones out when the strike ended at midnight.

At the Jomo Kenyatta International airport, Caylie spotted her sister immediately. White people stood out in Kenya, and there was no mistaking Jenny. She was the only single woman, taller than everyone around her, and she had wild red hair and a one hundred watt smile. She wore a red-printed, blanket-stitched jacket, a gold shirt and olive, khaki pants. To Caylie, Jenny looked unquestionably American.

After handing her passport and immunization record to the immigration *askari*, Jenny looked past him and saw her sister waving. Her face lit up. "Caylie!" As she waved back, Jenny suddenly jumped back when the *askari* stamped her paperwork.

Caylie laughed. She'd have to tell her sister that Kenyan people in positions of authority loved to stamp things with vigorous enthusiasm.

Within minutes Jenny had completed the passport check and customs and skipped toward her Irish Twin. Caylie threw her arms around her tall sister and both sets of eyes filled with tears. *"Jambo, dada yangu! Karibu!"* cried Caylie.

"I don't know what you just said, Caylie, but I'm so happy to be here. Let me look at you." She pulled back and they smiled at one another's tears. "Wow, you're so pretty. And look at your hair. It's longer than mine!"

Caylie ran her fingers through her blonde tresses. "Not too many stylists in the bush. I had to let it go." She extended her arm and pointed. "We have to go over there to get your bags."

"It shouldn't take long," Jenny said. "I was one of only six people on that plane because of the strike. And it was an Airbus! Would you believe I had four personal flight attendants catering to my needs?"

"Why doesn't that ever happen to me?"

"Well, it ended up being a good thing. But for about twelve hours I didn't know if I was going to ever get the fuck out of Frankfurt!"

Caylie threw her head back and laughed. "Oh my God! It's so good to hear American!"

Arm in arm, they walked to the baggage area. "Thank you for coming, Jenny. I was going out of my mind alone at the hotel with Robert up in Dagahale. I've only been able to talk to him on the radio once or twice a week."

Jenny stopped and looked at her sister's glassy eyes. "That's just nuts," she said. "How could he leave you alone to go off and live in a refugee camp?"

"Robert's found his passion with this work. He's the big man up there. The *bwana*. He wouldn't be able to find anything like this back in Grossdale. If he goes home, he'll probably just start working at a Home Depot or something."

They took a taxi to the Boulevard Hotel and never stopped talking. They hadn't seen one another in nearly three years and there was a lot of catching up to do. Caylie had kept in touch with her sister through aerogram letters and Jenny was good about writing back, and even better about sending cassette recordings of her favorite music. "Old volunteers love new music," was a motto they had in the Peace Corps. But Caylie never dreamed she and her sister would be together in Africa. During the weeks it took for Jenny to arrange her trip, obtain her visa, her shots, her malaria medication and arrange the time off work, Caylie planned a series of safaris they'd never forget.

The next morning they took a taxi from the Boulevard to the train station to get tickets to Kisumu, a city in Western Provence. Caylie wanted to show Jenny where she and Robert had lived and worked.

At the ticket station, they stood in a long line. Jenny towered over everyone, a solitary lighthouse beaming a white light. She had a fresh-off-the-boat expression, taking everything in, and Caylie knew what she was thinking. It was always odd for white Americans to be in a place where their skin color made them the minority. "There's a lot of waiting here," said Caylie. "And staring. You get used to it."

"Yeah, but will I get used to that?" Jenny pointed to a man who had his index finger jammed up his right nostril. "My God! His head's about to cave in!"

Caylie's eyes popped and she swallowed hard. *"Shhh!"* she scolded. "People do speak and understand English here." Then she couldn't help but smile. No one made her laugh like her sister.

It was very warm and the air was ripe with the smells of food and body odor. Jenny brought her hand to her forehead and swooned. "Geez, Caylie. How can you stand the smell?"

"What smell?"

"Oh my God, don't tell me you can't smell the B.O!"

Caylie sniffed the air and then shrugged. "Oh, that. You get used to it."

Jenny dropped her jaw in disbelief. She didn't think she could ever get used to a smell so sour—so permeating. She put her hands to her stomach, feeling nauseous. "Caylie?" Her voice was as small as a kindergartner's.

"What is it?"

"I'm going to vomit."

Caylie took her seriously at once, but after waiting in line for an hour, she didn't want to escort Jenny to the ladies and lose their place. "Okay. You need to go out those doors and to the right, and then into the area near the tracks. I'm pretty sure the bathroom is just on the right. But if you don't see it, ask someone for the 'ladies.' Like I said, everyone speaks English, but just in case, it's called the *choo*."

Jenny darted off, her ponytail wagging, and every set of eyes in the ticket office followed her out the door. Then they turned their gaze on Caylie. She simply smiled and shrugged her shoulders, and within ten minutes she had their tickets. Walking out the door, she wondered if Jenny was still throwing up. Poor thing. Caylie knew just how she felt. The long flights coupled with culture shock and the smell of African sweat could be overwhelming to sheltered suburban girls.

With the tickets in hand she walked into the dimly lit station. The slick concrete floor was freshly polished. A line of kiosks was before her, where Kikuyu men and women sold everything from newspapers and magazines to animal carvings and fabrics. Looking left and right, Caylie didn't see Jenny, and when she checked the ladies room, she wasn't there either. She approached a newsstand, operated by a *khanga*-clad Kikuyu woman, who had had her eyes on the yellow-haired *muzungu* the entire time she searched the station. "Did you see a woman who looks like me wandering around here?" Caylie asked her.

"Yes."

"Which way did she go?"

She pointed past Caylie to a large, potted palm. "Well, she vomited just there, and then she went over there."

Caylie didn't know whether to be horrified or to laugh out loud. "She went back outside?"

"Yes."

"*Asante sana*," she called over her shoulder as she dashed toward the door leading back to the ticket office. She found Jenny at once. She was standing outside the ticket office, conversing with a taxi driver. Caylie ran to her. "Jenny! Are you okay?"

"I am now," she said laughing. "I puked in a plant."

"So I heard." Caylie took her sister's arm.

"I think it was the smell. Or maybe the coffee I drank at breakfast."

"*Kahawa.*"

"Huh?"

"Coffee. From now on, sister, it's *chai* for you."

"*Chai*?"

"Tea. I see I'm going to have to teach you Swahili. C'mon. Let's go register at the embassy and get ready for our trip. It's a fourteen-hour train ride. It'll give me plenty of time to teach you enough to get you through this trip."

"But I thought you said everyone spoke English."

"Not in Western."

Boarding the train, which Caylie called "the Iron Snake of Kenya," they made their way down the narrow aisle until they found the door for their designated compartment. "Are you sure this is first class?" asked Jenny. "It's about a tenth the size of my freshman dorm room. And I described *that* as a shoebox!"

"What do you want for thirty bucks a person?" asked Caylie with a laugh. "These seats convert to beds. Trust me, this is definitely first class. We even have a sink."

"What about a toilet?"

"It's down a-ways."

"And hence the difference between first world and third world definitions of first class, I guess."

"Funny how often it comes down to a toilet," said Caylie. "If you're truly desperate, you can always pee in the sink. I'll never tell a soul."

The girls stored their bags and fell into the bench seat. Jenny pressed her face to the glass. She took in everything like a fascinated child. Shortly after the train began its long journey, Caylie watched as her sister's childlike enthrallment crushed into horrified disbelief at what she saw. Beyond the cosmopolitan glass and steel high-rises of Nairobi, the train passed through a ghetto known as Kibera. Crude, mud wall structures abutting the tracks fanned out into a sea of connecting, corrugated tin roofs. The train traveled at a slow pace as hoards of people cleared the path to let it by, and all the while, they whistled and called out to the passengers.

"*Mzungu! Mzungu*!"

"*Papayas! Mangoes*!"

"Jambo, Jambo! Hbari Yako?"

"Shilling, shilling shilling? Tafadhali?"

The noise was deafening. Children in mismatched clothing ran alongside the tracks, roosters fluttered, women held up fruits and vegetables, trying to pass them through the open windows of the rail cars. An electric color palate of clothing hung on lines between the dwellings. Plastic bags and wrappers kicked up by the breeze of the passing train were a snowstorm of trash.

"It looks like a garbage dump," said Jenny.

"That's exactly what it is. Almost all these people moved from the *shambas* or farms upcountry. They came to Nairobi looking for work and found nothing. They ended up here."

"Why did they move?"

"Because of immunizations."

"Mzungu! Mzungu!" cried the children just inches from the track.

"Immunizations?" asked Jenny.

"Kenya has the fastest growing population in the world. Look at all the women with babies strapped to their fronts and backs. Many of them are also pregnant. For years women have typically given birth to a dozen children. The difference is that half of them used to die. Since Peace Corps, Red Cross, CARE and even the missionaries came to this country and pushed immunizations, the children now live."

"But isn't that a good thing?"

"Certainly," said Caylie. "But in an agrarian society, families divide their farms among their children. There was only so much land to go around. They simply ran out of real estate. The children, even though many of them made it through form four educations, had no work. That's why they came to the city."

Jenny didn't understand what form four education was—four years of high school?—at that moment, she did understand how privileged her life in America had been. And this was something Caylie had completely understood for two years.

The train continued a slow ascent before picking up speed as it made its way into the Great Rift Valley. That night, Caylie gave her sister Swahili lessons. She taught Jenny greetings, how to count, and how to say things like, "May I take your photo?" and "No thank you." Caylie had an immediate sense of being in charge of Jenny, and for once it was she who knew more about the world than her older sister.

And even though they were on the other side of the globe, unlike that day in the forests of Mitten Lake behind Aunt Bee's cottage, Caylie never got them lost.

In Western they stayed with Caylie's Somali friends in Kisumu, Sikh friends in Kakamega, and then with the Grande Damme of Nandi Hills, an elderly British ex-patriot. Her name was Beatrice Jackson and she lived on a tea estate. The bedroom Jenny and Caylie shared in her guest quarters was similar to the attic bedroom they had shared in Grossdale. The twin beds were only three feet apart, yet they were further separated by individual mosquito nets.

On their first night there, they talked well into the night and Caylie explained Robert's life in the refugee camp.

"Robert's camp is swelling with new refugees," explained Caylie. "Truckloads arrive each day. He says he starts his day at around seven and goes straight for twelve hours, solving as many problems as possible. Because that's the primary purpose of his job."

As her sister's voice penetrated the dark, Jenny stared at the minute holes of the mosquito net encompassing her bed. It was like being in a dream.

"There are new problems each day and problems left over from yesterday, and the day before and clear into last week. You see," she said, "the Somalis—especially the warring factions—can be very demanding people. They have destroyed the country to the point where there's nothing left, and therefore, there's nothing really left to fight over. Yet the civil war continues and has become meaningless fighting and warring for sake of fighting and warring. There's been no room for compromise—no negotiations.

"As a result, innocent bystanders—the women and children—flee their villages with nothing while the young men get caught up in the battles. Most are nomads who are suddenly thrust into a semi-permanent living situation at the camps and want to be accommodated. They're living in squalor with no means to make a living.

"Robert says they can't begin to understand how complicated it is managing this forever-growing number of people and all their problems. His job is to turn chaos into order and walk a fine line between diplomacy and dictation. Frankly, I don't know how Robert's going to maintain the pace he's keeping."

"Doesn't sound like the Robert I knew back in Grossdale," said Jenny.

Caylie sighed. "I know. He's changing."

"I'll bet."

"He was in tears over his first death," she said. "He didn't tell me that, mind you. One of his colleagues told me this the other day. But he's growing harder. He has to. The man who trained him said he'll grow harder and harder, maybe to the point where we don't recognize him."

"Are you sure you want to join him in this camp? Sounds dangerous."

"You mean because of all the AK-47s?"

"Caylie!"

"Yes, it's dangerous! But I need to be with him—at the very least to comfort him and keep my eye on him so he doesn't go too cowboy."

Jenny didn't tell her sister, but she suddenly realized why she had come to Kenya. Jenny needed to keep an eye on Caylie while she worried about her husband and planned a very uncertain future.

Jenny's instinct was always to take care of her sister.

Following an afternoon nap the next day, Caylie emerged from her mosquito netting when Beatrice knocked on the door. The fragile old woman delivered a tray with tea and biscuits and suggested they take a walk before dark. Caylie took the tray, thanked her, and poured two cups of tea. "Well, Mom would like it here with all this tea. Sugar?"

Jenny held up her fingers in a peace sign. "Two please."

Caylie added two heaping teaspoons of sand-colored sugar in both cups. "Does Beatrice, our hostess, remind you of Mom?"

"Not at all!" Jenny took the white porcelain cup from her sister. "I think you've been away from her for too long. Mom would never be able to survive on her own out in the middle of a tea plantation. Not even if it were a cornfield in Michigan."

"You're right. There's no woman on earth more dependent on a man. If I depended on Robert the way she depends on Dad, my marriage would have been long over by now."

"Do you think you'll recognize Robert once you get to that camp?"

Caylie sat down on her bed, blew into her tea and shrugged. "I don't know. Actually, I don't want to talk about it. Say, do you think we'd ever get Dad to Kenya?"

"You're kidding, right?"

Caylie smiled and used her best British accent. "Right. We'll never get him to leave Mitten Lake." In spite of the sugar she'd added, the tea was bitter. "Can you bring me the sugar? Mom likes it hot. I like it sweet. Really sweet."

Jenny rose, crossed the room and shoveled a third teaspoon of sugar into her sister's cup. "How long do you think you and Robert will really stay in Kenya?"

"It depends. He only signed a three-month contract with the UN; but in a couple weeks he has to decide if he's going to stay on for another year."

She handed the cup back to her sister. "Another year? Is that how long your contract will be if you get the job with CARE?"

"I don't know. I'm not even sure we can be stationed in the same camp."

Jenny sat on her bed, across from Caylie, and placed her cup on the nightstand. She pulled her hair back into a ponytail. "Geez, Caylie. I never pictured you living in a refugee camp. It was hard enough believing you lived in a hut without electricity for your blow dryer for those two years in the Peace Corps."

"Well that just proves how little you know about me, Jenny. I mean, when Mom and Dad left me in Grossdale, I had no choice but to survive."

"They didn't just leave you, you know."

"Yeah, but you already had a year away from home without Mom cooking your meals and doing your laundry. And trust me, things didn't get much better with Dad after you left. He was even more into his middle-age misery than he was during your senior year. He constantly griped about how much he hated his job and how he wanted to get to Mitten Lake. He was wasted all the time. And, God help me, he rambled on and on about World War II."

"War stories and the Depression. It's all I remember about him from high school. Man, I still can't believe they left you on your graduation day."

"Yeah, well, I had to get over it." Caylie set down her teacup. "I can't drink this. I think it's my fifth cup today. Let's go for a walk."

It was raining lightly, but the girls didn't mind. They strolled along a red clay road between rolling fields of fluorescent green tea shrubs. In the distance men and women with large straw baskets strapped to their backs diligently worked their sections, plucking tea leaves and tossing them over their shoulders and into the baskets. The rain birds serenaded them with the song Caylie knew she'd forever associate with Africa. *It will rain. It will rain. It will rain.* "Listen Jenny. Kenya birds," she said.

Jenny smiled. "Like the blue jays. Michigan birds."

An old man with a gnarly walking stick approached them. He wore a Sammy Davis Junior fedora, a gray sport coat and a blue and black cotton *kekoi* tied around his waist. Caylie said fashion in the Western Provence of Kenya was a mix of tribal traditional and Salvation Army. "*Jambo mzee*," Caylie called to him.

He stopped and returned the greeting. "*Mzuri*." Jenny stood behind her sister, listening to their Swahili banter. He asked Caylie about the woman standing behind her and Caylie laughed, explaining she was her *dada*, or sister.

Jenny flashed him her big smile and they continued walking. "What did he say that was so funny?"

"He wanted to know if you were my daughter."

"No way!"

"It's because you're so much bigger than I am and so smiley. And since you didn't speak he probably thought you didn't know how. Also, you're wearing shorts. Only little kids here wear shorts."

"C'mon Caylie. Your daughter?"

"They have no clue how old we are."

The rain stopped. In the distance the puffy white clouds looked like mountains in the sky. Patches of rainbows were between them. "Much as I don't like the idea of looking old enough to be your mother, it's still a compliment to know my authority shows."

"Your authority?"

Caylie stopped and turned to her sister. "Jenny, do you have any idea what it was like growing up with you as my older sister?"

"What are you saying? I was bossy?"

"No, not that. Well, maybe a little. It's just that you were so damn good at everything. It was a real tough act to follow."

"Yeah, but nobody liked me. I was a gawky, freckle-faced strawberry! I mean, I was never voted queen of anything, and I wasn't the one collecting homecoming and Christmas dance corsages."

"Mom liked you. I think of all of us she loved you best."

"Not true. But if anything, she was just trying to compensate for the way Dad treated me."

"It was your red hair that bothered him." Caylie smiled, then reached out and pulled on a lock of Jenny's thick hair, frizzy because of the rain. "Actually, it's probably because you're a lot like him."

"And you're like Mom. You look just like her with blonde hair instead of brunette."

Caylie let go of Jenny's curl and it coiled back. "I may look like her, but I'll tell you this right now. If Robert and I end up having kids, I'll never leave them when they're still teenagers."

* * *

It was a hard swallow. I know Caylie believed what she had said, and I loved her for her youthful, naïve proclamation. Now that she had children, and one, Frankie, was a teenager, would she still feel the same way three years down the road when she shared a house with three high school students?

It's so much easier to judge the actions of others than to judge them—or perhaps justify them—for ourselves. We all lead lives with differing, unpredictable circumstances; however, sometimes, the shared and universal experiences of raising children causes history to repeat itself. In the meantime, we can't help but inherit whatever damage our parents pass onto us. It sets the course for our lives. Because my father left my mother—and Molly and me—my youthful proclamation was that I'd do everything I could to keep my marriage intact.

And I did.

I stared into the tea and the scene returned to Northern California, a place that often reminded Caylie of the Great Rift Valley of Kenya. She was sure it was why Robert and she came there to live after their years in Africa. Sometimes when driving north of San Francisco, she squinted her eyes and believed she was back on the other side of the globe. If it weren't for all the power lines, lack of wild game and lorries belching out black clouds of exhaust around every corner, she could sustain the fantasy for any length of time.

Caylie got a job with the San Francisco Zoo, designing exhibits, and Robert taught Swahili at San Francisco State University. They had three kids in three years. All boys. Irish triplets. And when their youngest, Zachery, was only three months old, Robert decided he had to go back to Africa. Caylie refused to follow him.

It was the beginning of the end of their marriage.

"Here's your wine," a voice called from the dock behind her. "Hope you like pinot grigio."

Caylie took the bottle from the redheaded woman's outstretched hand. "*Mmm*. My favorite. But it really wasn't necessary. No one came near your boat."

"Enjoy it! Be on vacation," she said with a high voltage smile just like Jenny's.

Aah, Jenny. They had spent five weeks together in Kenya that year, a trip that also included safaris in Amboseli National Park, an excursion to Mombasa where they snorkeled in the Indian Ocean, and horseback riding through the Great Rift Valley. They stayed at a magical tented camp at Lake Baringo, where they water-skied among the hippos and crocodiles. They cried together when Jenny had to leave. Somehow they both knew they'd never again have that kind of time together.

And they were right. When the kids came along, everything changed.

The redhead and her friends sped off in their boat and Caylie wondered what was keeping Albert and the boys. His kids, Joe and Savannah, were supposed to be dropped off by their mother at ten. It was pushing noon.

Within minutes, however, Caylie heard the unmistakable clomping of boys' feet parading down the dock toward their massive boat.

"Mom! We're back." She wasn't sure who said it. Before she knew it, all three, Frankie, Adam and Zachery, had issued their customary boy hugs, pressing a shoulder into her chest, and went about their business. Adam and Zachery whipped off their shirts and looked longingly at the water slide on the stern, no doubt counting the minutes until they were out of the harbor and once again on the open water. Frankie set down a bag of groceries and then stood before Caylie, frowning.

She put her hands on his shoulders. He was nearly as tall as she was. "What's the matter with you?"

"I think Albert's drunk."

A jolt went through Caylie's stomach, and heat shot up her legs. "What?"

"After we picked up Joe and Savannah, he took us to a bar."

"You . . . you and your brothers were in a bar?"

"Well, we sat at table and ate fries while they were over on the bar stools."

"But his kids aren't old enough to drink."

"They had beers."

"Oh, sweet Jesus."

Frankie hugged her tightly, with both arms. Something he rarely did since turning thirteen. "Mom? Albert's a tool. Please don't marry him."

"Frankie—"

He pulled back and looked into her eyes. "Can't we all just get out of here? Can we move to Michigan and live on Mitten Lake?"

CHAPTER 10

For the first time in a long while during my time in *Obr*, I wasn't holding a teacup. I wondered, would Caylie marry Albert Powell? And would she really consider moving to Mitten Lake? Perhaps she'd move in with her father and take care of him. She could start a landscaping business there. With the boys' father spending so much time on the other side of the world, it wouldn't much matter if she moved from California to Michigan. Would it?

Moving had become so commonplace in the world I had left behind.

It was Jenny who first pointed this out to me. When she was a junior in high school, she enrolled in an alternative American History course. It was called "Sem-Cen," which was short for the seminar-centered approach used by the team of three instructors teaching the class. Jenny always had an interest in contemporary history. I could tell by the way she sat up a little straighter and listened intently to her dad's stories about World War II and growing up during the Depression. At least she did at first—before he repeated the same stories again and again.

Most of Caylie's and Jenny's friends' parents were a lot younger than Michael and I, and I once heard Jenny tell a girlfriend that her mom and dad were like walking history books. I didn't share much with her about my life—other than about how Michael and I met at Virginia Beach, and about how I had only three days to plan our wedding—but that didn't stop her from asking questions, and from collecting as much information as she could about our era. Jenny didn't live her life as a sum of her own experience. She wanted to tap into her family history. I watched as she spent countless hours pouring through my photo albums, even taking time to paste the loose corners that had grown tired of holding the black and white photos in place. "Who is this woman?" she asked. "And who is this?" "Why do you all have so many flowers?" She wondered if we had done our own hair in the rolled, high-top styles that were fashionable then. She wanted to know what color the dresses were and whether or not they were short or long. "Did you wear high-heeled shoes?" "What was the music like?"

For Christmas one year, she bought me an eight-track tape of Glenn Miller's Greatest Hits. Soon, she knew every word to every song. It wasn't unusual to hear her humming, "Pennsylvania six-five-oh-oh-oh!" while dancing around the house.

Jenny's questions were easy for me to answer and my answers satisfied her. They allowed her to paint a romantic history of my life as a young woman and a War bride. It didn't occur to her to ask the more serious—more difficult questions. Her father's personal history book, on the other hand, was fascinating at first; however, soon she felt she'd read it too many times. It contained only two chapters: struggling to make ends meet during the Depression and the War. Her dad's history lessons ended with the end of the War. He rarely spoke of the ensuring chapters, those containing tales of marriage, family and fatherhood.

The first topic covered in Jenny's Sem-Cen history class was called "Transportation." I thought it would be about the growth of transportation systems in the United States from horse and buggy, to trains and automobiles, to planes and rockets. And it was to a degree. The focus, however, was about how the development of transportation changed the structure of life—particularly family life—in America. During the Twentieth Century, as the population grew and the country became more connected, it became far easier for people to move away from their hometowns.

How true.

I never dreamed I would leave Boston and move to Chicago. And I certainly didn't consider that all five of my children would eventually live nowhere near Michael and me. Marie, still in Grossdale, was the closest. Darlene was in Atlanta, Ronnie in Phoenix and the Irish Twins in California. Transportation was like the torpedo that shot through my family and scattered it across the country. But I supposed I started the trend by following my husband from Boston to Chicago, and finally, to Mitten Lake.

The biggest surprise of my life was that I spent my last days in Michigan. Michigan, of all places! Growing up, Michigan was merely a mitten on a map. As a young girl, I thought maybe I'd move one day as far away as New York. And then later in life, on the one or two rare occasions that I allowed myself to imagine a life without Michael—if he were to pass over before me—I'd have an apartment in a big city. Chicago perhaps?

Meanwhile, I think it was the biggest surprise of *his* life that he had to face his remaining years without me.

After he retired and in our last years together, Michael battled high blood pressure and arthritis. He'd even had a heart attack when he was seventy-seven. I, with the exception of those brief spells—those mini strokes as Darlene called them—was the picture of health. We didn't talk about it, but I know we thought we would somehow die together. Secretly, however, I think we both believed Michael would go first. Of course, he didn't.

I couldn't help but laugh a little. After all, people plan. . . .

My husband was alone again at Mitten Lake after making the rounds with our children. He was back in his dream house with the Michigan ball cap still perched upon the pillow where I had once slept. Most of my possessions were still surrounding him, although he had given my wedding band to Marie and my diamond to Darlene. I'd already given my mother's gold watch to Jenny. There was no jewelry left for Caylie. My jewelry was like limited Kenyan acreage, not enough to go around. The youngest of the surviving children faced an empty jewelry box. There was a lot of clothing; but none of my daughters was interested in having it. So it all stayed stored in closets and dressers.

Michael couldn't throw out anything. A child of the Depression, he never could.

Time slowed for him after I died. Days grew longer, and the nights were especially long. And yet, he aged more quickly. His walk was now a shuffle. He wore slippers all the time. There was a small hunch in his back, and he looked thin to me. Daily, he sat at the kitchen counter and sorted through the recipe cards I had painstakingly copied and recopied during the last years of my life. But Michael didn't venture further and break out the measuring spoons and cups and prepare himself more than an instant cup of coffee, or a can of Campbell's soup and a piece of toast.

Molly arrived with her now customary pot of tea. "He'll be okay," she said. "Your children—particularly Marie and Darlene—will take good care of him. They're grown up, responsible people. It's even possible that the Irish Twins will come around sooner rather than later. They held far less resentment toward him than he did toward them." She set down the pot on a glass-topped table. Through the glass I saw avocado green, shag carpeting. It looked like grass. "It's a funny thing about our children. We think love is defined by the way we love them. But there are many layers to how we love." She handed me the cup with the Michigan M and filled it halfway to the top. "I realize it was a difficult adjustment at first, but I think you've already learned that worrying isn't something you need to do anymore. You did enough of it during your life."

"I worried so much about *your* children after you . . . after you—"

"After I died."

"After you died. I suppose you know Michael and I took them in."

She took the cup from me and set it aside. "Yes, Anne. I know you did."

"I would have kept them forever. But with another baby coming, one I never believed I'd conceive . . . I don't know. Charlie's parents insisted they return to Boston. I think they were better off—"

"Yes. Ultimately, they were. It's because they weren't with *him*. The bastard."

"Molly!" I knew my sister was referring to her husband, Charlie, and was shocked at her language. I had never heard her utter such a foul word.

"I know. It's taken me a long time to forgive him, which is one of the reasons I'm still here."

"What do you mean?"

"Come here, sister," she said, calmly. "It's time to look into *my* tea—to hear *my* prayers."

Molly's delicate teacup had a shallow bowl. It was fine china white, with gold edging on the outside, along with what appeared to be Celtic symbols. There was blue writing, a message printed on the inner rim. It read: "Many curious things I see when telling fortunes in your tea."

I was taken aback. "Is this a fortuneteller's cup?"

"That's precisely what it is. My mother-in-law gave one like this to me shortly after we were married. She may have been Irish Catholic like the rest of us, but I swear she had a little gypsy in her. Mother wouldn't have approved, which is why I never showed it to her."

"Or me."

She nodded. "Or you."

The tea in Molly's fortuneteller's cup was very light in color, which made it possible to see the red images decorating the inside of the cup. They included a fish; a castle, a horseshoe, grapes, a drum, a candle, weighted scales, a butterfly, two hearts shot by cupid's arrow, a lovely two-story home, a baby's pacifier, and a myriad of other symbols.

"Look closer," said Molly. She used a teaspoon to stir the contents, and a small collection of tea leaves, which had been camouflaging the most ominous symbol, swirled about in a dizzying eddy. When the image was freed of its tea leaf burial, I gasped.

Molly brought the cup to her lips, pursed them and gently blew into it. The tea leaves dissolved. "That's right," she said, "my tea leaves landed on the skeleton skull. And thus my fate revealed."

"Goodness, gracious! Did he poison you?"

"No. Charlie wasn't clever enough for that. My death was by pillow. He held it over my face until I stopped breathing."

"Molly!"

"A skull was the last image I had while on earth. As I fought for my breath, my eyes hollowed out and everything went white. It was like looking at a backlit x-ray in a dark room. I fought as hard as I could, but it was no use. He was a strong man. And he was determined."

"I knew it! I knew you didn't have asthma!"

Molly smiled without showing her teeth, and sipped her tea. "Yes, but it certainly was a respiratory disorder that caused my death." She set her cup in a matching saucer. "Hmmm. Perhaps old Red was more clever than I gave him credit for."

"Well, he got away with it."

"Far away," said Molly. "And you, and everyone else seemed to let him. I know our friend, Mary Margaret Kerrigan, sure had her doubts."

"Molly, I—"

"Anne, I'll say it again. You lived your life quietly and with dignity. It was impossible for you to even imagine that I was murdered." She sighed and her expression softened. "See? You even cringe at the word.

You can barely hear it let alone wrap your mind around it."

"It's unspeakably awful. I never saw Charlie again. I never had to confront him."

"I know. He left Massachusetts and, as you know, he didn't even tell his parents where he was going. This was why they ultimately wanted their grandchildren to be with them. It wasn't that they didn't think you and Michael were suitable parents. It was more like we—Charlie and me—were both dead, and the children were all that was left of us."

I nodded, remembering.

* * *

Shortly after I lost our first son and Molly died, Michael made it a priority to get us out of his mother's home. He bought a small, Cape Cod-style house in West Grossdale and we made arrangements for Molly's children, Dorthea, Pauline and Matthew, to stay with us. I assumed it would be a permanent arrangement, but soon learned Michael had no intention of having them stay forever. He was far more confident than I that one day we'd have children of our own.

The West Grossdale Cape Cod had only two bedrooms, but Molly's children were still young, twelve and under, and didn't mind sharing a room. I don't think any of them understood that their mother was gone for good. They didn't ask questions about when she might be coming back, nor did they talk or ask about her. I think they sensed how upsetting her death was for me and, trained like true Monaghans, kept their deepest feelings to themselves.

The girls both had their mother's dark, curly hair and green eyes. They were quiet and helpful around the house. Dorthea, like her mother, loved to sew, and she had a vast collection of buttons, which she stored in a large cookie tin. It was one of the few possessions she had brought with her. Pauline spent most of her time reading. Matthew, however, the youngest, was a handful. Like his father, he had a fiery crop of red hair, and a temper to match. He wet the bed nearly every night and cried uncontrollably, unable to put into words what was bothering him. Was it his mother's death? His father's departure? Was it the move? Did he not like sharing a room with his sisters? I believed it was everything.

His second grade teacher, Sister Agnes, offered two suggestions. Number one, she told me to ask Matthew to "use his words," whenever he deteriorated into a tantrum. Secondly, she suggested we pray.

Neither seemed to work.

Michael did not treat Matthew like a son—he was cold to the boy, detached. But I couldn't say anything. I remained grateful that he was willing to take in the children at all, and felt I couldn't ask for more than that. But poor Matthew. He was the proverbial "red-headed stepchild." Michael called him a "malcontent." He said there were one-or-two so-called "malcontents" aboard ship and he knew the type. I was puzzled by his comparison of grown men at War and a young boy who had just lost his mother—not to mention his home. It worried me that Michael might not have the patience to be a father. Perhaps I was trying to prepare myself for the possibility that having our own children wasn't in our future.

Before the school year was over, however, I was expecting. And it turned out that my condition became our release ticket for custody of Molly's children. It wasn't just Michael's doing. I was highly cautious and even fearful that chasing after and fretting over Matthew wouldn't be healthy for me or safe for the baby. I admit I willingly relinquished my responsibility of taking care of Dorthea, Pauline and Matthew. The day after school let out, we put all three on a train back to Boston, where they met Charlie's parents and moved in with them.

Dorthea, the eldest, stayed in touch with me through letters, but I rarely heard from Pauline or Matthew. I often wondered about how Matthew turned out. Throughout my life, whenever I met an ornery little boy, I thought of him. So often, it seemed, that the most malcontent turned out to be the smartest and most likeable young adults.

Michael never talked about Molly's children, and on the rare occasion he brought up the subject, he referred to Dorthea and Pauline as "the girls," and Matthew as "that red-headed boy." I could only guess that his lifelong lack of patience with his own red-headed daughter, Jenny, had something to do with his feelings about Matthew.

"Molly, did you watch over your children from here?" I asked. "I mean, do you see them through the tea as I see mine?"

"Of course."

"And do you forgive me for letting them go? I always felt as though I had abandoned them."

"Anne, they were not your children to raise. And you may not have had the five healthy children to whom you ultimately gave life if you had kept them with you. Besides, it was obvious that Michael's heart wasn't in it."

"And Charlie? What about Charlie?"

"What about him?"

"Do you ever see him through the tea?"

"Him? Ha! Never." She took a large sip, filling her mouth with tea. She swished it like gargle and spit it out. "I'm told he immediately took a new wife, and have been assured that neither are anywhere to be found in *Obr*."

"He's like us?"

"You mean dead? I don't know if he's dead or alive. But I do know he's not like us. Charlie Red Murphy gave up the gift of judging his own life. He gave that up when he took mine."

"Molly, please tell me what happened."

She replenished the tea in her fortuneteller's cup and handed the cup and saucer to me. The tea was much darker, the color of soil. "See for yourself."

* * *

What I saw reflected in Molly's tea appeared to be a dining area in my daughter Marie's home. Marie had a distinctive style, with taste heavily influenced by *Country Living* magazine. The carpet was forest green, the table made of recycled barn wood. A large crock of dried flowers was the centerpiece. Next to the table against a dark paneled wall, sat an antique oak hutch, which we had left in Grossdale when we moved to Mitten Lake. Marie had asked me if she could have it, and since I intended to give up Early American décor and keep everything modern at Mitten Lake, I was happy to bequeath it to her. The moment our car wheels were northbound out of Chicago, she stripped the whitewash finish of the hutch and gave it a coat of clear shellac. This brought out the beauty of the quarter-sawn wood.

Marie filled the restored hutch with her extensive Hadleyware Pottery collection. Hadleyware were clayware pieces designed by a Kentucky artist named Mary Alice Hadley. The plates, cups, bowls, saucers and other pieces featured her simple, whimsical drawings of barnyard animals. Mostly they were blue and white in color. It was Marie's Aunt Marge, my sister-in-law, who inspired Marie's fancy for Hadley, and ultimate collection. Marge had family in Kentucky who knew Mary Alice personally and hence, the association began. It was very folksy—very Midwest. To me it was as definitive of regional style as an accent.

Marie's table was set for a guest. There were two woven, red placemats holding Hadley plates, one with a chicken, one with a cow. There were also two mugs, featuring a rooster on one, a farm girl on the other. A squat teapot with a house painted on it sat between the place settings.

A vision of my eldest daughter appeared and warmed me. Why, I wondered, was I seeing her in Molly's tea?

Marie, her blonde hair straightened, her makeup impeccable, opened her front door and momentarily studied the man standing on the stoop on the other side of the screen. "Matthew?" she asked.

"Marie?"

"Yes, I'm Marie. Your cousin." She opened the door. "Please come in."

The gray-haired man had a round face and brown eyes. He self-consciously brought his hand to face and stroked his auburn-colored, day-old whiskers. "You can call me Matt, if you want. But Matthew's fine. Say, is it okay if I leave my *caah paaked* at the curb? It's a rental I picked up just outside of O'Hare. Nice, Irish airport you've got here in Chicago."

"Oh my goodness, your accent!" cried Marie. "My mother would sometimes let a few Boston words like that slip now and again. I love the sound of it!"

"You don't say."

Marie laughed. She held the door as he stepped inside. "Your *caah* is fine there."

Matthew smiled. He wiped his feet on the mat, and at once extended his hand. "Do you think we should shake or hug?" he asked.

Marie laughed awkwardly. "How about we shake to start out. I've made us some tea and some cherry pie. We can get acquainted. Do you like pie?"

Matthew patted his round belly. "Does it look like I like pie?"

Marie laughed again and motioned for him to follow her through the kitchen and to the dining table she had prepared. "My mother taught me how to make pies," she said. "Sometimes I cheat and buy a frozen crust at the Jewels, but I didn't do that today. I wanted to make it for you the way your Aunt Anne would have made it. Did your mother make pies?"

"I don't remember," said Matthew. "But I do remember Anne—er, Aunt Anne. I'm sorry for her passing, by the way. It's *haard*, I realize."

"Thanks."

"You know, I spent second grade not too far from *heeh* and went to a Catholic school. They made us wear a blue tie. I'm pretty sure I wore the same tie every single day."

"Really?" asked Marie. She pulled a ladder-back chair from the table. "Was it St. Teresa's? My brother and sisters and I all went there."

"No, that wasn't it. May I sit *heeh*?"

"Yes, of course. But you did live in Grossdale, right?"

"West Grossdale. It was a white house with a fireplace."

"Right. That was my parents' first house. It was where they were living when Darlene and I were born. You must have gone to St. Cletus. That's the parish on the other side of town."

"Yeah, that's it. St. Cletus." He shook his head a little then drummed his stubby fingers on the table. "I gotta tell ya, Marie, that time in my life is pretty much one, big blur. It's kinda one of the reasons I came back *heeh*. I've been in therapy, see, and it's really stirred my memory."

Marie cut into the pie and put a generous-sized wedge onto Matthew's plate. "I made tea. Would you like some?"

"Sure." He picked up the rooster mug and looked inside. "The End? How do you like that? It says 'The End' in the bottom of this cup. Does it say something else when the tea gets to the top?"

"Excuse me?"

"Nothin'. Say, I'll take some honey if you got it."

"I have honey. Just a minute." Marie darted into the kitchen and pulled a plastic bear from the cabinet above the stove. She placed it in front of Matthew and then filled his rooster mug. "I can't believe it's taken us this long to meet. We always knew we had first cousins in Boston, but well, I guess we never had the opportunity to get together. Mom didn't really talk about her sister or her life back there."

"There's probably a reason for that." Matthew used his fork to cut into the pie. Deep, maroon-red cherries oozed from between the soft, golden crusts. "Jesus, I'm pushing sixty. You can't be too far behind, can ya? But you look great. Where'd the blonde hair come from?"

"My father. Well, it used to be from my father. Now it comes from Lauren, my hairdresser. Only she knows for sure, right?"

He shoveled the forkful of pie into his mouth and his large eyes popped open. "Mmmm. This is good. Man! If you grew up with pies like this it's a wonder you're not as big around as I am. My Nana wasn't much of a cook. Irish Stew. That's about it. Maybe corned beef and cabbage. I don't know."

"So Matthew," said Marie. "What do you do for a living?"

"Call me Matt. I'm a lawyer. But I'm taking some time off. I told you I've been going to these therapy sessions and they've really made me come to terms with some pretty important stuff."

"Like?"

"Well, like I'm pretty sure I witnessed my old man kill my mother."

Marie dropped her fork. "What did you say?"

"I think you heard me." He filled his mouth with another large bite of pie and continued speaking with his mouth full. "Marie, I'm sick I didn't get the chance to discuss this with Aunt Anne before she died. I know you said she didn't talk much about my mother—her sister—but did she tell you anything about how she died?"

"Well, not really," said Marie. She squirmed in her chair, clearly uncomfortable. Clearing her throat, she picked up her fork and used it to cut into her pie. "It was asthma. Um, yeah. I'm pretty sure Mom said she had a severe asthma attack. That's all we ever knew."

"Right. I don't suppose you have any ice cream to go with this pie, do you?"

Just then, a sliding glass door opened, and into the room from an outside patio walked one of Marie's sons, her youngest, and the last still living at home. His name was Lincoln. "Oh awesome!" he bellowed. "Cherry pie! Mom, can I have a piece?" He looked from the pie to the man sitting in front of a half-eaten piece and then looked at his mother. "Who the heck is this?"

I raised my eyes from the teacup for the first time during this scene and at once, the images faded. The tea had gone cold. Molly's teacup now held only the fortunetellers' images.

I looked directly into her feline green eyes and had no words.

"He did see it," said Molly. "Matthew saw it all and I knew it. I knew he was still awake that night. I'd let him stay up with me to listen to 'The Thin Man' on the radio. Les Tremayne was back in the role as Nick and my little boy just loved that show. He didn't even care that Nora actually solved most of the murder cases. I'll say I wasn't surprised to learn that he turned out to be a lawyer. But I think Matthew was always a detective at heart. So, it's fitting he's solving this mystery, isn't it? I mean, of course, the mystery of my death."

"He never said anything to me during the time he lived with us. But, my word, he was in such a bad way. He cried all the time, and I didn't know what to do or how to talk to him."

"No one did. He held it all inside. Carried it around with him for his whole life. It's probably why he never married."

"He didn't. No, he didn't. That's very sad."

"What Matthew saw that night was suppressed very, very deep inside."

"So, why is it coming up now? After all these years?"

"I think it was your passing that brought it on. He'd always meant to contact you, Anne, but didn't. And then it was too late. He tried to talk about it with his sisters, but they didn't believe him. Neither did his grandparents, of course. Parents always have a hard time believing the worst about their children. I didn't blame them. Obviously, he's finally turned to his cousin—your Marie."

"I wonder if *she'll* believe him. She may not have been the best one to contact."

"Are you thinking Jenny? I'm thinking Jenny."

"Yes, my red-headed Jenny. She would have made a fine lawyer too. Or a detective—as you say about Matthew. Even Caylie would have been a better choice. They turned out far more sophisticated than the others."

"To use my son's words, there's probably a reason for that."

"Perhaps. They were forced to grow up rather quickly. But Molly, what really happened? Why did Red do this to you? Why?"

"Why does any man kill?"

I looked away. "I'm afraid I don't know."

"And why do young couples elope?"

I shrugged, and Molly sipped her tea, keeping her eyes on me, and hoping for a response.

"We met and married when we were very young," she said. "In spite of the times—remember the Hoover pockets? None of it mattered to us. We were optimistic, and had our whole lives ahead of us. But when the War came and he couldn't go off to fight like all the other boys with whom we grew up, well, that was the turning point. He quickly grew disappointed. And he lost control. Charlie lost control."

"Surely, Molly, everyone becomes disappointed with his or her life at some point. I know Michael did."

"I didn't," she said. "I didn't get the chance. The truth is, Red doesn't even remember doing it. What he remembers is what he constructed when he sobered up and found me no longer breathing."

I sighed and shook my head in disbelief. "So he came up with asthma."

Molly took the now empty fortuneteller's cup from my hands and set it aside. "Anne, do you know what happens to souls who have not been able to undergo judgment? To souls like mine, murder victims for example, who have not received vindication for their deaths?"

"Molly?"

"They stay here in *Obr.*"

"You mean, *Obr* is . . . Purgatory?"

Molly smiled. "Call it that if you like. Given our Catholic upbringing, it's a natural assimilation. As I tried to explain since your arrival, the gift of God you have received may or may not be a torture sentence. Is it a purification process? For some. Do we rely on the prayers of others to move us through? Absolutely. It's the prayers of our loved ones that you hear and see through your tea that guide you to the right hand of the Father."

"So, Matthew's coming to terms with what he witnessed is his way of praying for your, uh, purification?"

"Our children help us define our love. Our love defines our lives. We can't help but to judge our lives according to the lives of the children we have loved. It's our legacy. And it's why you're so focused on your Irish Twins. Neither one of them was ready to let you go. Not when they were teenagers and not even now."

"But Molly, is there something that comes after *Obr?* Is there a Heaven beyond this?"

"My dear sister," she said. "I'm actually still trying to find that out. And you are helping me and much as I'm helping you."

CHAPTER 11

Why do we have children? Molly said we judge our ability to love through our children. From the moment I passed from my life to the Light of *Ohr*, I knew I was surrounded by not only the love—a feral, unbridled love—I had for my children, but also by the love they had for me. So, I supposed there was truth in Molly's proclamation.

But was it *my* truth? I had always believed that children were a gift from God. And yet my understanding was terribly shaken when the gift of my first son was snatched away the moment I cut the bow and unwrapped the fragile tissue paper. Was his death some kind of test? Or was it a punishment?

I had lived my entire adult life with the weight of those unanswered questions. And then, to be granted the gift of five healthy children, and especially with the unexpected births of the final two—the Irish Twins—and the challenge they presented to my marriage and to everything I understood as "right," I had difficulty judging my role as Mother.

Did I love my children as much as they loved me?

I held a plain, colorless cup. It was empty, and no matter how hard I stared into it, it didn't hold the answer to this question. I raised the cup to eye-level, a clear blue sky as a backdrop, and examined it. Was it made of china? Porcelain? Ceramic? Stoneware? And what was that color? Was it the color of an unanswered question?

I said the question aloud: "Why did *I* have children?" I knew only the God in me was listening, and it was my job to answer.

I had children because I married Michael. It was what I was supposed to do.

Of course, my entire life had been about what I was supposed to do.

Without a doubt, raising children was the most challenging job I'd ever had. My offspring consistently showed me both how much and how little I was worth. I lost myself a tad more with each of their births, and my sense of self continued to diminish as I raised them and watched each one leave me. And ultimately, upon my death, I brought very little "self" with me to the other side. I then completely gave myself over to a mysterious form of judgment I'm only beginning to understand.

My cup took on a pinkish hue.

Having children made me stop estimating my value in the eyes of our Holy Father—of God. Instead, I estimated my value in the eyes of *their* father, my husband. Naturally my outlook of marriage and family stemmed from our father leaving Molly and me. But he left our mother too. And she let him go. Could she have stopped him? Could she have done anything differently to have made him stay?

It was a topic we didn't—couldn't—discuss.

Because our father left us, I was certain of one thing: My children would grow up in a house *with* a father. Their experience would *not* be a repeat of my own childhood. I wanted to do a better job.

My teacup took on an even pinker hue. Nevertheless, uncertainty kept floating before me, like steam:

Why did I have children?

Once I was married, there was no question in my mind about whether or not Michael and I would eventually start a family. We never entertained the idea of birth control. And it wasn't simply because it was against our religion. Birth control, or Planned Parenthood as it came to be known, was a concept that didn't penetrate our realm. It was like a vocabulary word we'd never heard. Or perhaps, we hadn't bothered to learn the meaning.

Meantime, it took me years to get pregnant.

"Pregnant." I said the word aloud and it echoed around me. It was another word we didn't use. We referred to this condition as "expecting." Michael called it "P-G." Regardless, we weren't having much success. First we were apart while he was still at sea, and then, well, I didn't know what was going wrong. I do know I wasn't very skilled in the bedroom—I didn't feel comfortable in—goodness, I can barely express—sexy lingerie or revealing nightgowns. I simply wasn't raised to be a seductress. Where I came from, any woman referred to as a "Jezebel," was on a par with the Devil himself. Even pierced ears were a symbol of promiscuity, which is why we never allowed our daughters to have them.

Michael had more experience than I, although he never shared the details of his premarital indiscretions. And, bless his dear heart, he was patient until finally—finally—I received the good news.

The news *was* joyous. Finding out I was expecting for the first time may have been the most joyous moment of my life.

Everyone is happy for a young, married couple expecting their first child—especially a Catholic couple with every intention of following the directive to be "fruitful and multiply," and for whom it had taken over five years to conceive. I remember there were women at the baby shower that my sister-in-law threw for me whom I had never even met. Prior to that day, I didn't understand why such parties were called showers. When I had heard the mothers-to-be were "showered with gifts," I took the meaning literally. I thought the experience would be painful! But that was hardly the case. With each gift I opened and passed around the room, I pictured my baby wrapped in that blanket, or wearing that cap, or playing with that toy.

I listened to everyone's advice, marveled at their knowledge, and for the first time in my life, I felt like I was in the right place and my life was on the right track.

And then I lost him.

They called it a "stillbirth." It was a word I could never bring myself to utter aloud. There was a sibilant hiss to it, which reminded me too much of the word "sin." They say a stillbirth differs from a miscarriage because stillborn babies are generally to term and die during labor. I didn't know what happened to my son and I don't know when he died. Had it been during the two weeks when I stopped feeling him kick me? Or did he die in that room where I was left alone to bask in my pain? How I wished I had insisted on seeing him. If I had seen my lifeless child, perhaps it would have been easier for me to accept.

Instead, I fell into a dark tunnel, isolated by grief. I was consumed by an overwhelming sense of failure.

Michael couldn't find a way to comfort me. He had not asked to see his son at the hospital that day, nor could he talk about his death. All he told me was that the baby's body was delivered to the cemetery, and buried next to Michael's father. His tombstone read only the words: "Baby Shields." There were no dates because he never actually lived. I saw this pathetic slab of rock for the first time some twenty years later. It was at Belle's funeral. My children saw it, too, and one of them asked about it. Funny, I can't remember which of my five living children asked, but I remember that I responded by shrugging my shoulders. "I've never seen it before," I said. It was the most truthful thing I could say without revealing or reliving my pain.

Meanwhile, after it first happened and I grieved for Baby Shields, I certainly couldn't turn to Michael's mother or even my sister-in-law, Marge. Neither would look at me, let alone speak to me. Had Molly been with me on the day I delivered him, I know she would have gotten to the bottom of the situation. She would have demanded answers—and demanded that they bring my child to me. But she was too late. She came to me as soon as she could get away, and had been my only comfort.

Then I lost her too.

I had married into a strong Chicago family—a family that didn't tolerate wallowing of any kind. There was an unspoken time limit placed upon me for my grief, and I had nothing left but prayer. Through prayer and faith—and what I also believe was a lot of luck, miracle after miracle were ultimately bestowed upon me.

How could I not have anything but love for my children?

I don't think it's possible to fully grasp the miracle of birth until you've had a child, however, when you couple that with the experience of having lost a child, well, it humbles you to the truth of the random fragility of creation and how easy it is to take it all for granted.

Michael was as much a devout Catholic as I ever was—perhaps even to a greater degree. He felt the same about children being the natural result of marriage. The difference was that he may have seen our children not as a gift from God, but instead as a gift from *him*. I've come up with no other reason for why he grew resentful toward them—particularly the last two—when he had to continue paying for his "gifts" by climbing telephone poles in the harsh Chicago weather.

Instead he wanted to spend his days retired next to the relaxing waves of Mitten Lake.

Michael was a hard worker and he came home every night. He was a good husband. But was he a loving father? Was it enough to just be there and to provide the home and the food? For Michael, I think giving me children was like giving me a bouquet of flowers. He brought home the bundle, deposited it in the kitchen and then expected me to arrange the flowers in the vase, keep them watered and tended to, until they no longer smelled sweet.

Did Michael ever change a dirty diaper? Not one.

His eye may have wandered toward the glamorous blonde-woman down the street once or twice, but he never actually strayed—at least not physically. During those last years in Grossdale, Jenny and Caylie's high school years, he spent more time in the basement with his seventy-eight RPM records and his drink than he did with us. While there he lapsed into a maudlin, unhappy world where he focused only on his miseries rather than his successes.

Too bad he never learned to live vicariously through his children—to have a form of father-love on a par with mother-love.

"Michael will, one day, face his own judgment," said Molly.

"There you are," I said. "I was beginning to think you abandoned me."

"Impossible. Are you ready for some tea?"

I didn't have to respond. My cup, now as red as a Valentine's Day heart, was full.

"Keep your focus on your children, dear," she said. "For now."

"Yes, Molly. I will."

From the eldest, Marie, to the youngest, Caylie, my children were ten years apart. If anyone—relatives or neighbors—commented on the growing brood of the Shields family as being abnormal or worthy of conversation, it didn't matter to me. I do recall our next-door neighbor in Grossdale telling us about their expectation of child number four. "We're just trying to catch up with you," said the proud papa-to-be. And eventually they did have a fifth child as well. I now wonder if people then described my neighbor as "the woman with all the kids," the same way I was described? And what about the other Catholic families in the neighborhood, those with not only Irish names, but also with Polish and Italian names? Those with nine and even twelve kids?

Surely they made our brood of five seem meager.

"Did you know that most families are larger than anyone ever anticipated or planned?" asked Molly. "I would have had many more children had I lived. As a matter of fact, it's what ended my life. I was trying to fight off the drunken sot when he smothered me to death."

"Oh, Molly!"

"It's neither here nor there at this point. What I'm saying is that most children are unplanned—like your Irish Twins, Jennifer and Catherine. You know they weren't planned. It had been four years since Ronnie, and you thought that stage of your life was over. And yet, how many pregnancy scares did you have after they were born?"

"Yes, after Jenny and Caylie, I suppose you can call them 'scares.' I fretted through one doctor's visit when the first test came out 'neutral.'"

"Neutral? There is such a thing? I thought either the rabbit died or it didn't."

"Believe me, I never quite understood it either. But in the doctor's words, it was neutral. Regardless, I wasn't as concerned about another pregnancy and another baby as I was about telling Michael. He didn't react the same way when he heard the news when he was in his forties versus his thirties."

"Your husband wasn't unusual in viewing a child as something to support rather than to love," said Molly.

"Well, I never regretted the birth of my girls. Truly they were the joy of my life."

"Then why did you leave them?"

Molly drifted away. I watched her fade into the Light and then watched as the color faded from my cup.

"Why did I leave them?" That was a question I *could* finally answer with confidence and justification. I left them because of Michael. I went with him to Mitten Lake because my place was with him, and it's what he wanted me to do. I had made a vow to him on that September day back during the War. I wore the long satin gown and stood before God and promised to "love, honor, and obey this man until death do us part."

Death has done its part.

I closed my eyes for a moment, and when I opened them, my teacup had become a silver goblet—a chalice. Reflected inside was not the image of my husband. Instead it was of my girls. My Irish Twins.

* * *

Jenny stored her wine glasses in a hand-carved hutch, a collectible piece of furniture from the Works Progress Administration—the WPA. She had discovered the furniture at an antique store in La Jolla, shortly after she and Don moved to southern California. Given her affinity for contemporary American History, the story behind the hutch interested her as much as the intricate basket weave and rosette carving design of the piece.

The WPA, a program initiated by President Roosevelt during the Great Depression, was an economic stimulator meant to provide jobs. Although it was controversial, it was a successful program. I didn't pay much attention to politics at that time in my life, but I did know that the WPA mostly involved big, infrastructure construction projects like roads and bridges. It also employed writers and artisans. WPA furniture at this time was constructed clear across the country in the Southwest. It was completely out of my realm. The Southwest may as well have been a foreign country. According to Jenny, New Mexican artisans called *carpinteros* built the pieces. Their creations were made without nails, screws or braces and there was extraordinary attention to detail. Funded by the WPA, the highly skilled *carpinteros* took on students and taught them the craft of traditional furniture making.

Jenny fell in love with the hutch the moment she saw it. It sat in her kitchen, against a wall perpendicular to the cabinet housing Don's massive collection of travel coffee mugs. She reached inside and took out two cut crystal wine glasses. They were Waterford—fine Irish crystal—a gift from her sister-in-law. Jenny rarely used these glasses; however, it was a special occasion.

Caylie had come to visit.

It was the eve of Caylie's birthday. She was turning forty. Her boys were with their father for the weekend, and she and Albert drove to San Diego from San Francisco. They planned to stay for two nights. Jenny thought it was unfortunate that Caylie brought Albert Powell with her, but for the time being, he and Don were out in the guesthouse watching an NBA game on television. It gave the sisters a chance to visit.

Jenny filled both glasses with cold, white wine and pushed one toward her sister. "So," she said, "how does it feel to be forty?"

"You should know. You've had fifty weeks to come up with an answer to that question."

"Ha, you're right. I guess I haven't given it much thought. I've never really paid that much attention to my age."

"Oh, I have," said Caylie. "It's because I'm always the youngest. Or at least I was."

"Yeah, me too. But you had the distinction of being the baby of the family. I didn't have a distinction besides, what? Number Four?"

Caylie smiled. "One of the 'squirts.' "

"Squirt! *Aaaargh*. That stupid moniker always sounded like diarrhea to me!"

"Moniker? Boy, Jenny. Will you ever stop being the rhetoric major?"

"I suppose not." Jenny smiled and sipped her wine.

"Do you prefer 'Freckle-face Strawberry'?" Caylie asked.

Jenny threw her hands to her cheeks. "Please! You know, someone called me that just recently. Now *that* made me want to squirt in my pants."

"Gross. Your freckles will always make you look young, Jen." She leaned over the bar counter and squinted her eyes. "But I can hardly see them anymore. Looks to me like they've all faded."

"Right. I paid good money to have these blasted freckles blasted off my face. It had to be one of the most bizarre things I've ever done. They put goop all over my skin and then zapped me with laser beams."

"How much did *that* cost?"

"Plenty."

Caylie shook her head. "It was worth it. You look great, Jenny."

"I've got our dear sister, Darlene, to thank for that. She underwent the same treatment, and I had to pry it out of her to find out what she had done to make her skin look so good. Didn't you notice her face at Mom's funeral?"

"No. I was preoccupied," said Caylie. "I can't believe we haven't seen one another since Mom's funeral. Is it the longest we've gone?"

"No. It was longer when you were in Kenya."

"Kenya. Right. Another world. Another time." Caylie released a slow, wistful sigh. "I loved it there. Who knew it would turn out to be the bane of my existence?"

"What do you mean? Robert?"

"Yes, Robert. He's going back again next month and wants to take the boys with him. Something about returning them to their roots."

"*Their* roots? In Africa? Is he cracked?"

"Yes. He's definitely cracked. He thinks he's Alex Haley or something."

Jenny rolled her eyes and held up her wine glass. "Well, I can't drink to that. How about to my Irish Twin on her last day of being in her thirties," she said. "I'm so glad you came."

"Albert did all the driving. Cheers," said Caylie with a raise of her glass. She didn't take a sip. Instead she set it down.

Jenny sipped the wine and cocked her head. "You don't want any? I bought this just for you. I thought pinot grigio was your favorite."

"It is. Was. Yes. It absolutely is."

"So? It's after five o'clock. Haven't you usually had half a bottle by now?"

Caylie bit her lower lip and squirmed a little on her bar chair. "Well, aside from my birthday, um, that's what I came to tell you about."

Jenny set down her glass, placed both hands on her kitchen bar counter and leaned toward her sister. "You're kidding me. You are *fucking* kidding me. Caylie, are you— "

Caylie cringed, pursed her lips and nodded her head. "Fraid so, Sissy."

Jenny slapped both hands on the granite countertop. "No!"

"I'm nine weeks along. I wanted to tell you in person."

"Jesus, God! And I thought Robert was the one who was cracked. A fourth kid? At forty?"

Caylie shook her head. "Once again, not the reaction I was hoping for. Damn, you're good at that."

"Oh my God. What do you want from me?" Jenny dug her fingers into her scalp and clutched thick clumps of red hair. "Are you purposefully trying to do a repeat of Mom?"

"Not really. It's not like I'm planning to have *two* babies after forty. And you might recall Mom stayed married?"

"Wait a minute," said Jenny releasing her hair. "You told Don you were marrying Albert a long time ago. On his birthday, right? And yet you're only nine weeks along?" She raised her hand and counted on her fingers. "Three, four, five— "

"May. My due-date is at the end of May."

"So, you're not just marrying him because of the baby?"

"The baby was an accident. It happened on the houseboat while we were on vacation. And you can't say anything to him. Or anyone right now."

"Albert doesn't know?"

"No. And I'm not marrying him."

"What? Oh my God. Are you telling me you're not keeping the baby?"

"No! NO! Not at all. You know I've always wanted to have a girl."

Jenny dropped her face into hands and shook her head. "A girl? You think it works that way? What, did you take special X chromosome seeds or something to guarantee yourself a girl?" She lowered her hands. "What if you end up with a fourth boy?"

"I'll name him Shirley," said Caylie with a deadpan expression and a shrug.

Jenny couldn't help but laugh. They both had heard their father, the youngest of the three Chicago-born Shields boys, tell the story of how his mother, Belle, wanted him to be a girl so badly, she almost named him "Shirley." According to Shields family lore, the old man—the grandfather they never knew—put down his foot on that one and gave him his own name, "Michael."

"Caylie, I don't understand. You're pregnant and you're not marrying Albert? You're already struggling to raise three boys with little financial help from their father. How will you manage?"

"Oh, Albert will help with the finances. He's got bucks, you know. And to be perfectly honest, that was probably the only thing that really interested me about him. I know that's terrible. That *is* terrible, right?"

"Aah geez. It's too much to swallow. Mom is probably rolling over in her grave."

Caylie groaned. "Don't say that. I *hate* that expression."

"Right. Impossible because of the cremation."

"Shut up, Jenny. This has nothing to do with Mom. I *can't* marry Albert. For one thing, he's an alcoholic. When we were on that vacation he took my kids to a bar, and let his own kids—who are underage, by the way—get drunk with him."

"What?"

"I know. I tried to break up with him after that but then this happened." She placed her hands on her stomach. "Between my age and his pickled sperm, I'll be lucky if this baby doesn't come out with a pointed head."

"Caylie! Man, you're flip. What's happened to you?"

"Just a long series of bad choices, Jenny. But I promise I didn't make them to disappoint you. Although that's all I ever seem to do."

Jenny shook her head. "Caylie, I think you know I can't stand Albert. And it seems you can't either. At least not now. But you're obviously still with him, and you're willing to have his baby?"

"I told you. It was an accident."

"Sounds more like a case of drunk driving to me. Not to mention a lifelong prison sentence to follow."

Caylie's eyes filled with tears. She stood up and looked around the room. "Can't you just support me on this? Can't you—for once in your life—react the way I need you to react?" A clear stream escaped from her nose. "Shit! I need a tissue."

Jenny quickly reached for a tissue and handed it to her sister. "Just give me the script, Caylie, and I'll say the things you want me to say. But is that really what you want? Do you want me to just agree with all the decisions you make to continually fuck up your life?"

"Can you *stop*?"

Jenny took a large swallow from her wine glass and returned it to granite counter top with a loud clank. "Caylie, do you know that was the one thing she asked of me?"

"She, who? Mom?" Caylie blew her nose.

"It was before I was married. I don't remember if I'd even met Don yet. But one day, out of the blue, Mom looked at me very seriously and told me that she wanted me to be married before I had a child."

"I don't remember you being in any kind of a hurry to have a baby."

Jenny snorted. "I wasn't. When she said that to me I just laughed because I wasn't considering either—marriage or a baby. To this day, I don't have a clue why she said that to me."

Caylie dabbed at her eyes. "I do."

"Yeah? Why?"

"Maybe," she said, "it was because one day you'd say it to me."

CHAPTER 12

Every painter begins with a blank slate. He constructs the frame, stretches out the bare, white canvas, pulls it taut and staples it in place. He sits and stares at the empty portrait, hoping the light is right. He waits for inspiration and then picks up his paints and begins. Life as he sees it covers the canvas. The painting is then hung and either admired, abhorred or ignored. But anyone who does look at it, judges it.

It can be argued that true artists paint from within as a need to express themselves, and what others think is not important. Taking one's art to a commercial level, however, is a different story. If the critics don't admire the work, if the reviews aren't good, the artist is not a commercial success. I have no doubt; however, that the artist is no different from any other human being. He is his harshest *and* best judge.

Toward the end of my life when the culture in which I lived obsessed over celebrities—what they wore, how much they weighed, to whom they were married or divorced—I often wondered why anyone would want to live under such an intense spotlight. Seeking fame was never a consideration for me, and thankfully, my children were the same way. They had enough judgment about their choices coming from their own siblings to want to further invite the world's opinion.

No one is as honest as a sibling.

I drank every last drop of my tea. It burned my tongue. I had just learned my youngest daughter was expecting another child. She hadn't yet told the father and didn't plan to marry him. As I swallowed this information the taste lingered. It tasted of Caylie's fear and insecurity. They were what made the flavor sweet. Jenny's strong judgment and disapproval, on the other hand, were what made it bitter.

Everything about my Irish Twins defined the word "bittersweet."

The cup I held now showed no sign of ever having been filled, and I stared into a plain white emptiness. I thought of a painter's barren canvas. What now? Was I waiting for inspiration? Perhaps I was waiting to hear the prayers of my children? I couldn't help but wonder how long I'd been away. And I wondered if there was a time limit on my ability to see and hear them. Were there stages of judgment just as there were stages of grief?

After I lost my mother, my child and my sister, for far too long my emotions were tangled inside me. I couldn't understand them. I couldn't express them. Then I gave birth to five children and didn't have time to think about my losses. I chose, instead, to focus on my gifts. As the children grew older, however, as one-by-one they ventured into adulthood, I had more time to myself. For years I had only an hour before breakfast to contemplate my thoughts over a hot cup of tea and a buttered scone before the morning routine kicked in. I listened for the gushing sound of water running through the pipes to know Michael was up and showering. Then I made his breakfast—a chocolate milkshake with a raw egg—and packed his lunch. After he was out the door, the children descended from their bedrooms to the kitchen one-by-one. I prepared their breakfasts, packed their lunches, and kissed them goodbye. Then the hours stretched before me.

When only Jenny and Caylie were left at home, while they were at school, I took up reading magazine articles. Monthly subscriptions to *Family Circle*, *Redbook*, *McCalls* and *Ladies Home Journal* provided far more information about coping with the changing world of the 1970s than my previous bible, *Hints from Heloise*. Since I spent hours each day standing at the ironing board in the basement, I hung a sizeable bulletin board above it. Upon the cork surface I tacked articles I had clipped from the magazines so I could reread them while steaming the endless parade of cotton wrinkles from my family's clothing.

It was during this period when I learned of Elisabeth Kübler-Ross's five stages of grief—Denial; Anger; Bargaining; Depression; Acceptance. I thought it was a fascinating concept and tried to place my grief experience on this tidy chart. At the time it didn't help. I simply couldn't see how the stages applied to me.

I knew I was depressed when I lost the baby, but I never denied it happened—at least not to myself. And yet, I didn't tell my children about him. Was this a form of denial? This baby, after all, was their brother. Even though he never took a breath, he had lived inside of me for nearly nine months. He even had a name: Barry.

His death didn't make me angry. It made me sad. But I never forgot the sound of the harsh voice belonging to the nurse who, after what felt like hours, finally came to me in that dark room where I had been left alone with my cutting labor pains. With seemingly little sympathy for my pain, she barked the words "Don't push!" Every instinct urged me to push. Apparently Nurse Negative was too weak to share the news that the baby had no heartbeat, and she was incapable of delivering a dead baby.

I don't remember anything after "Don't push!"

I put a hand to my stomach and felt a churning well up inside me. Was it this nurse who injected the drug to silence me and take the birth experience away from me? Was it she who decided I didn't have the right to see the child I'd carried for forty weeks?

Someone knew my baby was dead.

How did they conclude it would be better not to tell me anything? To leave me alone in a cold, unfriendly room, and scold me for trying to act upon my natural instincts? I held both hands over the sharp pain of realization.

I *was* angry.

I was so angry, that I swore I'd never have another child. It wasn't because I didn't think I was capable of having children—that was my sadness speaking—it was because I was angry about the pain, and I was angry at the nurse for not telling me the truth about the pain. Any woman expecting a child knows, without question, there will be discomfort—and yes, pain involved in the delivery. But the world's mothers assure you the pain is forgettable and worth it once you hold your newborn baby in your arms. Before the experience, "labor" is just a term. But when you actually feel that low moan from within, which over the course of a minute grows from a whisper to the blast of an air horn, you understand the true definition.

It was neither forgettable nor in the case of my stillborn son, worth it.

Ultimately, did my unrealized anger subside? Did I bargain by praying to God for another child? Did I accept my loss when the first of my five additional children lived?

Perhaps. Perhaps the article I read and reread about the five stages of grief were more on target than I realized while I was still alive.

There were articles and guidelines on nearly every subject imaginable. I lived through a time of information explosion, which was coupled with what they called the self-actualization movement—the ME generation. Even though I wasn't of that generation, my children were. And as I lived vicariously through them, I did experience a stage where I finally had time to turn inward.

But it was an uncomfortable place to be. I'd grown so accustomed to having my opinions not matter that I never believed my feelings mattered either. So, as Jenny and Caylie spent less and less time at home—because of their many friends and activities, and their desire to get away from their father's tirades—I did two things. I started working outside the home *and* I shifted my primary focus to Michael. Like their three siblings before them, I knew my Irish Twins were about to leave me too. I didn't want to leave them first; however, I understood my place was with my husband. That's another thing the mother's of the world will tell you—whether it's over a cup of tea or through a magazine article. Children will grow up. They will leave. The articles call it an "empty nest." But just like labor pains, you don't know how it actually feels until you experience it.

For me, it was awful. And because of my inability—actually, my reluctance—to focus on myself and my feelings, all I had left was Michael.

The atmosphere around me became as white as a puffy, cumulous cloud, and as large as a world-sized mural canvas. And soon, a new image of my Irish Twins formed upon the canvas. Jenny and Caylie shared an upholstered chair in Jenny's San Diego living room. It was an oversized chair—called a "chair-and-a-half" by some, a "mother-daughter-chair" by others. Their legs stretched before them on a matching ottoman, and each held a cup of tea. It was like old times for them—old as in the brief period after college when they shared their Oak Park Victorian:

Before Caylie announced she was marrying Robert.

Before Africa.

Before children.

Life was good for them at the time. Uncomplicated. Everything they took on had been as simple for them as steeping a tea bag. Of course, they didn't know that then. Since the day Michael and I moved to Mitten Lake, neither ever again had the feeling of being carefree. Their childhoods had come to a screeching halt, with no true weaning involved. They both felt they had struggled through college. And yet the truth was, they breezed through. Each knew how to apply for scholarships and financial aid, and each was successful. Their grades were good. They found desirable entry-level jobs in their fields. They were healthy, strong young ladies, far more sophisticated and educated than I had even hoped.

My Irish Twins were everything that I could have been had I grown up in their day.

When we left them, the girls were given the opportunity to sink or swim. And like their Shields family ancestors, they proved themselves strong swimmers. That's what they inherited from their father. From me, both Jenny and Caylie inherited the unending feeling that their lives were flying by at a rapid rate.

We never truly saw what was right in front of us.

When we were young, we constantly looked toward the life ahead of us, and wondered what we had to do to make it better. I don't remember at what point my thoughts turned from the future to the past. But they did. Alone with Michael at the lake, nostalgia was my constant companion. Did I ever have an interval when I was simply present in the moment?

I could see, now, that my youngest daughters were in the in-between. Jenny had made most of her notable life decisions and was content with her choices. As the mother of two adolescent daughters; however, she looked toward the future through *their* eyes and marveled at how quickly *they* were growing up.

Caylie felt the same way about her boys; however, the difference between the Irish Twins was that Jenny knew her childbearing years were behind her. Caylie, on the other hand, wasn't quite ready to let them go.

"A baby at forty," said Jenny. "Who'd a thunk it? You of all people."

"Me of all people?" asked Caylie with a slight sneer. "What's that supposed to mean?"

"You think you can hang in there for another eighteen years doing the hands-on mommy thing? Your own mother couldn't do it, and she didn't have a career to think about."

"Yeah, but I'm younger. She was forty-two when she had me."

"I've got news for you. The doctors start referring to you as 'an advanced age mother' the day you hit thirty-five. And aside from that, at least Mom was married."

"Right. Well, I don't remember Dad doing all that much. I mean aside from bringing home the bacon."

"That's some pretty important pork, Kiddo."

Caylie laughed. She loved it when Jenny called her "Kiddo." All her siblings had called her by that nickname for her entire life; however, she hadn't really noticed it until she and Jenny were together in Africa. It was at a point during their long, wandering safari, when they were staying at a remote guest ranch on the equator, at the foot of Mt. Kenya. It was a district called Laikipia. After experiencing a series of dusty, tented safari camps, Laikipia offered what felt like luxurious accommodations. The sisters stayed in a stone cottage with a grass-thatched roof. Hand-woven rugs, created by Kikuyu women in a mill on the property, covered the floors and the walls. Evening meals were served on the terrace of the owners' home, where fuchsia bougainvillea curtains framed the golden rolling hills leading to the majestic mountain. They dined with the family, a young couple with two small daughters. During each of the three nights they were guests, a gray and black striped civet cat found its way to the terrace and meandered between all the feet parked below the table. Caylie, accustomed to mixing with wildlife, was unfazed by the civet's presence. Jenny was startled at first; however, she adapted quickly, once she learned the small cat was harmless. As for the family, they considered the civet a pet, and had been contemplating a name for it—something other than the Swahili names *fungo* or *ngawa*. And on the third night when one of them overheard Jenny call Caylie, "Kiddo," the civet's name was decided.

"I know Albert would support this child," said Caylie. "That's actually the least of my worries. I'm more worried about Robert. He isn't going to like it one bit."

"And you care what he thinks?"

Caylie stirred her tea. "How could I not? He won't approve of his kids having a half sibling. It'll just give him more ammunition to throw at me. He's so unpredictable. He'll go for weeks when he's really nice to me—the old Robert—like the cool guy he was when we were growing up. Or when we were in Kenya. And then bam! Something sets him off and he just yells at me. And most of the time he yells at me in Swahili. My friends think he's a freak."

Jenny laughed and nodded her head. "*Ndio*," she said.

"Oh! *Dada yangu*! You still remember your Swahili!"

"A bit," she said.

"A bit. But not enough to bite," they said together, impersonating Meryl Streep's Danish accent in the film *Out of Africa*. They both knew the movie by heart. Jenny had first seen it while Caylie was still in the Peace Corps and watched it several more times before flying to Kenya. Knowing how much her sister loved the story of Karen Blixen's years in Kenya, Caylie showed Jenny many of the places where it had been filmed, including Lake Nakuru—always filled with pink flamingos—and the town of Karen just outside of Nairobi. They went to the house where the Baroness lived while trying to sustain a coffee business. A tourist destination, the house was open for viewing. "Hello the house!" they called to it when first stepping upon the hallowed grounds.

"We're about due for another viewing," said Caylie. "Do you have the video?"

"Better. I have the DVD. Ah, you should hear the music! I'd love to have my girls see it with the both of us. But Don would rather stab himself in the eye than watch it again—or even be in the same room when it's on."

"Hopefully he'll keep Albert occupied out in the guest house with an endless series of sporting events on the tube. He's got beer out there, right? If there's beer, we might manage to avoid seeing Albert for the rest of the weekend. Got any vodka? We can really anesthetize him."

"Caylie, you've got to tell him about the baby."

She sighed. "I know."

Jenny placed her hand on Caylie's forearm. "Why don't you do it before you go back to San Francisco? I'll be right here by your side if you want."

"Do you think I can get away with *not* telling him?"

Jenny snorted and placed her teacup on a small table. "Sure. Until you have to explain the basketball sticking out of your gut, and then later when the kid needs a new pair of shoes. Or braces. Or, uh, a college education?"

Caylie leaned her head on her sister's shoulder. "I know. I know

I have to tell him. The baby isn't even the hardest news. He can be pretty volatile."

"What do you mean? Like violent?"

"I don't know. I don't think so. But it's the not wanting to marry him part that keeps me from telling him anything. It all just scares me."

"It should!" Jenny exhaled an exasperated groan. "This is serious shit, Caylie."

Caylie abruptly lifted her head. "You think I don't know that?"

"I don't know what you know or don't know, Caylie." She removed her hand from her sister's arm. "I still don't understand why you agreed to marry him in the first place. You can't tell me it was love. In fact, you really didn't tell me anything, did you? You told Don."

"Get over it already! I admitted to you it was more about security. You have no idea what it's been like for me these past five years since my divorce."

"I have no idea? Are you kidding me?"

"It's hard, Jenny. And it's lonely." Her voice grew thick. "Sometimes I just want someone to take care of *me* for a change."

Jenny squeezed shut her eyes and slowly shook her head. She couldn't believe her ears, and she wondered how her sister could discount everything she'd done—everything she'd contributed to her survival and wellbeing over the years.

She didn't know what to say.

The edges of the canvas—my viewing screen—began to curl. I watched Jenny's expression carefully and felt her confusion. She wondered if Caylie simply hadn't noticed how much she'd taken care of her, or if she'd grown so accustomed to it that it was expected.

With a sharp stab—an arrow to her heart—it dawned on Jenny that she really didn't care. She had her own daughters to think about. She obviously hadn't been a good enough sister, but she was confident that she had done the best she could do where Caylie was concerned.

It was time to focus on being a good enough mother.

Jenny swung her legs from the ottoman and turned her back to Caylie. It hurt to learn that her sister had placed so little value on her emotional and financial contributions over the years—particularly the last five years—but she didn't do it in order to gain her sister's gratitude. She did it because it was the only way she knew how to behave.

She rose and sighed. "Caylie?"

"What?"

"Plain and simple: You've made a mess of your life."

"Well," said Caylie. "Thank God I have you to constantly remind me of that."

"You don't need me to remind you. You already know it. But I just want to make sure you also know, that I can't—nor could I ever—fix it."

"Are you telling yourself that? Or do you think you're just telling me?"

Jenny let out a deep breath and then smiled. She leaned over and pressed her index finger into Caylie's nose. "Both, Kiddo," she said. "Both."

CHAPTER 13

"What was that you said about siblings?" asked Molly. "No one is as honest?"

"Jenny is a truth-teller. She always has been. She's like Michael."

"Caylie's more like you. She's better at keeping things inside."

"Yes, you're right, Molly. But I never blamed you for anything."

"I don't think Caylie's blaming Jenny. And you certainly didn't blame me for anything. After all, you were the one whose life turned out well. ***I'm*** the one who married a scoundrel."

We were seated in upholstered, wingback chairs, across from one another at a small wooden table with a worn butcher-block top. Three unlit, tapered white candles rose from a polished silver candelabra at one end of the table. Next to it were a bowl of green apples and a white porcelain teapot. Behind Molly was a long window seat lined with half a dozen green-striped pillows and a matching pad.

It was our mother's kitchen—a setting I had recreated in many dreams throughout my life. I knew every inch of it—from the solid oak, hardwood floors to the elongated cream-colored cabinets. To our right was a pale yellow Martha Washington gas stove. It had green handles, the same green color in our wingback chairs and window seat pillows. Atop of the stove sat an iron skillet holding what was no doubt—according to the aroma surrounding us—freshly baked Irish soda bread. A simple recipe of flour, sour milk, salt and baking soda, we ate it with every meal, and also had it for afternoon tea.

This time I reached for the teapot and filled our cups. "Molly, does it all come down to whom we choose to marry?"

My sister laughed. "Certainly not! Your place at the right hand of the Father is not based upon marriage. It's based upon love: Of course, that may include the love of and for a spouse; but it's also about my love for you; your love for your children; Jenny and Caylie's love for one another. Our love is tested while we live. It's judged when we die."

I dropped a spoonful of sugar into Molly's teacup. "I'm not sure you and I ever had what Jenny and Caylie have. We were close for a while—at least I thought we were. But we lived through such different times. We didn't share our feelings because I don't think we were taught how to do it."

"It's funny you should say that, Anne."

"Funny? What do you mean?"

Molly rose and walked to the stove. She removed the towel, which covered the soda bread, then leaned over and pressed her nose to the golden crust. "It's the same thing Mother told me during my early time in *Obr*."

"Mother? Mother was with you?"

Removing the loaf from the skillet, she placed it on the towel, gathered the four corners to form a sack, and carried it back to our table. "Who else did you expect would meet me?"

"I don't know, Molly. I suppose I hadn't thought of it." I closed my eyes and took a deep breath. "I'm sorry. Have I been horribly selfish?"

"Not at all. I understand this is your time—*your* judgment journey. Slice of bread?"

"But . . . Mother!" An image of her filled my thoughts. "I would love to see her. May I see her and talk to her the way I see and talk with you?"

Molly produced a bread knife and sliced the round loaf right on top of the butcher block, just as we'd always done in this kitchen. "You will be with her, Anne. I promise. As you may have already learned, in *Obr*, there are few limitations, and infinite possibilities. Hold your hour, my dear."

I believed her. Molly had used not only our mother's expression, but also her voice. And with these words and the taste of the warm bread on my tongue, our mother's image grew clearer, and I felt her presence.

Her name was Grianne. Grianne Ellen Lane Monaghan. Everyone called her Anne, which is why she gave me that name. Grianne, she said, was her parents' version of an Irish name, a variant of the name Grace, meaning "love."The true Gaelic origin of this name is "Grainne," (pronounced GRAWN-ya), which was from the word *gran*, meaning "grain." Mother once told us the legend of Grainne, who was said to be the most beautiful woman in Ireland. She was the daughter of a king, and because of her great beauty and her wit, all the princes and chieftains of the land wooed her. Ultimately she was promised to an old chief named Fionn MacCool; but at the feast celebrating their pending nuptials, Grainne was repulsed by Fionn, who was even older than her father. So she set her sights upon a warrior named Diarmuid and fell in love with him. Diarmuid was Fionn's friend and best warrior, and he refused Grainne, remaining loyal to Fionn. Grainne had her mind made up, however, and to win Darmuid's love, she cast a love spell—or a *geis*—upon the handsome warrior. Under her power, together they ran off. And as an angry Fionn and his men chased them, they hid out in remote corners all across Ireland. Eventually they married and, according to our mother, Grainne had five children.

That was where the story ended for our mother. Later in my life I learned the mythological tale of Grainne and Diarmuid had a tragic ending. Fionn was relentless in his pursuit, even after the couple believed they were in the clear. Fionn had placed his own *geis* upon Diarumid, and prophesized the traitor warrior who stole his bride would be killed by a wild boar. He was.

When I was a child, the only part of the story that was important to me was the part about Grainne being the most beautiful woman in all of Ireland. I believed this because I thought my mother was the most beautiful woman in our neighborhood of Melrose. She had lustrous black hair, which she had never cut. At night when she let out her tortoise shell combs, a single braid cascaded down her back and occasionally she'd allow Molly and me to watch her unravel and brush through the rippling waves. We begged her to just once, wear it in a different style other than the coiled braid wound into a massive bun behind her head. But she refused. A proper woman pinned up her hair, she said.

Mother was a small woman and very quiet. She always wore black. Because our father didn't live with us, many thought she was a widow;

however, this perception didn't concern her. The church did not permit divorce, and separation was too painful to speak of in polite company. So, our mother never had reason to affect anyone's opinion. If she were the topic of any congregational or neighborhood gossip, she was unaware.

Our mother was trained as a classical pianist, and our Victorian-style home was often filled with the sounds of Bach (her favorite) and Chopin, which she played on a Howard-Baldwin baby grand. I was six years old when she received this beautiful, mahogany piano as a gift from her uncle, and I remember how she quietly directed the movers to place it in the far corner of our main parlor. Neither my sister nor I were musically inclined and Mother didn't encourage us to pursue piano instruction. The Howard-Baldwin belonged to her and for the first several years it was in our home, she had exclusive rights to it. By the time we were in our early teens, however, Father was gone, and as the Great Depression blanketed us with the need to survive, Mother relied on her talents to earn money as a piano teacher. Every day after school and all day on Saturday, we had a constant stream of children coming and going out of the house. Because of this, for the rest of my life, I cringed whenever I heard various études, scales, or the opening notes to Beethoven's "Für Elise."

Mother kept up the lessons until her hearing gave out. That happened during the War. Molly had already married and was living in Lynn and I was earning a decent wage as a telephone operator—enough to support us. Each day I sat in a hard-backed chair wearing headphones and asking into a small microphone, "what number please?" At the end of my shift, my ears were sore and my throat was tired, and I thought, perhaps, I was speaking too softly when my mother constantly asked me to repeat myself. It wasn't until she accused me of mumbling, which I never did; that it dawned on me her hearing had deteriorated. She must have noticed the muffled tones of her beloved piano keys; however, she refused to let me take her to see someone about it. Luckily, my friends Lolly and Mary Margaret Kerrigan were the daughters of a general practice physician, and we arranged for their father to make a house call one Sunday after Mass. That day Dr. Kerrigan and his daughters showed up with a device he called a "vacuum tube," which was a battery-operated hearing aid. When he placed it on the brunch table, I thought it looked like something that belonged under the hood of a car. We didn't own a car and I'd never driven one at that point; however, our great uncle had one he called a "Roadster," and once, he showed me the inner workings.

"What's this?" Mother had asked.

"It's going to help you hear," said Dr. Kerrigan.

"How's that?" she asked.

"It'll help you hear."

"My ear?"

"Precisely, Mrs. Monaghan."

Mother looked at me and knit her eyebrows. "What's he mumbling about?"

The Kerrigan sisters stifled giggles as their father shot them a stern look. He picked up the heavy, rectangular amplifier, which had a long, thick cord attached to two large batteries. One battery was bright red, long and tubular like a stick of dynamite. The other was flat, with squared-edges, just like a Schilling spice tin. Side-by-side, the batteries were larger than the actual hearing aid. "The girls are going to help fit this to you," he said.

Mother took two steps backward, and Dr. Kerrigan turned his gaze to me and spoke too loudly—as if I were the one who was hard of hearing. "She'll need to wear the amplifier on her chest. She can attach it to, pardon me, her undergarments." He patted the center of his own chest. "With the batteries she has a choice. They can be strapped alongside the device, or she can strap them around her leg. In either case, the battery holder is somewhat cumbersome and weighs as much as the amplifier. She'd probably be more comfortable with everything up top."

Mother practically barked. "I'm not comfortable with any of this."

Lolly frowned and commented out of the side of her mouth. "Well, she heard that!"

Mary Margaret nudged her sister. "Let us help you, Mrs. Monaghan. Lolly and I have done this before. We know what we're doing and we'll make sure you're comfortable."

Mother smiled at Mary Margaret and took her arm. The Kerrigan girls, like towering bookends on either side, escorted our mother to the first floor guest room. My mother had always found the Kerrigan sisters, particularly Mary Margaret, to be irresistibly charming. Behind the closed door she allowed them to strap the hearing aid to her, and for the rest of her days, walked around with what appeared to be an Amazonian breastplate under her black dress and an earphone attached to her left ear.

"Did Mother greet you like you greeted me?" I asked Molly. "With a cup of hot tea?"

"No," said Molly. "It wasn't the same."

"Well what was it like? Was she wearing her hearing aid? Or was she young and beautiful? Was her hair down? Did she give you something from which you could view your life? Or to view your children? Maybe some chicken broth? I know you always loved your soup."

Molly smiled and I heard the soft sounds of a piano rising in the distance. A minuet played in the parlor—the well-appointed room next to the kitchen. "That's clever, Anne. But it wasn't soup. Nothing like that. Mother handed me something entirely different."

"What? What did she give you?"

Molly's face took on a radiant glow and the piano music grew louder. I listened, discovering it was no longer a minuet that I heard. There was no mistaking it.

It was "Brahams Lullaby."

In sync with the melody, the light from the bay window behind my sister flickered with hues of gold and violet, and everything smelled as fresh as rain. I recognized the scent. It smelled just like—

Molly touched my hand. "Our mother handed me your son, Anne. It was your baby boy."

A tremble rose from within. For a moment, I wasn't sure what she meant. "My baby?"

It was the scent surrounding us that answered me. It was the unique smell of a newborn, which for me was a combination of soft rain, talcum powder, toasted bread and cream cheese.

Within seconds, it dawned on me, of course, that she could only be speaking of my first child. Barry, the son I had lost. "Mother handed you my baby? Was he—?"

"He was sleeping. He was born sleeping, and it's how he came to *Ohr*."

"He was born sleeping," I repeated. I liked the sound of that. It was far gentler than that awful term, *stillborn*. I looked left and right—over and around Molly.

"He's no longer here, Anne."

"In *Obr?* You mean I won't see him?"

"You already have," she said.

"I have?"

"Yes, my dear. You saw him in each one of your children during all of your days on earth. He was there, and you saw him, felt him, smelled him and loved him every day."

I shook my head. "I don't know what you mean."

Molly smiled. "He was in the eyes and in the touch and in the love of Marie, Darlene, Ronnie, Jenny and Caylie."

The Light around us grew very bright, as bright and warm as a spotlight. In an instant, I was filled with an overwhelming sense of love and understanding. And for the first time since I had lost this child, I knew that I had done nothing to cause his death.

On the contrary, my love for him had allowed him to live.

I looked into my white porcelain cup, and reflected in the tea, I saw him—a fully formed infant inside my womb. He was curled like a ball with fists tightly clenched. Tiny eyelashes protruded from his closed lids and his lips formed a soft line. His head was as round and bald as a cue ball, and I imagined him a blond, just like his father. And Marie. And Caylie. His eyes would have been green, like mine. And like Darlene's. I knew this. As I studied every detail of his features, my eyes traveled to his extended oval belly and then I focused upon his umbilical cord. There I saw a knot, exaggerated like the twist of a pretzel. It jumped out like a kindergarten illustration.

"He had a knot in his umbilical cord."

I wasn't sure if I said it aloud or if Molly had said it. But it didn't matter. What mattered was that I understood. He died; but he had also lived.

My! How simple everything seemed the minute I embraced this understanding.

Molly reached across the table and dipped a teaspoon into my cup. She stirred away the image of my baby and in its place, another formed. It was another fetus. This one was far smaller, although the features—the fists, the mouth, the round head—were identical.

"This is Caylie's baby, isn't it?" I asked.

"Yes," said Molly. "This baby's soul is now present with your daughter," said Molly.

"Does that mean— "

Molly closed her eyes and prayed. "*He is not far from each one of us, for in him we live and move and have our being.*"

"Are you speaking of God?"

She opened her eyes. "I'm speaking of all of us."

CHAPTER 14

When Caylie was a student at the University of Illinois, she bought a pair of overalls at a used clothing store.The shop was called Second Hand Rose. From the first time she saw the wooden sign, carved block letters painted metallic gold and surrounded by a wreath of pink and purple roses, she felt the store sang out to her. As the baby of the Shields family, Caylie spent her life wearing second-hand clothes, riding second-hand bikes, and taking second-hand advice from all four of her older siblings. Having saved very little money for college as a teenager, she soon learned how far five bucks could get her in a store like Second Hand Rose.And even though most of her wardrobe came from this packed, dusty establishment during her four years of school, the only thing still remaining in the forty-year-old woman's San Francisco closet were the overalls. She'd never get rid of them.

Caylie's overalls, Oshkosh Bgosh, had become a work of art.They were a landscape of her life. Originally a shade of deep blue denim, countless washes caused the color to fade. Underneath patches of velvet and leather and a rainbow of embroidery, the once rich denim had turned to the color of an overcast sky.The knees were patched with a deep purple and rawhide brown, and a meticulous blanket stitch outlined the random geometric shapes. Embroidered designs worked their way up from the foot holes through the pant legs and to the bib and shoulder straps, like flowering vines climbing a trellis. Using a book from one of her early landscape architecture courses, she followed an alphabetical list of flowers, sewing the seeds of her garden from pale yellow anemone to crimson zinnia.

With plenty of room in the waist and the legs, Caylie's beloved overalls had seen her through her first three pregnancies, and she trusted them to help get her through her fourth. As her unborn child entered the twentieth week of gestation, her colorful overalls, once again, had become her favorite item of maternity wear. No one knew there was a baby bump beneath the bibs.

Not even the father.

I didn't see or hear Caylie end her romantic relationship with Albert Powell, although my understanding was that she broke off the engagement on their drive north from San Diego. My youngest daughter had not taken her sister's advice. She didn't tell Albert about the baby. And because she abandoned all forms of prayer over the matter, Molly explained that my observation and influence from *Ohr* were limited.

Shortly after their weekend together celebrating Caylie's fortieth birthday and her revealing the expected baby, the Irish Twins once again went their separate ways. Their thoughts, as always, were with one another; however, these thoughts were clouded with confusion. I could tell by the murky reflections in my tea.

When the girls were in junior high, I remembered they listened to a pop song on the radio over and over again about a woman looking through clouds in her coffee. At the time, I didn't understand what the lyric meant; however, I didn't understand most of the lyrics to their music. But Molly explained what the clouds in my tea signified.

"Your observations are based on two things," she said. "Love and prayer. You see the people whom you love and love you, and you hear them through their prayers."

"Perhaps that's why I've yet to see anything of Caylie's Albert."

"He's *not* Caylie's Albert and, my dear, and it's not because he doesn't pray."

"I know. She doesn't love him."

"But she does love the baby she's carrying. Unfortunately, she's so wrapped up in hiding the truth from his father that she's thinking primarily of the pregnancy rather than the child."

"Is it a boy?"

"It is a baby, Annie," said Molly.

My tea remained cloudy.

God grant me the serenity to accept the things I cannot change; courage to change the things I can; and wisdom to know the difference.

I looked into my sister's green eyes, a reflection of my own. "What does it mean she's thinking primarily about the pregnancy rather than the child?"

"She wants to be able to support all her children without relying on their fathers. And she doesn't want to depend on her sister either."

When I finally saw Caylie again, Molly was not with me, and I was seated in a white wicker chair in the midst of the most beautiful English tea garden I'd ever imagined. The table at which I sat was on a red brick patio. Feathery, florescent green moss lined each brick. Bordering the patio, the garden took shape with purple lobelia and alyssum, mixed with two-toned coleus, bachelor buttons, stargazer lilies, and black-eyed Susans. I could make out lavender, coneflowers, phlox and tall, full foxgloves. A cardinal, red as the blood of Christ, whistled from the branch of a dogwood tree filled with white, fragrant, cross-shaped flowers. It was all far more beautiful than any garden I had ever produced—I didn't inherit my father's or grandmother's green thumbs. And yet I knew one of my daughters had. That daughter was Caylie.

Since she was a young child drawing pictures of buildings and floor plans on everything from napkins to paper plates, we believed our youngest child would be an architect. By the time she was in seventh grade, however, her interest had turned to plants. The first plant she brought home was a variegated spider plant. Daily, she checked it for offshoots. Once they were formed, she clipped them and put them in water-filled plastic cups in order to root. It wasn't long before Caylie had collected about as many baby plants as the spider Charlotte had in *Charlotte's Web*. Her interest grew into an obsession and by the time she was a junior in high school, our Grossdale living room resembled a terrarium. Michael and I took a few of the larger plants—the dracena, dieffenbachia and hibiscus—with us to Mitten Lake, and Caylie took a few with her to decorate her first college dorm room. The others she gave away as graduation gifts to all of her many friends.

When Caylie declared her major to be landscape architecture, everyone who knew her believed she had found her calling.

I poured green tea from a porcelain teapot, one with bright pink hibiscus flowers on either side. Through the reflection, at last I saw her. She was wearing her overalls. All the colors of the garden around me were contained in her embroidery. Beneath them she wore a sky blue, collared shirt. She, however, was not in a garden. Caylie was in an office and seated across from a woman wearing a navy blue suit and a tidy French twist in her auburn hair.

"Well then, Mrs. Cotrell," said the woman, we're so glad you could make it back over the bridge to this side of the bay once again."

"It's not a problem. And please, call me Caylie."

"All right, Caylie. I must say, your references were glowing. And with your reputation, it's hard to believe you're actually available for this position."

"Oh, I'm available all right. After the Zoo and all the commercial landscaping work, I changed to residential during the dot-com boom. But now it isn't what it used to be since the real estate market tanked. I'm just lucky I got to ride the rollercoaster during the upswing."

"Is your company still in business?"

"Barely," said Caylie. "It's why I really want this job. Not only do I need the steady income, but also the benefit package. I have three boys to support. They're in school in the City, but I've wanted to move all of us to the East Bay for quite a while."

"Well, the current site is pretty far east—it's practically Sacramento." The woman smiled and then sipped from a paper Starbucks cup. "Not really, but it's out there. It's not a difficult commute from here in Walnut Creek. Really, you could even find something in Dublin or Pleasanton and take the 580 out there."

Nothing in California ever felt too far away to Caylie. To the west was the coast, the east the mountains; to the north was the redwoods and to the south, her Irish Twin. The freeways may have been crowded, but they were in good shape, and they could transport her anywhere. Caylie smiled. "At least it's not in Africa."

"Excuse me?"

"Oh nothing. Sorry. My ex spends a lot of time overseas. I, in fact, lived in Kenya for several years."

"Yes, I saw that on your resume."

"You should have seen the gardens in the rainforests of Western Provence. Just beautiful." Caylie looked to the windows beyond her interviewer's auburn hair and spied the golden hills in the distance. "If only we had that kind of rain here in California."

"Yes, well, any given El Niño." Again she sipped her coffee. "Okay, listen. You're obviously very passionate about your work. I like that. I know the department assistant, Allison, took you for a tour of the site during your previous meeting. So, I assume you're aptly familiar with it and have begun formulating a few ideas?"

"Oh, absolutely," said Caylie. "I'm very familiar with the site. It's a gorgeous backdrop—like something out of a Western painting. I already have an idea for the plan and drew up a few initial specs. They're rough, of course, but I think they'll convey the general idea." She reached down and unzipped the black portfolio case at her feet. "Even though it's by far the biggest hotel property I've seen, I'd like to use my expertise in creating atmospheres at the boutique hotels and bed-and-breakfasts I've done up and down the coast." She unfolded a large sheet of paper and revealed a blueprint of her plan.

The woman glanced at it, pursed her lips, and made a brief notation with a mechanical pencil. Gathering her other papers, she tapped them on the desk and checked her wristwatch. "Excellent. I'll give this a thorough review later this week and there'll be a few more steps before it's presented to the Board. By the way, Caylie, are those overalls your design?"

Caylie's smile lit her face, already a little fuller than usual. She placed her thumbs behind the straps. "Yes," she said. "I know it might seem unusual to wear them to a job interview; but I'd say they're as much a reflection of me and my work as that resume you have in your hands."

"I agree. And even though we're a large corporation, we don't have a dress code. I know it's hard to tell by looking at me," said the woman. She smoothed the right side of her head, took in a deep breath through her nose and exhaled. "But I'm just a square executive. Not an artist like yourself. So, when can you start? After Christmas? Say, the first of the year? That should give you enough time to square up any open contracts you may have and maybe even find a new place to live."

Caylie sprung out of her seat. "I've got the job?"

"You've got the job. We'll start you at eighty-five thousand. There's a bonus on the first property if you come in on time and manage to have the plan executed by the soft opening; however, that's still nearly two years away. Also, the benefit package is decent. It includes health insurance and a lot of perks."

Caylie raised her eyebrows. "Perks?"

"You bet. For example, you'll get to stay at our hotels for free all around the world. And that includes Africa."

Caylie's palms were on her warm, rosy cheeks. "Rest assured, I'm not going back anytime soon. The idea of malaria medication—" Caylie abruptly stopped. Her thought and her sentence were interrupted by a sharp kick from inside her womb. During the interview, Caylie actually forgot she was expecting a child. She placed her hands over her stomach, frowned and sat back down. It was her baby's first kick and she wanted to cry out with a strange mix of joy and regret.

"Is everything okay?" asked the woman. "I can go as high as ninety."

"Really?"

"Really. It's all that's been approved by the Board."

"Well, I'll take it. For sure. I'll have to start looking for a house right away. We're going to my sister's in Atlanta for the holidays. I'll be back by the new year, but that's not what concerns me. There's something you need to know. And I completely understand if—"

"Does this have something to do with malaria? Are you ill?" Caylie was taken aback. "Malaria? No. I mean, I have the virus—in my system—but it hasn't flared up in years." She sighed. "Geez. Even that might be less complicated."

The woman furrowed her brow. "What's going on?"

"What's going on is a baby."

"A baby? You're pregnant?"

"Fraid so."

"Well, you can't be that far along. You're not showing."

"These overalls are multi-purpose. I'm due in May."

The woman bit her lower lip and shook her head. "Hmm. Well . . . honestly? I really don't see it as a problem. I'm a mother myself and I know that carrying a baby doesn't make any woman incapable of doing her job. Not this job, anyway."

"You're right about that," said Caylie. "I even did the physical work during all three of my last pregnancies."

"Pregnancy is the easy part, right? It's raising the kids that muddies everything up. But obviously this isn't your first child. You already know what you're in for. Hell, I don't care if you're carrying twins. As long as you meet the deadlines. You'll have a big staff, and Allison—even thought she's a little funky—is a crackerjack assistant. The bonus deadlines are completely up to you." She touched the corner of Caylie's drawing. "From the looks of your initial blueprints, you're already way ahead of the game. I'd even venture to guess that you'll be celebrating the little tyke's first birthday around the same time you're celebrating the completion of Cielo Grande California."

The baby kicked her again and Caylie smiled. She stood and extended her hand. "I believe that means you've got yourself a landscape architect. I'll meet those deadlines. You won't regret giving me this job."

Caylie closed the office door and immediately pulled her cell phone from the bib pocket of her overalls. She couldn't wait to tell Jenny the good news.

CHAPTER 15

My dark-haired, green-eyed daughter, Darlene, who resembled my looks more than any of my daughters, specialized in internal medicine. When she wasn't off helping hurricane victims in the southeast or volunteering time at the Jane Fonda Center at Emory University, she managed a successful private practice. Darlene had a keen talent for diagnostics and for making her patients feel comfortable. For Christmas, she focused on making her family comfortable in her large Atlanta home.

The mug I held was a Santa Claus head. His red cap bent into a handle. As the aroma of nutmeg and cinnamon wafted through my senses, in the tea I saw my husband, Michael. He sat in an upholstered recliner in Darlene's parlor, with his feet, clad in tan corduroy slippers, upon the extended hassock. A frosty mug of beer was at his side, reading glasses hinged with black electrical tape rested low on his nose, and the *Atlanta Journal-Constitution* newspaper was open before him. He had flown to Atlanta the week before and planned to stay in Darlene's guest quarters through the holidays. Caylie and her boys bunked in the other spare rooms and Marie and Jenny's families stayed at the Ritz hotel downtown. Only Ronnie declined the holiday invitation, claiming his wife had made mandatory plans with her family.

Darlene and her teenaged daughter, Meghan, lived together in the historic Druid Hills neighborhood of Atlanta. Divorced for some ten years, she got the house, and custody of their only daughter. The ex-husband, a professor of medicine at Emory, got the condo in Captiva and a new wife. It was a stately home, Tudor Revival, set upon a sizable lot with several enormous red oak trees surrounding it. Caylie had designed the gardens as a wedding present, but Darlene had little time or interest in keeping up the work involved, and resorted to hiring a landscaping maintenance company to tend to the grounds.

On the afternoon of Christmas Eve, Caylie's younger boys were busy decorating a gingerbread house in the breakfast room, and filling their mouths with frosting and gumdrops. Her eldest son, Frankie, was in the office next to the parlor, wrapped up with a hand-held video game. Periodic curses punctuated his play. Words like "shit!" or "piss!" or "balls," kept wafting from the room, and each time he heard one, Michael frowned and looked over the top of his glasses at Caylie. Her back was to her father as she stood at the picture window, her hands thrust deep into the pockets of her overalls. She was studying the growth of Darlene's thuja hedges.

"I don't like the language coming out of that kid," said Michael. "He should be reading a book, not playing with that toy. Not if it makes him talk like that."

"He's fine, Dad," she called over her shoulder. The light reflected off her blonde hair. "It's winter break."

"Well, I don't like it."

Caylie put her hands on her hips and walked toward her father, seated in his throne like a dowager king. She sat on the arm of his chair, leaned over and kissed his cheek. He was freshly shaven and to Caylie, his essence was a combination of mouthwash and Miller beer. "What are you reading? Anything interesting?"

Michael lowered the paper. "Oh, just a bunch of nothing about the goings-on in this city. Have you ever heard of environmental racism? Honest to Pete, the blacks have taken over."

"Dad! That's the kind of language *I* won't tolerate. I'd rather hear my kid swear than hear anything remotely prejudiced."

"That's not prejudiced. They want to be called blacks. Looky here." He pointed to a headline. "Black Atlanta. See? There's a group called Black Atlanta."

"The preferred term here is African-Americans, Dad. Skin color is important and definitely an acceptable way to describe a person, but we never referred to anyone as 'black' in Kenya. When referring to race, we used African, Asian or European. But it's not that anyway. It's the *they* thing." She shook her head, knowing better than to get into a discussion about race with her father. He wasn't paying attention anyway.

"Go get me another cold beer, will you Kiddo?"

Caylie glanced at the half-full mug sitting next to them. "Why don't you finish that one first?"

"Have one with me."

"No thanks, Dad."

"Oh come on," he said with a scolding tone. "Have a drink." He returned to his article.

He was just like Albert, she thought. Drunks preferred company. Caylie quietly thanked God that Albert was no longer in her life. She had managed to avoid him after breaking it off on the drive home from Jenny's. It hadn't been that difficult. He was a busy man, and she no longer went out to dinner or to any of the San Francisco hot spots where they had once gone together. Studying her father's profile, his sharp, Roman nose, his downturned mouth, she frowned. Caylie wondered how important it would truly be to have her child's father around. She no longer needed his financial assistance now that she had the job waiting for her back in California.

Caylie continued looking at her father and I studied his face along with her. His pale pink mouth was stretched so tightly it looked like the drawing of a sad-face. His once sharp jaw line had collapsed into heavy, sagging jowls. He looked thinner every time I saw him, and the vertical line between his brows was deeper than Caylie or I remembered. His hair was as white and as wispy as a cirrus cloud.

Losing me had truly aged him.

Caylie felt the baby inside her roll and knew the stomach camouflaged by her colorful overalls was changing shapes like a giant, three-dimensional amoeba. For a moment, she thought about telling her father about the baby. But she quickly erased the thought. He wouldn't understand.

The baby offered another kick and she let out a gasp.

Michael looked up. "What's the matter?"

"Nothing!" she said. "Say, did you know this community was designed by the grand daddy of landscape architecture?"

"Frederick Law Olmsted," said Darlene, entering the room with a Santa Claus mug filled with eggnog in one hand, and a bottle of Miller Genuine Draft in the other. "This neighborhood was his last project. In fact, the actual development didn't begin until after he died. He also designed New York's Central Park."

Caylie took the Santa mug from her. She sniffed it. "Does this have booze in it?"

"No," said Darlene. She furrowed her brow and narrowed her green eyes suspiciously.

"Olmstead Senior," said Caylie.

"That's right," said Darlene. "Here Dad." She handed him the beer.

"Thanks, Mommy," he said. He put the bottle next to his mug and continued reading.

Darlene looked at Caylie and smiled.

"Olmstead designed lots of things," said Caylie. "Like the Chicago World's Fair, and—did you know—the town of Riverside?"

Michael bent the corner of his newspaper. "Riverside, Illinois?" he asked. "As in the town next to Grossdale?"

"That's the one."

"Godforsaken curving streets," he hissed. "That town had the highest taxes in the western suburbs."

"Olmstead really got around," said Caylie. "You can't become a landscape architect and not know about him and his philosophies and designs. He was all about following the natural topography of the land. He was a revolutionary."

"G.D. radicals," spit Michael under his breath.

Darlene made big eyes at Caylie. "Marie's sister-in-law lives in Riverside. She still gets lost driving around those curvy streets when trying to get to her house."

"I always wanted to live there," said Caylie. "But I had a few friends from school who did, and at least I got to see the insides of those beautiful houses. Darlene, did you know Olmstead designed the Berkeley campus, too?"

"I know," said Darlene. "And Stanford. He did a lot of work in Boston, too. Last time I was there for a conference I actually visited his house and office. It was fabulous. Hey Caylie, did you ever ask Mom if she knew about him?"

Caylie sipped her eggnog and stood up. She licked her lips, put her hand on the arch of her back and stretched. "No. Never asked her. Probably not, though. But then you never know about Mom. She may have learned about him in school the same way we Illinois kids focused on Abe Lincoln or Jane Addams."

Crossing the room, Darlene sat in the middle of a leather sofa, then reached over and took a handful of almonds from a bowl on the coffee table. "Too bad she never talked about Boston."

"Yeah, too bad."

Caylie walked toward her, and Darlene stared at the bibs of her sister's overalls. Her green eyes slowly made their way from the silver buttons, scanning down to the bottom of the heavily embroidered pocket, and to the top of the legs. Caylie realized her sister's diagnostic radar was in high gear. She sat next to her and put up her feet.

"Get your feet off my table," barked Darlene.

"Bite me," said Caylie. She left her feet in place.

Darlene frowned. "Are you feeling okay Caylie?"

"I'm fine."

"Whatever you say, Kiddo." They held each other's eyes for an extended moment.

"Guess what, Dad?" asked Darlene.

Caylie shook her head. "Don't, Dar."

Darlene frowned. "Don't nothing, little sister. You don't know what I'm going to say. I was just going to tell Dad that I got a Christmas card the other day from one of Mom's old friends from Melrose."

Caylie's eyebrows shot up. "Really? Who?"

"Someone named Mary Margaret Kerrigan. I'm not sure how she got my home address, but she knew I was a doctor. She said she found me because she hadn't heard from Mom for two Christmases now, and feared she was dead."

Caylie grimaced. "Wow. How would we have known to contact her?"

"Apparently she and Mom were quite the pen pals," said Darlene. "Say, Dad, put down the paper for a second and listen to this. Did you know her? A woman named Mary Margaret Kerrigan?"

Michael lowered his paper as instructed, and took off his glasses. "Did you say Mary Margaret Kerrigan?"

"Yeah. The return address was from Melrose. Ring any bells?"

"Well I'll be damned," said Michael. He twisted the top of his new bottle of beer. "I did know her. And she had a sister." He pursed his lips and hummed. "What was her name again? Funny, I can't think of it. Was it Lily? I don't know." He scratched his head. "But yeah. Yeah, I remember the Kerrigan sisters. They were both with Mommy the day I met her."

"At Virginia Beach?" asked Darlene.

"Yes, that's right. Virginia Beach. I didn't know you knew that."

"It's one of the few things we do know," said Caylie.

"I was ashore in service school then. It was like college." He tilted his mug and poured the beer. A frothy head rose to the edges and he immediately sipped it, then licked a white foam mustache from his upper lip. "Right after that we took off for Casablanca. No. Lisbon. It was Lisbon, of course. That's when we painted the ship gray. Now that was something. We painted everything. Even the brass and teak decking."

He turned and looked out the window, a wistful moment. "I was in Casablanca just before our wedding. That's why my hair was so blond in the photos." He took another sip of beer and winked at his daughters.

Darlene and Caylie exchanged knowing, patient smiles with one another. They knew their dad had been in service school in Virginia Beach. They knew about how he and his shipmates painted the ship gray. They knew he'd been in Casablanca just before our wedding. But their dad never talked about the early days of our courtship. When he spoke of that time, of World War II, it was only about the service. It was about his combat cutter ship, the *USS Ingham*, and how it led convoy missions across the Atlantic. He spoke of the swelling, rolling seas and waves crashing over the bow. He spoke of German U-Boats and enemy aircraft—of cramped sleeping quarters and how the officers doled out cigarettes to the enlisted men. It was the only time in his life that he smoked. And when he was in Iceland, it was the only time he ever wore a beard.

Each of his five children had heard the tale of the December, 1942 "U-boat kill," about fifty times. He said they dropped depth charges in a diamond shape and were sure they took out a German submarine; however, they weren't given credit for it until after the War. There was something about that episode that caused him to carry a bitter feeling about it for the rest of his days.

Before he could tell the U-boat kill story again, which he was, no doubt, about to do, Caylie turned the subject back to how he met me. "How did you and Mom get to know one another if you were always at sea?" she asked.

"Things were different back then. They happened quickly," Michael said. "There was a port in Boston and that, of course, is where Mommy lived. Well, Melrose anyway. She worked in Boston. We came back there from Lisbon right after we painted the ship. We overhauled the whole thing. New armament—weapons for war—and this was even before Pearl Harbor. We went from three bunks to four. The whole way back we had the ship blacked out at night. Then the supply convoys started. We went in and out of Boston. Of course, you know the story of how we escorted the convoy ships."

"Right," said Caylie. "But tell us about Mom."

Michael sipped his beer. "I sent telegrams to Mommy every time we'd come to port, and then I met her when we had liberty. We'd get our pay and, I'll tell you, we felt like rich men. So, I spent all my money on flowers and taking Mommy out to hear music and to dance. She loved to dance."

"Mom always said you weren't much of a dancer back then," said Darlene.

Michael laughed. "I was a fast learner. And Mommy liked me so she was patient. Aside from that, I think she liked all the flowers. We never knew if we were coming back, so we spent everything we had before we left to be shot at again. . . ."

Michael continued talking as Darlene rose and removed the screen from the fireplace. She poked at the logs, stirring up the flame, and then placed another split log on top of the pile. Just as she replaced the screen, they heard the sound of car doors slamming. Within moments, Marie and three of her sons, along with Jenny, Don, and their two girls strode through the front door.

"We're here!" cried Jenny, her arms full of wrapped presents. "The fun can start."

Caylie's boys, with gumdrops puffing out their cheeks, ran into the room. Meghan sauntered down the staircase, her long hair swinging in front of her face. Marie set a large ham on the dining room table, and her tall, grown boys threw their jackets into a pile near the front door. Everyone exchanged hugs and kisses, and wished one another Merry Christmas.

The noise level made it sound like a parade.

Watching so many of my family members together filled me with warmth and joy. I felt as though I were present in every part of that room—from the souls within each of them to the sparks jumping off the flames of the fire. I was a part of the Christmas tree in the corner, covered with ornaments from my children's and my own childhoods. I was wrapped inside the colorful gifts beneath it, and I was inside each Santa mug, replicas of the mug I held while viewing them.

Did they know I was there? Could they feel me?

"Marie!" called Caylie. "It's so good to see you. I love your hair!" Caylie hugged her eldest sister, holding her tightly, until Marie pulled away.

"Hey, Kiddo," she said. "Look at you." She kept her hands on Caylie's shoulders and looked her up-and-down. "You're wearing your overalls. I can't believe you're still wearing these. They're amazing."

"Thanks."

"Honestly! Do you think you have room for any more embroidery?"

"There's always room for more."

"Why, I don't think I've seen them since—"

"Hey there Cay," interrupted Jenny. She hooked her finger under one of Caylie's straps and pulled. "Come with me this minute. There's something I'm dying to tell you about what I got Marie for Christmas."

"You brat!" cried Marie.

Marie loved receiving presents more than any of my children. The kids always teased her about it and ever since they grew up and moved to different parts of the country, they sent her things well in advance of her birthday with notes reading: "Don't Open until . . ." She never waited.

The Irish Twins giggled, linked arms and left the clamorous living room. They walked through the kitchen and into the library. Jenny closed the door. "Oh my God, Caylie, you are so obviously pregnant. Has anyone said something?"

"Darlene knows. She hasn't said anything yet, but she definitely knows."

"She would. You can't sneak a thing past her keen diagnostic nose. She's like a blood hound."

Caylie nodded and laughed. "Blood bitch! And one more second with Marie and she would have blurted it out in front of everyone. Thanks for pulling me away."

"No problem. I've been taunting her about the present for a week. It's only a scarf, but she'll love it. Has Dad noticed?"

"He hasn't said anything. And he's usually the first to comment about my weight; but he's barely taken his nose out of the newspaper. He was talking about the War, though, when you guys showed up."

"Oh God, you're kidding," moaned Jenny. "More War stories?"

"Well, yes and no. For a brief moment he was actually talking about Mom and when they met and stuff. It was kinda sweet."

"What brought that on?"

"Darlene said she got a Christmas card from one of Mom's old friends. Someone named Mary Margaret."

Jenny screwed up her face. "Sounds like a nun."

"Who knows? Could be. But Daddy knew her. He said he met her on the same day he met Mom. I think they said her last name was Kerrigan? Like Nancy Kerrigan, the skater."

"Hmm. Is that why the name sounds familiar? Any relation?"

"No clue." Caylie sat in a leather chair and placed her hands on her belly. "Just one more element to the mystery of Mom's life."

Jenny walked across a lush, burgundy and gold Persian carpet, and toward a wall filled with books. The built-in shelves were deep mahogany, and the books, hardbound and old, were mostly collectibles. Jenny ran her finger along the titles and then stopped at a bright red spine with raised bands of metallic gold. A black, rectangular box on the spine read, "Charlotte Brontë, *JANE EYRE*." She pulled it from the shelf. "This was Mom's," she said, opening it and flipping through the delicate pages. "She actually read this to me."

"Lucky! I don't remember Mom ever reading to me."

"Lucky nothing. I was totally traumatized when the girl with natural red curls had to get all her hair cut off." Jenny ran her fingers through her hair. "Hmm. I should read it again."

"I'm sure a lot of these books were Mom's. Darlene came to the Grossdale house and took boxes of them before Mom and Dad moved to Mitten Lake."

"She did?"

"Two weeks before my graduation. She wasn't there either, by the way."

"Geez, Caylie. Will you ever forgive me for missing your graduation?"

"Will you forgive me for booting you out of the Oak Park house when I got married?"

"*Touché*. Water under the bridge. I promise." Jenny sighed. "I'm more disturbed to learn that Darlene knew Mom and Dad were moving to Mitten Lake before I did. It's not like she ever had any plans to return home again. Wasn't she in med school by then?"

Caylie shrugged her shoulders.

"Whatever. She knew well enough in advance to get all the way there from freaking Georgia so she could take things from the house."

"Mom didn't want to move the books because she wanted only modern things at the lake house. I sure couldn't do anything with them, and Marie only wanted furniture. She had no interest in the books."

"No one asked me," said Jenny.

"Where would you have stored them? In your dorm room?"

"No. I suppose not. But man, this *Jane Eyre* is really valuable. If anything, it's valuable for the memory of hearing Mom's voice read it to me. I don't think I remember her reading any other book to me."

"I wonder why she chose that one," said Caylie.

There was a soft knock at the door and when the Irish Twins turned, they saw their sisters step into the room. "Hey you two squirts," said Marie. "What's going on in here? I know you're not talking about my present."

"No, you're right," said Caylie. "We're not. You better watch out though, Darlene. Jenny's going to steal that *Jane Eyre* book from you."

"Take it," said Darlene, waving her hand.

Jenny gasped. "Really? You mean it?"

"Sure. You're the one with the Liberal Arts degree. Have it. Take anything you want."

Jenny raced to Darlene and hugged her. "Thank you!" she cried.

"Hey, no sweat. Mom wanted us to be generous with one another. And I know you didn't get the chance to take anything from the house."

Jenny nodded. "That's true."

"She did give you that gold pocket watch, though," said Marie. "Have you worn it since her funeral?"

"No," said Jenny. "I keep it in a box next to my bed. I should have brought it with me—just to have a piece of her with us."

"A piece of her *and* her mother," said Marie. "Have you had it appraised? Who knows how far back that watch went?"

"We'll never know now," whispered Caylie.

"I don't need anyone to tell me the value of that watch," said Jenny.

All four sets of eyes grew glassy, and within moments, my four daughters stood in the middle of the library with their arms around one another. It was the first time they'd all been together since my funeral, and the power hovering over their grief was palpable.

My tea tasted of tears.

But the grief quickly turned to joy. They were so happy to be together. I couldn't take my eyes off the image of the four of them together, holding one another and sharing a mixture of grief and joy, and a lifetime of shared memories and emotions.

"Say you guys, listen," said Darlene. "I told Marie about the Christmas card from Mom's friend, and she had a scathingly brilliant idea."

"GIRLS!" They all shouted. "TAKE OFF YOUR BINDERS!"

They threw their heads back and laughed, recalling a scene from the movie they'd all seen countless times, *The Trouble With Angels.* The Haley Mills character, Mary, who was a trouble-making Catholic schoolgirl, was always coming up with "scathingly brilliant" ideas.

"We should all go to Boston together," said Darlene. "There's a conference I try to get to each year—it's required to keep my board certification—and this year it's in Boston. We can stay at the Plaza, where Mom and Dad stayed on their honeymoon. I'll pay. I can write it off on the business."

"That *is* a great idea," said Caylie.

"And we can get together with this Mary Margaret person," said Marie. "Plus you guys might be able to meet our cousin, Matthew, if he's there. What a case that guy is! You'll never believe what he told me when he came to Grossdale."

"What?" they asked in unison.

Marie looked only at Jenny. "I tell you later. But only if you tell me what you got me for Christmas."

"You're nuts," said Jenny. "Do you guys think we should invite Ronnie to go with us?"

"Let's make this a girl's trip," said Marie.

"Yeah," said Darlene. "His wife will probably have mandatory plans for him anyway."

"Hmm. Bitter, are we?" asked Jenny.

"A little," said Darlene. "I wanted all of us to be together. When's the last time we were all together for Christmas?"

"My house," said Marie. "The year we got Mom and Dad a new dishwasher."

"That was B.C.—Before Children—for me," said Jenny.

"Me too," said Caylie. "It was right after we got back from Kenya. Listen, I'd really love to do this, but I start my new job after the first of the year. I'm not sure if I can manage a long weekend, unless it coincides with President's Day or something."

"The conference is the first week in April," said Darlene. She looked at Caylie, who was unaware she had her hands resting on her unborn child. "Your new job, huh? Is that really your biggest concern right now?"

Caylie immediately shoved her hands into her pockets. "What do you mean, Dar?"

"I mean, little Miss Obviously Pregnant—when's the baby due?"

Caylie dropped her head and Jenny nudged her. Marie's jaw dropped open.

The Irish Twins both looked up and spoke with one voice.

"May," they said.

CHAPTER 16

April in Boston was a weather forecaster's challenge. It was highly unpredictable. Snowstorms were as common as seventy-degree days. Darlene, the only one of my daughters to have ever been there, instructed her sisters to pack a little of everything.

It's odd. I hadn't been in Boston since I left there in 1945. And when I thought of it, I rarely thought about the weather. Regardless, I was happy to see my girls were enjoying a lovely spring day.

To me, they looked like movie stars strolling over the suspension bridge at the Public Gardens. They walked as a foursome with linked arms. Darlene was on the outside with Marie next to her, then Caylie, then Jenny. They all wore sunglasses. Their hair was long and loose, the curls—a spectrum of color from deep brunette to auburn to blonde—happily bounced with each step. Everyone noticed them.

Weeping willows with small, florescent buds reflected in the pond. The willows were the first to bloom, a harbinger of spring. A host of mallard ducks, males and females, swam and splashed nearby. I looked for, but didn't see the swans or the swan boats. It was still too early in the season. The swan boats, foot-propelled paddleboats, had been operating on the lagoon since the late 1800s. I never rode on one. We believed they were for the tourists. Even though my daughters were certainly tourists, they'd have to come back another time if they wanted to ride the swans. They did, however, pose for several photos while on the bridge, and a kindly passerby was good enough to use each of their cameras.

"Did you know this is the country's oldest botanical garden?" asked Caylie. She stashed her tiny camera back inside her shoulder bag. "There are a hundred trees. Fourteen willows, I think."

"You would know that," said Marie. "I'm not all that interested in the trees. I promised the boys I'd get pictures in front of the 'Cheers' bar. The map shows it right over there."

"Do you think they'll let a pregnant lady in?" asked Jenny.

"She's with her doctor," said Darlene. "It'll be okay."

"We're not going there before we see the Japanese pagoda tree," said Caylie. "It won't be flowering yet, but I've always wanted to see it. It's the largest of its kind."

"There's plenty of time to do everything," said Darlene. "We don't need to be in Melrose until four o'clock. Mary Margaret is having us for tea."

"How are we getting there?" asked Jenny.

"We're taking the T."

Jenny laughed "Taking the T to tea?"

"That's right," said Darlene. "Mary Margaret is picking us up at the station because the train doesn't go as far as Melrose. Apparently she's got a great big car. A caddy."

"Ooh!" said Marie.

"How old is this woman?" asked Caylie. "She must be in her eighties."

"Eighty two," said Darlene. "But she's a spry old broad. We've spoken on the phone twice now. She's a physician, too. Retired, of course, but she didn't actually go to medical school until she was in her late fifties. She worked in medicine all her life—started out as her father's assistant."

I could tell by the looks on my daughters' faces, as clear as though I were standing with them in Boston Public Garden next to the pagoda tree, that Mary Margaret Kerrigan impressed them.

They were about to meet my oldest, and perhaps dearest friend.

"Do any of you remember Mom ever talking about her?" asked Marie.

Caylie shook her head.

Jenny shrugged. "I may have heard her name—or seen pictures of her in Mom's photo albums. But I don't remember."

"I think Mom once told me she had a friend who was a doctor," said Darlene. "I don't know. I was probably in med school or doing a residency at the time—or something. I wish I had listened."

"Do you think Mom actually told us more about herself than we realize?" asked Jenny. "I mean, as kids, were any of us really listening? Do our kids listen to us?"

"Mine don't," said Marie. "But they're boys."

"Mine either," said Caylie. "Whenever Robert or I bring up anything about the Peace Corps days, they sigh and roll their eyes the same way we did when Dad talked about the War."

Jenny horse-rumbled her lips. "The way he still talks about the War."

"I don't know," said Darlene. "But if I'd known about Mary Margaret, I would have looked her up a lot sooner."

"At the very least, we would have contacted her after Mom's stroke," said Jenny.

Caylie snapped a photo of the massive tree. "Jenny thought she was a nun."

Darlene smiled. "When the letter first came I thought so, too. After all, what Catholic schoolgirl didn't have at least one nun named 'Sister Mary Margaret?' "

My Latin teacher's name was Sister Mary Margaret. I admit she was my favorite nun, probably because she shared the name of my best friend, Mary Margaret Kerrigan. I might not have done as well in Latin class had it not been for this coincidence. I was in her class during my sophomore year when I experienced my first menarche. I had no clue what was happening to me; however, Sister Mary Margaret knew before I could even mention the word "blood." Without hesitation, she put Edwina Logan in charge of the class, and escorted me to the nurse's office. Before leaving me in the nurse's care, she told me I was lucky to be Catholic.

"Jewish girls get slapped when this happens to them," she said.

I was relieved to know I wouldn't be slapped; however, it didn't take away from the shame and humiliation I felt because of what was happening between my legs.

I often recalled certain milestones and events that happened during my life with great clarity. These events were so big, that they triggered a heightened sense of awareness. I couldn't help but remember details like colors and smells and the sounds of the voices of those who, in some cases, relayed the news: news both good and bad. I was with Mary Margaret Kerrigan, the younger of the two Kerrigan sisters, on several momentous occasions in my life, including the day I met Michael. When we were much younger, we were together when we first heard the news of Amelia Earhart successfully crossing the Atlantic. We were in her kitchen and the smell was of cinnamon sugar cookies. She called them "snickerdoodles." How thrilled we were to learn that while bound for Paris, Amelia Earhart ended up on a farm in Ireland. As young girls, we didn't even know any women who drove cars let alone flew airplanes. Mary Margaret, Lolly, Molly and I used to sit on the street corner at the end of Grove Street and count the number of women we saw behind the wheel of a car. Some days, an entire afternoon would pass without one sighting.

We were also together when we learned the news of Franklin Delano Roosevelt's death. Michael was still at sea then, and Mary Margaret and I were volunteers for the Red Cross. My friend, who had spent her life in a doctor's office and at her father's side as he made house calls, suspected the president was in ill health. So, she wasn't as surprised as I, and seemingly the rest of the country, when the radio reported our beloved President Roosevelt had died from a cerebral hemorrhage. And when my mother died, when I was preoccupied with adjusting to my life in Chicago with Michael's mother, Belle, and our sister-in-law, Marge, it was a phone call from Mary Margaret that relayed the terrible, heart-breaking news. "She died in her sleep," Mary Margaret said through the static in the phone line. "Natural causes." It was the first personal, long-distance call I'd ever received, and for the rest of my life, I associated long-distance calls with bad news.

The next one I received came from not from Mary Margaret, but from Charlie "Red" Murphy, who told me that Molly had died. I knew then that I never again wanted to receive another long-distance phone call.

I also never wanted to return to Boston. And I didn't. Not while I was alive.

In spite of my work as a switchboard operator, I was more of a letter-writer than I was a phone-caller. I continued a regular correspondence with Mary Margaret until the summer I died. She was the only person from my past—from my life in Melrose—with whom I stayed in touch. During my last years, because I was so busy keeping up with my children and grandchildren, my letters to Mary Margaret weren't as frequent. I always remembered her birthday and, of course, I wrote at Christmas as well. My letters were newsy. They included updates about my children, which was truly, the only news in my life once we moved to Mitten Lake.

Mary Margaret knew more about me than anyone—perhaps even Michael.

"She knows all your secrets, Annie," said Molly.

I narrowed my eyes and scowled at my Irish Twin. "You and Mary Margaret are the only two people I'd let get away with calling me Annie."

My sister smiled softly, and handed me a fresh cup of tea. Resting on a matching blue and white saucer, the cup was Wedgwood, the pattern "Countryside." I had spent many afternoons as a teenager drinking tea from Countryside cups in the Kerrigan's kitchen.

"Thank you, Molly. And you're right about Mary Margaret. She knows things I didn't want anyone to know."

Molly sat at a table with a lemon yellow tablecloth and pointed to the chair across from her, suggesting I sit. Her voice was a whisper. "She knows my secrets too."

The girls arrived at the Oak Grove station at the end of the Orange Line. A quick ride, they made it at precisely four o'clock. All four of my girls were always punctual. It's how they were raised. I taught them that it was impolite to keep people waiting. Each of them listened to me more than they realized.

They stepped into the parking lot and looked around.

"What color's the Caddy?" asked Marie.

"White," Darlene said absently as she stood on her toes and craned her neck. "I see her!" She pointed past her sisters to a tall, slender woman standing curbside next to a shining, white Cadillac. One hand held onto the passenger door handle, the other was extended high in the air and waving at the girls. Her hair was as white as the Cadillac, and she wore thick, black eyeglass frames. A chain dangled from the temples and went around her neck. Her posture was amazingly erect. She appeared to be six feet tall.

As the girls neared Mary Margaret, it was apparent she was not that tall. Jenny, my tallest, towered over her. "Hello Shields ladies," she called. "I'd recognize you as Annie's daughters any day of the week." She reached for Darlene first. "Doctor Shields I presume?"

Darlene accepted her hug. "Dr. Kerrigan. So nice to meet you in person."

She pulled back and smiled, her teeth yellow with age, her lipstick bright cranberry. "Call me Mary Margaret. Now don't tell me your names. Let me see." She put her bony hand on Marie's shoulder. "You're Marie. The eldest, and definitely the most blonde. You have your father's hair but your mother's figure. Lucky gal."

Marie gave her an awkward hug. "Hello. I love your accent. You sound like the Kennedys."

"Oh, I imagine my voice sounds rather familiar to you. After all, your mother had the very same accent."

"Not really," said Marie. "She held onto it a little bit, but Chicago definitely flattened it."

"Yes, after all those years, I suppose it must have. She probably talked a bit like you."

"Marie has the most profound Chicago accent in the family," said Jenny. "It's because she was the only one to stay there. When you live in California and you meet people who are from everywhere else, you get to be a bit of an accent expert."

Mary Margaret shifted her gaze. "Hmm, is that so? Now let's see. You two are the Irish Twins." She looked up at Jenny. "You're first. Jennifer. Annie always wanted a redhead."

Jenny saluted. "Right. Hi."

"And this means you must be Caylie." She grabbed Caylie's hands and looked at her swollen belly. "Oh my! And what do we have here?"

"Just your average forty-year-old pregnant lady," said Caylie.

"It looks like you're darn close to having that baby. Your doctor said it was okay to travel?"

"I've got nearly eight weeks to go," said Caylie. "And my first three, bless their hearts, were late. So, I doubt this one will be in any hurry either."

"Do we know if it's a boy or a girl?" asked Mary Margaret.

Caylie shook her head. "No. I didn't want to know with any of my children. There are just too few surprises left in the world, ya know? But it feels the same as the others."

"Boys, right?"

"Yes," said Caylie. "Three. How did you know?"

Mary Margaret looked from one girl to the next. "Your mother told me all about all of you."

"I'm afraid we can't say the same thing about you," said Jenny. "Mom almost never talked about her life here."

"No. She probably didn't." The old woman opened the front passenger door of the Cadillac. "Jennifer, dear, you've got the longest legs. Why don't you sit up front with me? Ride shotgun."

Jenny stuck out her tongue at her sisters and quickly lowered herself into the front seat. She breathed in the Armor All aroma. The car was old, but the white leather interior was impeccable. A small statue of the Virgin Mary clung to the dash. Her sisters climbed in back and closed the doors. Mary Margaret fired up the engine and cleared her throat. "Melrose is the next town over. Before tea I thought I'd take you by your mother's home. It's right around the corner from mine."

"I'm so excited to see Melrose!" said Jenny.

Mary Margaret checked her mirrors and pulled into the street. "Well, that is indeed the plan. I've lived in Melrose almost all my life. It's a lovely town, really. Some folks call it 'Mystic Side,' because it's in the valley of the Mystic River. It used to be a part of Malden, the town we're in now. It didn't become Melrose until the B&M Railway came to town."

"That's a Monopoly property," said Jenny.

"It certainly is," said Mary Margaret. She made a left turn. "The road we're on now is Main Street."

"There's the sign," cried Caylie. "Welcome to Melrose!" She nudged Marie, who was sitting to her left. "I saw it first."

"Good for you, Squirt!" said Marie.

They all let out small laughs and then stared out the car windows, looking for me—any signs of me. What they saw instead were things I had never seen before in Melrose: Starbucks, CVS Pharmacy. Modern shops. It could have been any New England town. Stretching their necks, they looked down the side streets off Main, which were tree-lined and filled with new, Spring growth.

"Oh look!' cried Jenny. "A lake."

"That's Ell Pond, actually," said Mary Margaret. "We used to swim there until the 1950s. We still skate on it. Your mother loved to ice skate. Did she skate in Chicago?"

"Yes!" All four girls had answered.

"One of my patients started calling it 'Golden Pond' after that movie with Kate Hepburn came out some years back. We've even seen loons out there. And I don't mean crazies. I mean diving birds."

"Yes, we know," said Jenny. "They're actually not on Mitten Lake, but there are a lot of loons in the U. P."

"Yep," said Marie. "The You-pers have all the loons."

"Tell you what," said Mary Margaret. "I'm going to loop around the pond and then head back to Annie's place."

"I like that you call her Annie," said Jenny. "No one called her that in Grossdale."

Mary Margaret's penciled eyebrows raised above her glasses. "She didn't really like it. She'd always say, 'I'm Anne with an e, not Annie.' But her mother went by Anne, so everyone referred to her as Annie. Pretty Annie Monaghan."

Within minutes, they turned on Grove Street, and for me, it was like being transported back in time. Everything looked the same. The houses were large, mostly Victorian, with front porches close to the street. I'd forgotten how pretty it was.

Mary Margaret pointed out the quaint, white church where Michael and I were married. She tapped the glass. "Right over there, down the block," she said. "Good old St. Mary's."

"We'll need to go in and make three wishes," said Darlene.

Again, Mary Margaret smiled. "That was from your grandmother. I don't remember any of us ever going to new churches, but I remember her saying that about making three wishes." She tightened her grip on the steering wheel and checked her speed. "Hmm. Why would I remember that?"

"I'm not sure it works," said Caylie. "The three wishes thing. Never worked for me."

Mary Margaret slowed the car. "Who's to say?"

"God," said Jenny absently.

Mary Margaret glanced over at Jenny and pursed her lips, nodding in agreement. "Yes. God. I suppose you're right, dear." Then she called over her shoulder. "Caylie, you're still young. Your wishes may come true yet. Keep the faith."

"I've wished about a thousand times that I'd have a girl," said Caylie.

"Well, there you go then," said Mary Margaret. "See? We'll be sure to stop in and maybe all your sisters can make that wish on your behalf. Girls?"

From the backseat: "Sure!" and "Why not?"

"It'll be a boy," said Jenny.

Caylie slapped the headrest behind her sister's head. "Thanks, a lot Jen."

"Oh, Cay! I'm only kidding."

"The house is right up here," said Mary Margaret. "I don't know who's living in it these days. It's sold a few times after your cousin, Teddy, passed." She pulled over in front of a large yellow house and parked against the curb. "Here we are. We can get out and knock on the door."

The girls climbed out of the white Cadillac slowly, and stood on the sidewalk staring up at the house. It was tall, three-stories, and six wooden steps led to the front porch. To them it was like a foreign castle—something out of a fairytale.

To me, it looked exactly the same as I remembered.

Molly took my hand, and together we watched and listened, as each of my girls was filled with her own thoughts. None of them had ever seen a photograph of this place, nor had they heard me describe it. They were amazed at its size—far bigger than our Grossdale home.

The breeze picked up and the sweet smell of hyacinth filled the air. They looked around, trying to locate the origin of the aroma. At the foot of the house, in front of white lattice and bright yellow forsythia bushes, they saw the lilac-colored hyacinth flowers. Behind them were rows of tulips, wide green leaves and tall, narrow stems, their buds not yet in bloom. Black-capped chickadees sang and called to one another, and bounced around from tree branch to tree branch.

The girls took it all in. And for a moment, my daughters, more than ever, felt my presence. They knew I was with them.

Finally, Jenny spoke. "So, this is where our grandparents lived."

"Well, your grandmother lived here," said Mary Margaret. "Your grandmother *and* your mother, of course. And Molly until she moved over to Lynn with her husband Red Murphy. Now he was a piece of work, that boy Red. Left town for good after Molly passed."

"What year did she die?" asked Jenny.

"Oh, I'd say it was 1949—after the War. Poor Molly. It was the mistake of her life marrying that good-for-nothing."

"Yeah," said Marie, exchanging a look with Darlene. "I had a visit from her son, Matthew, not too long ago. He was hoping to get in touch with Mom to ask her some questions about his mother's death."

"Suspicious at best," said Mary Margaret. "How he got away with asthma is beyond me. Your Aunt Molly did *not* have asthma."

"That's what Matt said."

Mary Margaret cleared her throat. An eyebrow arched above her glasses. "Did he?"

Marie nodded. "He said he saw his father put a pillow over his mother's face. But he was so young he didn't really know if it were the truth or if he dreamed it. His sisters didn't believe him."

"I'm not surprised," said Mary Margaret with a sigh. She grabbed the handrail and ambled up the steps. "I regret not getting involved. But I was taking care of my father at the time—advancing Alzheimer's. Better to let sleeping dogs lie, I suppose." She scratched her head. "Hmm. There was always something about the Monaghans that kept them silent. I will say, though, that Molly was more of a talker than your mother. She was older and certainly more outgoing than Annie. Annie was content to hide in her sister's shadow."

The girls exchanged looks as Mary Margaret called "hello" into the screen porch. She rapped on the door, and then pressed the doorbell. "I wonder if this thing works."

"Would you say they were close?" asked Caylie. "Mom and Molly?"

Mary Margaret looked over her shoulder. "Close as Irish Twins can be. I'm one, too, ya know. Got a sister named Lolly. She's old, though. Eighty-three. Lives in New York." She winked and pressed the doorbell once again.

There was no answer.

"It was pretty hard on your mother when Molly ran off with Red. She spent a lot of time with my sister and me, but when their mother's hearing failed, Annie had to work to support them both—even after she married your Dad. He was still at sea, of course."

"We never met our aunt," said Darlene. "Or our uncle."

"Oh, Annie didn't like that Red Murphy. None of us did—except for Molly. At least she liked him enough one night. The bastard knocked her up. Poor girl really didn't have a choice but to marry him."

All the girls spontaneously sat on the stairs—as if they had the right—and no one spoke.

Molly looked up from the tea and into my eyes. "All our secrets," she whispered.

"You were expecting when you married him?"

"It was a miscarriage," said Molly. "Nothing close to what you went through when you lost your baby. I was actually relieved. I wasn't very far along, and the only reason Mary Margaret knew is because I went to her father to help me."

"But then you were married."

"I made a lot of mistakes, Anne. But I didn't live long enough to regret them."

"And now?"

"Now, you ask? Now my existence isn't about regret. It's about understanding."

I nodded, and I understood.

Returning my gaze to the blue and white teacup, I watched as Mary Margaret sat with my girls. She was remarkably agile. Dressed in a black leather jacket and khaki trousers, with Nikes on her feet, she could have been one of them. She put her hand on Caylie's knee. "Your mother inherited a lot of damage," she said. "Things I don't think she even realized. When she left Melrose with her new husband—your father—it was a new life for her, which she vowed to dedicate to him. She never wanted to look back. Especially after she lost her mother and her sister so close together. I think part of her believed they died because she left."

Caylie felt her baby kick. She reached for Jenny's hand and put it on her stomach. "It's a shame we knew so little about her. And that she'll never get to meet this child."

"Ooh!" cried Jenny. "That was a good kick. I think the baby agrees with you, Cay."

They all smiled. Caylie's smile was through tears forming in her blue eyes.

Jenny removed her hand from her sister's stomach. "Mary Margaret? What did you mean this was where our grandmother lived? What about our grandfather? Was he already dead?"

"Your grandfather? Why, no, he wasn't dead. He also lived over in Lynn."

All four jaws dropped open. *"What?"*

Mary Margaret put her hand to her mouth. "Oh my goodness. None of you knew that?"

There was nothing but stunned silence.

"Well, you obviously don't need to answer. I can tell by the ghastly expressions on your pusses, you didn't know." She shook her head slowly and clucked her tongue. "That was just like Annie."

Darlene let out a small snort. "Well, *I* didn't know." She looked at her sisters. "Did any of you?"

They all shook their heads.

"Well then, I guess I let the cat out of the bag." Mary Margaret took off her glasses and cleaned the lenses with a corner of her shirt. "Close your mouths, girls. I know you have this romantic notion about your parents, but life was far from perfect for any of us. And I suspect all of you are old enough—and wise enough—to understand that. The plain truth is that the Lane family always thought the match with Monaghan was beneath them. The Lanes owned this house, you know." She stood up. "And it doesn't look like we're going to get inside." She dropped the glasses, allowing them to hang like a necklace, and clapped her hands. "Tell you what, let me take a photograph of all of you on these steps." Again she took the handrail and slowly stepped down to the sidewalk. "Which one of you has the camera? It'll be a nice picture for your Dad."

The girls were still stunned. They didn't move.

"Our grandparents were divorced?" asked Caylie.

"For all intents and purposes," said Mary Margaret. "They were separated." She returned her glasses to the middle of her nose and looked above them. "We Catholics not only got married when we unexpectedly found ourselves in the family way, we also didn't get divorced. And if you were a lesbian, like my sister, you moved to New York."

"I'll be damned," said Darlene. "How times have changed. I don't think we have any lesbians, but we do have both divorce *and* unwed mothers sitting right here on Mom's front steps. I can only imagine how our dead ancestors would feel about that."

"It's why I became an Episcopalian," said Jenny.

"It's why I became a doctor," said Mary Margaret. "I'm not a lesbian, mind you—I've had sex with men—I just never found one I wanted to marry. People overlooked the fact that I was a spinster once I was in medical school."

Darlene chuckled, Marie sighed and rolled her eyes, and Caylie was still feeling shocked. Jenny reached inside her jacket pocket and pulled out her camera. As her sisters moved closer to one another to pose for the picture, I focused in on my redheaded daughter, and could see her thoughts. She wasn't conjuring up images of dead ancestors, lesbians, divorced couples or pregnant girls. Instead she thought of the FOR SALE sign stuck in the front yard of our Grossdale home, and she remembered what it was like to walk inside the house and have all the furniture, as well as her parents missing. She knew at that moment, sitting on the front steps of my childhood home, what she didn't know while standing in the hollow chamber of her own childhood home when she was just eighteen years old.

Jenny knew her dad wanted to leave and that her mother, I, wouldn't let him leave without me. It felt like abandonment at the time; however, it was actually a lesson in what it meant to be married—and to stay married.

Rising, she handed her camera to Mary Margaret and then turned and looked at her sisters. "Well then," she said. "That explains a lot."

All the girls nodded their heads in agreement.

CHAPTER 17

Michael didn't leave Atlanta after the holidays. He wasn't well enough to travel—to make the rounds to his children's homes throughout the country as he had done the previous year. Darlene's house was the most logical place for him to stay. She certainly had the room, and she had the ability to keep him alive.

And this is exactly what she did.

Darlene had diagnosed her father with congestive heart failure, complicated by severe anemia. First she explained that anemia caused a low level of healthy red blood cells, and that red blood cells carried oxygen to body tissues. Because of the lack of oxygen, or hemoglobin, their dad was often fatigued. It's why he slept like a teenager. His heart further failed to pump what good blood he did have in a manner to sustain an active, healthy lifestyle.

Her sisters believed their father was dying of a broken heart, which wasn't untrue; however, Darlene assured them that this had been a long-term, chronic condition. For years, she said, he'd had high blood pressure and wasn't properly medicated. It had caused his heart to grow and grow. She was certain that the stress of losing me hadn't helped.

She monitored her father closely with regular echocardiograms and blood transfusions, prescribed ACE inhibitors, and did her best to take sodium out of his diet. But for a man who regularly sprinkled salt into each glass of beer to "make the head foam up," it was tough. She couldn't keep watch over him twenty-four hours a day.

But I could. I had always believed that my husband and I would somehow die together.

Michael was dying, yet far from dead. It was because Darlene was a good doctor.The transfusions would keep him going for a long time. Unlike my mother, who Mary Margaret Kerrigan had told me, died of "natural causes," modern medicine rarely let nature cause death anymore—at least not without a good fight. It appeared to me, however, that Darlene was more interested in keeping her father alive than Michael was committed to being alive.

In *Obr*, there was mostly darkness all around me. Regardless, I couldn't help but focus on the Light. I sat next to a calm body of water and spotlights from afar reflected in the peaceful, subtle ripples. I had always loved the look of lights on the water. Fainter, distant stars twinkled and a sliver of a moon, a distinct 'C,' hovered above. I knew it was waning. Shaped like a C, which stood for Christ, we had learned to determine the moribund moon as waning by comparing it to Christ dying on the cross.

My life as a Christian continued to shape all my thoughts and guide me through my judgment. I had always believed that Michael was the more loyal Catholic than I, as he was far more intolerant of other religions. I, for example, embraced my Jenny's religious evolution as she moved from the Catholic to the Episcopal Church. I was simply pleased to know she had maintained her faith. Michael, on the other hand, refused to attend the Episcopal Sunday services when he visited her in San Diego. "Catholics," he said, "are forbidden to attend Protestant churches or receive the Eucharist."

I wondered, would Michael have the same—or even a similar experience as I in *Obr*? Would I be here for his arrival like Molly was here for mine? Or perhaps it would be his mother, Belle, who would greet him. Would it be his father, Michael? Would he see Mrs. Bowers/Aunt Bee? Or would he instead meet an old shipmate or someone with whom he had worked? I learned enough to know that every human's judgment path was unique; however, it wasn't until I arrived here that I truly understood how we, as human beings, had a single origin and one ultimate end.

Everything begins and ends with God.

Through the light of the crescent moon reflecting upon the water,

I saw it was a dreary May evening in San Diego. A storm had come in, soaking the thirsty coastal shores. Jenny sat with her younger daughter, Ariel, in the same large, upholstered chair where she last sat together with her Irish Twin on the eve of Caylie's fortieth birthday. In her hands was the book, *Jane Eyre*, which she had eagerly taken from Darlene's library at Christmas.

"My mother read this to me when I was your age," she said. "I might have been a wee bit older than you, though. I don't remember exactly."

Ariel leaned her head against Jenny's chest. "I hardly even remember what Nana looked like anymore."

"That's why I keep her picture on the fireplace mantle. Right up there." She pointed across the room. "It's so you can look at her anytime you like."

"But that's not what she looked like. Her hair is black in that picture. Nana's hair was salt-and-pepper."

Jenny laughed. "Salt and pepper? Where did you hear that?"

The little girl shrugged her shoulders, and she pushed away straggling strawberry tresses. "I don't know. Keep reading, Mama. Start where we left off last time. If we have to wait for Sissy, we'll never get through this story."

"I don't think your sister's much interested in it anyway."

Ariel's petite yet adamant index finger tapped upon the open book. "Read!" she commanded.

Jenny continued the story with Chapter Four. In a soft voice, she read aloud the words of Charlotte Brontë, telling the story of the homely, abused girl, living in the home of her intolerant Aunt, Mrs. Reed. I read with her, and she thought of me through every sentence. It caused her voice to take on my inflections—and a hint of my Bostonian accent. After spending a weekend in Boston with her sisters, Mary Margaret Kerrigan's voice resonated in her memory. It enabled her to pull off a noteworthy imitation of the girl I had once been.

In spite of not understanding many of the words in the story, Ariel loved listening to her mother. As the stars twinkled around me in *Ohr,* I knew my granddaughter would remember this experience as clearly as Jenny remembered when I read *Jane Eyre* to her.

Perhaps one day, Ariel would read it to her own daughter as well.

The idea of this notion increased my joy. I understood it wasn't necessary that I share all of my life—my painful secrets—with my children. What I did share with them, and what they ultimately learned about me—they would bequeath to their own children. Jenny, the child I held in my gaze, would share tips on how to execute mundane household chores—from how to separate the lights and the darks in the laundry room to the art of loading the dishwasher properly. She'd write notes to her children and slip them into their lunch bags. Occasionally, she'd write inspiring words on their bananas, like "have faith," and "Mom loves you." She'd tell her daughters about how I water-skied until the day I died. She'd tell them I was a good dancer, a loyal wife. One day, she would even have to choose which one of her daughters would receive the gold pocket watch, which had become our version of the Claddagh, an Irish friendship ring traditionally passed from mother to daughter.

One thing neither Jenny nor any of my children would hand down to their progeny was my grief. No one needed to pass on grief. It was a feeling that couldn't be explained or even understood. And there would always be enough opportunities for individual grief to go around.

She continued reading: *" . . . My Uncle Reed is in heaven, and can see all you do and think; and so can papa and mama: they know how you shut me up all day long, and how you wish me dead . . ."*

Ariel sucked in her breath.

"What is it?" asked Jenny.

"Is that true?"

"Is what true? That Jane Eyre's aunt wished her dead?"

"No," said Ariel. "About heaven. Can Nana see everything we do and think from heaven?"

Jenny placed her thumb in the book and closed the cover. She leaned her head back in the chair and looked upward. She took in a deep breath and slowly exhaled, contemplating the question. "I'm not sure about that, Ari. What do you think?"

The little girl vigorously nodded her head. "Yeah. I think she can."

"Really?"

"Yeah. But I don't think she wants to see *everything*. Like, I don't think she wants to look when we're going potty or anything."

Jenny laughed. "No, I don't imagine she's much interested in that. She changed enough diapers in her lifetime that's for sure." Jenny stretched her arm around her daughter. "No, my darling, I think Nana's heaven is poop-free."

"Poop free! That's gross, Mama!" Ariel put her hand to her mouth and giggled.

With a smile and a shrug of her shoulders, Jenny pressed the tip of her finger to her daughter's nose. "You're right. Poop is gross."

Ariel was a stunning child. The first thing everyone noticed about her was her strawberry blonde hair. It wasn't thick and frizzy like her mother's, but rather, it was long and silky and hung in soft ringlets. The second thing everyone noticed was her eyes. She got them from her dad. Big and blue, they made her look like a Precious Moments figurine. She was very petite, only in the tenth percentile on infant and childhood growth charts monitoring height and weight, and she was timid and soft-spoken. Ariel's mannerisms often reminded Jenny of me. It took a long time after my passing for Jenny to stop herself from punching in my Michigan phone number just to tell me about something Ariel did that brought me to mind. Things like how she always covered her mouth when she laughed, or like no matter how hard she tried, she couldn't turn a cartwheel. I could never turn a cartwheel, and Jenny—a talented acrobat—couldn't understand why.

It was rewarding to see my daughter learn things about me through her own daughter.

Ariel took the book from her mother's hands and stared quizzically at the words she couldn't read. She ran her finger up and down the page, looked up and sighed. Casting her eyes across the room to the black and white photograph of me on the fireplace mantle, she sighed again. "I wish I knew more about Nana."

Jenny pulled her daughter a little closer. "Me too, Sweetie. Me too."

* * *

Caylie turned the dial on a small, tabletop stove, silencing the high-pitched whistle of a black, cast iron teakettle. She peeled away the paper lid of a Styrofoam Cup of Noodles and filled it with boiling water. She had just eaten lunch an hour earlier; however, during the homestretch toward delivery, her hunger was insatiable.

Her embroidered overalls had run out of room. So did the baby, thought Caylie. It had become far less active during the past few days. With two weeks to go and thirty-five pounds added to her middle, she was clad in khaki maternity pants and a plain yellow, short-sleeved tented top, adorned with a necklace of large turquoise nuggets. She filled a spoon with saturated noodles, brought the spoon to her lips and blew. Steam clouded her frameless reading glasses and a kernel of corn dropped to the counter. She continued blowing, determined to get the spoonful to a suitable temperature.

There was a soft knock on her office door. Allison, her assistant—a sandy-haired girl in her mid-twenties—poked in her head. "Caylie, there's a man here to see you," she said. She stepped inside. "He says his name is Albert Powell, but he doesn't have an appointment. Said it was personal?"

Caylie dropped the spoon. Noodles and broth splattered on the counter. She swore under her breath. "Shit, not now."

Allison closed the door behind her and rushed to the counter. She tore off a paper towel and soaked up the mess. "Not a good personal visit I take it?"

"No. Not good." Caylie whispered. She bit the inside of her cheek. "How did he find me?"

"Are you kidding? The phone's been ringing all week. Ever since that article appeared in *The Examiner* about Cielo Grande."

Caylie leaned against the counter. "Damn! I should have never let them quote me."

"So, who is this guy?" asked Allison. "He's pretty good looking! I like a little more hair than that—it's like, totally retro—but he's wearing a nice suit."

Caylie rolled her eyes. "He's no one, really. Just some guy I was supposed to marry."

"Marry? Is he—?"

"Yes. He is." Caylie walked to her desk and sat down. "But he doesn't actually know he's the father." She rolled herself toward the desk, hiding her stomach. She looked downward, then back up at Allison. "What do you think? Can you tell I'm about to give birth at any moment?"

The girl raised her perfectly plucked eyebrows. "Well? Hmm." She cocked her head and put her hands on her hips. "I don't know if your boobs were that big before you were pregnant, but if they weren't, they're a dead giveaway. Same thing happened to my sister."

"Albert was more of a leg man," said Caylie. She put the heels of her hands to her forehead and bent forward, resting her elbows on top of an unfurled blueprint.

"Here!" cried Allison, moving toward her. "Try this." She moved a tall stack of files in front of Caylie, and then stepped back and squinted. "Could work."

"Oh my God!" moaned Caylie. "This is ridiculous."

"So let me get this straight," said Allison, scratching her head. "This man—this Albert Powell—is the father of your baby. You were supposed to marry him . . . but he doesn't even know you're pregnant?"

"That pretty much sums it up."

Allison sucked in her cheeks and whistled. "Seriously, Dude. That's some disturbed stuff."

"Right," said Caylie. "Listen, I'm not about to go into life stories or anything right now, but I know it's disturbing. Don't think for one minute that I don't realize this. Just go back out there and tell him I've only got a minute before I have to be in a meeting. And tell him I've got a cold—or something—so he shouldn't get too close to me."

"Aye, aye," said Allison, and she clicked her tongue.

"And if he's still here in five minutes, come back in with a pot of tea and point to your watch about the meeting. Okay?"

"So, like, you seriously *don't* want this guy to support the baby?"

"Allison!"

"Sorry! Right! I'm all over this." She turned and headed toward the door.

"Wait!" cried Caylie. "I have another idea."

Allison stopped. She turned her head and called over her shoulder. "Yes?"

"Will you get my sister, Jenny, on the phone? Patch her right through if she picks up."

"You bet." Allison scurried out the door, closing it behind her.

* * *

The lights on the lake went out. The moon hid behind a cloud. For the first time since my arrival, I was thrown into complete darkness. Only the stars remained. Was I still in *Obr*?

I heard something stir. "Molly?"

The voice came from behind me. "No, Anne. It's not Molly."

I turned around, away from the water, and focused on a shadow.

"Tis I," said the voice. "Your mother."

CHAPTER 18

I took my mother's hand and the Light returned. We were surrounded by lush greenery. In the distance we heard the sound of running water—a waterfall—and a symphony of singing birds. Chickadees, robins, blue jays, cardinals, common loons, and even African rain birds. "The birds of Paradise," she said. "The Paradise you have created."

She led me through a field of wild flowers. I watched her long, single black braid swing gently back-and-forth across her torso, like the metronome atop her beloved piano. As I silently wished for her to "please wear it down," the braid slowly and unceremoniously unraveled. The reedy tones of a Bach minuet, the same piece I had heard while taking tea with Molly in our Melrose kitchen accompanied the chatter of the birds.

A cobblestone road appeared beside us and I heard the soft rumble of an engine. It came from a yellow car with white-walled tires and red-spoke wheels. The top was down. It was a Ford, Model A Roadster, and behind the wheel, waving vigorously, was Molly. She wore a flat, brimmed cap made of tweed, and a white, fringed scarf around her neck. She pointed to the sky. And when I followed her direction, I saw a yellow streak coming our way. It was a bird of a different kind—a giant canary. A biplane with parallel wings and a spinning propeller flew in slow motion. The pilot was Amelia Earhart. "I'm off to Ireland," she called. Then she lowered her goggles, smiled, and raised her thumb, disappearing into the horizon.

Before us was Mitten Lake. In the distance I spied a Coast Guard cutter ship, painted white and red. It cruised by on a steady course. Sailors dressed in white uniforms with loose black ties and tilted caps stood at ease on the decks and waved to my mother and me. At the tip of the bow was my handsome cousin, Lt. Theodore Lane, in his blue dress uniform, which is what he wore on my wedding day, when he gave me away to Michael. He nodded to us and then pointed to the east as the ship sailed forward. I saw Mrs. Bower's white wooden cottage with green-trimmed windows across the bay. Then Aunt Bee herself appeared. She steered the wooden, Milocraft boat that had once pulled all of my children and me out of the water and onto the waves. A ski-rope trailed behind the boat, and the handle danced, popping up and down between the waves of the wake.

When the waves cleared, the tip of my solitary ski rose from the water, and the cracked, crescent moon ski-belt floated beside it, along with a perfect white water lily, which smelled like a gardenia. We glided past this fateful spot on Mitten Lake without effort, making our way to the shore. I recognized the large dock belonging to our neighbors, the Stantons. The round table at the end, the place where Freda and Henry took their morning coffee and waved every time we rode by, sat with two empty, shellback chairs.

My mother and I stepped onto the T-shaped dock in front of our home. A weathered whisky barrel filled with cascading, bright orange and yellow nasturtium flowers sat next to a wooden bench. The flowers looked artificial, like tissue paper, and felt out-of-place. They were not spring flowers. I remembered they bloomed late in the season.

"There are no seasons here," said Mother. "And nasturtiums were always your father's favorite—probably because they're edible. He had a green-grocer's approach to gardening."

"My father?"

Across the expanse of the lawn leading to the wrap-around deck of our house, I saw a man on his knees. In his hand was a silver spade with a green handle, and he concentrated on digging a small hole. A burlap sack of lily bulbs sat beside him. He wore denim overalls with colorful leather patches on the legs. His hat was made of straw. As we drew near, he sensed our presence and looked up from his chore. He furrowed his brow, his heavy dark eyebrows coming together, and then smiled broadly. He dropped the spade and put his gloved hand to his mouth. Slowly, he rose to his feet and removed the muddy gloves, placing them in his back pocket.

He looked past my mother as if she weren't there, and focused his twinkling green eyes upon me. "Hello, Anne," he said in a soft, low voice. It was a voice I remembered hearing in my dreams. "I was told you wanted to see me."

"By whom?"

"By me," said Molly. She was standing behind him, on the deck next to the sliding glass door leading to Michael's and my bedroom. "Tea is ready."

The heavy door squealed as Molly slid it open. She moved aside and I stepped into the room. My feet sunk into the shag, avocado green carpeting. The bed was made, the covers perfectly smooth. Upon the exposed pillow on my side of the bed, sat the blue Michigan ball cap, the golden M glistening. I smelled Michael's aftershave. Looking around, I noticed all of the framed photographs on the walls were sun-bleached and faded. I walked toward the door, spying a slim, silver crucifix with a sharp green palm leaf behind it, hanging above the light switch.

Exiting the room, I was at once in the kitchen. On the cluttered counter sat my open recipe boxes. Notepads and index cards filled with my tiny, tight handwriting were strewn about. It appeared as though someone had been looking for something—some kind of recipe.

"Come, sit," said Molly. "Mother? Father?" She pulled an iron-back chair away from a glass-top table set with four, avocado teacups and matching saucers. "Anne, this seat is for you. I made soda bread and snickerdoodles, your favorites. Drink your tea while it's hot."

Bless us, O Lord, for these Thy gifts, which we are about to receive from Thy bounty, through Christ, our Lord, amen.

With the four of us—my mother, my father, my sister and I—seated at the table, our teacups filled, I felt as though I were home. Filled with the peace of the Holy Spirit, I understood I was in Heaven. My judgment journey was over. I had reached this place through the prayers of my children and those whom I loved and loved me during my life. The presence of my father—a man I believed I scarcely knew—was like the final puzzle piece, completing my vision. I felt his love for me deep within my soul. Without actually touching me, he had put his arm around my shoulder and the palm of his hand penetrated my being and warmed me. I didn't need to ask him why he left us. It wasn't important. What was important was that he was there, in *my* Heaven. By his presence and the God within him, I understood that his leaving had not been about me. I understood that *all* of our lives did not necessarily go according to the plans we may have hoped for or expected. And our parents couldn't always be the people we expected or felt we needed them to be. Life offered a constant series of unpredictable events: economic downturns, wars, deaths, murders, miscarriages, stillbirths, accidents, alcohol abuse and, of course, abandonment. It's so easy to make mistakes. But God does forgive us.

And so do our children.

I took the seat my sister offered and looked into my tea. My vision expanded.

For the first time, I saw Albert Powell, the father of my unborn grandchild. He entered Caylie's office. He was tall and broad-shouldered. His hair was chocolate brown with a hint of red. It was cropped short in what we had always called a "crew-cut." It was the way my son, Ronnie, had worn his hair until eighth grade—until the 1970s dictated he grow it longer and part it down the middle. The cropped style must have made a comeback.

Fashions, like history, often repeated themselves.

Albert's suit smelled of money. It was deep, charcoal gray. A stiff, white pocket protector protruded from his left breast pocket. His shirt was crispy, as white as his bleached teeth, and the bright red tie knotted at his neck felt both powerful and a little threatening.

He looked around the room. "Nice office. Looks like you landed yourself a pretty sweet setup out here in the Boonies." He unbuttoned his jacket and put his hands in his pants pockets.

Caylie remained seated at her desk behind the stack of files rising as high as her left shoulder. She watched Albert's eyes as they bounced from wall to wall, from counter to window to drafting table. There was a light blue sofa, two chairs and a coffee table in one corner, and several tall plants in terra cotta and cobalt blue pots. Albert soaked it all in, seemingly looking at everything but her. She crossed her ankles under the desk, linked her fingers together and sighed. She wanted desperately to sound causal, but felt herself trembling. "What are you doing here, Albert? It's not like you to venture out to the—what did you call them? The Boonies?"

At last he looked at her. Narrowing his eyes, he took in the change of her features—her fuller face, her longer hair. "Did you do something to your hair?"

"I grew it out," she said, gripping her hands together a little tighter.

He moved toward a chair stationed in front of her desk and placed his hands on the back of it. "Notice anything different about me?"

"You've lost weight," she said.

He straightened and patted his stomach. "Yep. Gave up drinking during the week. Ever since you called me 'a drunk,' I thought I'd do something to prove you wrong."

"Albert, I—"

Her phone buzzed and a light on it blinked. She pushed the blinking button, picked up the receiver and held up her index finger. "Excuse me for a moment."

Albert raised his hands in surrender. "Go ahead. I'm sure you're very busy and important." He turned his back to Caylie and muttered under his breath. "Too busy to even bother getting up off your big ass to greet me."

Caylie placed her hand over the mouthpiece of the phone. "What was that?"

"Nothing," he said. "Go ahead. Take your call."

Caylie closed her eyes. "Catherine Cotrell," she said into the phone.

"It's me. Jennifer," said Jenny. "Your secretary said Albert's there. Is he in the room with you?"

"Yes, that's right."

"Put the phone on conference—or something—so I can hear what's going on. I won't say anything. Allison knows she may need to get help and she's waiting on the other line."

"Oh, I'm sure it won't come to that," said Caylie. "These plans are pretty well-laid out."

"Right," said Jenny. "Well, you know what they say about plans. Just because you've managed to avoid him for all these months doesn't necessarily mean he's spent all that time moving on with his life. Is he sober?"

"I'd say so." Caylie took a deep breath. "Listen, I promise you, I know what I'm doing. In fact, I have a meeting scheduled about this in five minutes."

"Fine, fine. Just be sure to use the code phrase, okay?"

"I will," said Caylie. "Wait, which one is that?"

"About liking your tea *hot*, you idiot!"

"Right. Okay. Thank you for calling." Annoyed, Caylie pushed a button on the phone and set down the receiver. She could almost hear her sister's heavy breathing coming through the telephone line. She quickly glanced at the clock. It was just before two. Albert didn't appear to be drunk. He said he gave up drinking during the week. She wondered, did that include Fridays? "So, Albert," she said.

He turned around. "So, you go by Catherine now?"

"It's actually my name. What did you say you were doing here? Did you come all this way just to see me?"

"Yes and no. I had an early lunch meeting in Orinda. Last Sunday I saw your name in the paper, and I figured since I was on this side of the bridge, I'd stop by. I went all the way out to kingdom come—to the construction site—but they said you were spending most of your time back here in the office these days."

"Oh? They?" Caylie felt a slight twinge low in her abdomen. It wasn't a kick. It was something different.

"He, actually. Some *beaner* in an orange vest and a yellow hardhat said it was better for you to be off your feet."

Caylie sucked in her breath. *God, what did I ever see in him?* she thought. "You mean a Mexican man, of course. It must have been Hector. He's my right-hand man out there."

"Right-hand man?" asked Albert with a sneer. "Is that what they're calling it these days? What *else* is he?"

"Albert— "

"Listen, Caylie," he said. He put one hand on his hip and then rubbed the top of his crew-cut with the other. "Game over. I know what you're hiding behind that desk. Señor Hector told me you're pregnant. Is he the father? Is that who you hooked up with after you dumped me?"

"No! Wait— "

"You sure didn't waste any time, did you? Or was he the reason?"

"Hector?" Caylie grimaced. "Don't be ridiculous. He works for me and I only just met him, like four months ago."

"CAYLIE!" Jenny's tinny voice warned through the telephone. Caylie quickly sneezed, trying to cover the sound. She pushed the phone aside and into the stack of files, which caused two manila folders to fall from the top. Their contents—pink and yellow carbon papers—spilled onto the desk.

Albert made his way toward her with heavy steps. He put his hand on the left armrest of her chair and pulled it back, away from the desk.

Caylie looked down at his fingers. They quickly turned from pink to white as they gripped the chair. Oddly, she focused on the individual hairs below his knuckles. She wondered if her baby would have hairy fingers. He then grabbed the other armrest and forcefully turned the chair. His brown eyes zoomed in on her stomach and he let out an astonished gasp. She smelled alcohol on his breath.

Albert straightened as though shocked, and took a step back. "Jesus, Caylie," he said, "How pregnant are you?"

"A hundred percent," she said softly.

"But it looks like you're ready to have it any day." He closed his eyes and held up a hand, counting on his fingers. "May, April, March . . ."

"End of August. Lake Barryessa," she said.

He closed his fist.

"It was before you brought my boys to a bar to watch you and your underage kids get drunk."

"*What?*"

"Yeah, that's right. Back when I still believed I was going to marry you."

Once again she heard Jenny's warning come through the phone line. It was the voice of counsel, authority—the sister voice she'd heard all her life: "Careful, Caylie!"

Albert narrowed his eyes. "Wait just a minute. Are you trying to tell me this is *my* child?"

Caylie rose. "I'm not trying to tell you," she said. "I *am* telling you."

"You're telling me now? *Now?*" Albert's face grew red. He placed both his hands to his head and clutched his scalp. Turning his back to her he shouted. "Bullshit!"

"It's true, Albert. You're the father."

A rage welled up within him. His skin turned from red to purple. He spun around, took one step toward her and stopped. "Were you planning to tell me at all?"

Caylie stepped back. "It's bad enough my boys are dealing with a broken home. Marrying you wasn't the answer. Don't you see?" She gripped her bulging stomach. "I don't want this child dealing with anything close to what I went through."

Albert shook his head furiously. "What are you talking about? I thought you said your parents had the perfect marriage." He turned again, walked to the sofa and thudded into it.

Caylie followed him. "The perfect marriage? I don't even know what that means."

"Because it doesn't exist. It's just one of your naïve fantasies."

"Well maybe it is! I don't know. But what I do know, is that if anyone's goal is to have the perfect marriage, than you've got to give up something else."

"What the fuck, Caylie?"

"Albert, just listen to me for a minute. My parents were in their forties when Jenny and I were born. We weren't exactly planned either." She sat next to him and paused a moment as he took in deep breaths through his nose. Sweat beaded on his forehead and above his lip. "I think my parents did their best to give us a good childhood, but by the time we were teenagers, our dad was over it! He wanted out and didn't do a thing to hide his disdain for us."

"So that's what you're doing? You're comparing me to your father just because I'm in my forties?"

"Albert! You barely have anything to do with the two kids you already have. God knows you could care less about *my* boys."

"That's ridiculous!" he shouted, his breath toxic. "What right did you have to keep this from me?"

Caylie stood up. "You're drunk! And you're a liar! Don't tell me you gave up drinking during the week. I can smell it on you." She moved quickly toward her desk. She looked at the phone, face down next to the stack of files. She knew Jenny was there—as she always was—listening and ready to protect her. Staring at the receiver, she spoke to her sister. "When we were teenagers, we had a drunk, disinterested father who pulled our mother away from us when we needed her the most. She shielded us from his alcoholism when she could, and we were too stupid and innocent to realize what was going on anyway. All we knew was that he was miserable. And ultimately, when it came time to make a choice, in spite of everything, she chose him."

Caylie turned around, still clutching her stomach. "Well, when my husband wanted to be in a Third World country more than he wanted to be here, I didn't follow him. I chose my ***kids***. And I choose this child."

Albert slammed his hands on the coffee table. "How could you? And how dare you compare me to them?" He loosened his tie, rose and stomped toward her.

Caylie squirmed. She felt something tingle between her legs. She moved behind her desk for protection, and sensed a wetness, a discharge. It wasn't dramatic, like when her water broke in the middle of the Africa exhibit at the Zoo when she was expecting Frankie. But it was something. She looked down just as Albert took another step toward her. He stretched out his hands and was about to grab her shoulders, when the office door opened and Allison appeared. She carried a tray with a Cielo corporation signature teapot, sky blue, along with stacked teacups and saucers. "It's time for your meeting," she said urgently.

Caylie looked up. Albert stopped in place. They both focused on Allison.

Her voice was chirpy. "I've got the tea all ready. It's nice and hot. Just the way you like it. I prefer my tea hot, too." She set the tray on the coffee table next to the sofa. "Do you prefer your tea hot as well, Mr. Powell?"

Albert frowned. "What the hell are you talking about? I don't drink tea."

The door pushed open again and a blue-shirted security officer stepped inside.

"CAYLIE!" Jenny's voice came through the phone. "Are you all right? What's happening?"

Caylie picked up the receiver. "I'm fine, Jenny," she said. "But do you think you can call Southwest airlines and get here right away? I don't know if my water just broke or it was merely the mucous plug coming out, but something just happened, and I might be going into labor."

CHAPTER 19

Jenny pushed the OFF button on her phone. Her heart beat rapidly. She called Don at work and told him Caylie needed her.

"Go," he said. "Do what you have to do and be with your sister. I've got everything covered here. We'll be fine. But don't take Southwest because I think you'll have to go through Vegas to get to Oakland. Let me get Nina to find you a direct flight. Pack—or whatever—and I'll call you back."

"God bless you! Boy, did I ever marry the right man," said Jenny. "Thank you!"

Jenny hurried to her bathroom, trying to ignore the dirty dishes piled in the sink, the piles of laundry practically pouring from the laundry room. She washed her face and pulled her hair out of the ponytail atop her head. Red curls cascaded over her shoulders. She changed into a fresh pair of jeans and a purple tank top. From her nightstand drawer, she pulled out a small white box containing her prized, gold watch, and hung it around her neck. Jenny only wore the heirloom I had given her on special occasions, and she felt this qualified. She folded it into her hand and held it to her heart. "Please make everything be okay," she prayed.

As she pulled together her clothes and cosmetics, Don called back. He instructed her to leave for the San Diego airport immediately in order to make her flight. He had even arranged a rental car for her to drive from Oakland to the town of Dublin, where Caylie lived.

"The car has GPS," said Don. "So, just plug in the address before you drive and you won't get lost. You'll be there at the tail end of rush hour on a Friday night. It'll most likely be pretty busy."

She didn't know if Caylie would be at home or at the hospital; however, she had faith she'd get to her sister in time.

* * *

"Is everything okay in here, Mrs. Cotrell?" asked the security guard.

"Yes, thanks Jackson," said Caylie. "Mr. Powell was just leaving. Would you see to it that he gets safely to the BART station? Or you can call him a cab if he prefers. But he really shouldn't be driving."

"Yes, Ma'am." Jackson kept one hand on the door handle and extended his other toward Albert, still standing next to Caylie's desk.

Albert knit his brow and threw up his hands. He was clearly confused. "You called security on me?"

Allison crossed her arms and shifted her weight. She narrowed her eyes at Albert and tapped her foot. "Dude," she said, "you just got your walking papers. Time to hit the road with our man, Jack."

Albert wiped the sweat from his forehead with the back of his hand. He bit his lower lip. "Fine," he spit, and walked toward Jackson's outstretched arm. He stopped, turned and looked at Caylie. "You are one crazy bitch," he said. "You know that? Go ahead and have this baby without me. It's probably not even mine anyway. Just don't come crying to me when you're dealing with four kids and feeling sorry for yourself."

Jackson scowled and put his beefy hand on Albert's shoulder. Albert shrugged it off and walked out of Caylie's office. When the door closed, it felt to Caylie like all the air went out of the room with them. A sharp pain stabbed her lower abdomen. She cried out, grabbed her stomach and fell back against her desk.

"Holy crap!" shrieked Allison. "Are you in labor?"

"I don't know," said Caylie. "I don't remember having a pain like this. I have to go to the bathroom."

"I can drive you to the hospital. Or should I call you a cab? What do you want me to do?"

"Call my sister again. Make sure she's on her way."

* * *

Jenny was the last one on the airplane. She found her seat, stashed her bag in the overhead bin, and just as she closed the compartment, the flight attendant secured the main door. She fastened her seatbelt and reached for the in-flight magazine. Jenny was a nervous flyer and used a ritual to calm her nerves before takeoff. It was her goal to have the magazine crossword puzzle completed by the time they were airborne and the wheels were folded back into their storage compartments. She flipped to the back pages, only to find the crossword already completed in red ink.

"Not a good sign," she said to the man seated next to her in the window seat.

"Here, have mine." He handed her his copy of the magazine. "I'm not much of a crossword guy anyway."

Jenny flashed her brilliant smile. "Thanks." She looked at him for an extra moment. He was handsome, with kind blue eyes. "I'm Jenny," she said, extending her hand. "My sister's having a baby. I hope I can make it in time."

"How exciting," he said. "Is this her first?"

Jenny looked down and shook her head. "No," she said. "Hopefully, it's her last."

* * *

Once she was in the bathroom, Caylie checked the discharge and didn't think her water broke. She didn't know what was happening, which surprised her. Going through three previous pregnancies made her believe there were few surprises. It was one reason why she didn't want to know the baby's gender. She phoned the office of her obstetrician, Dr. Wolfe, and described what had happened to his nurse. When he finally called back, he said it was probably brought on by the stress of dealing with Albert, and it sounded like the mucous plug released. Because of the pain and her "advanced age," he suggested she make her way to the Medical Center to be checked. It was just down the road from her office.

Allison drove her in a tin can Toyota, an old, faded model covered with Grateful Dead emblems and a host of bumper stickers with sayings like "Question Authority," and "Visualize World Peace." A crystal snowflake hung from the rear view mirror and swung back-and-forth, emitting hypnotic light beams. Allison apologized for the broken seatbelt, but figured it would be okay since the hospital was so close. "Are you having any more of those sharp pains?"

"Not really," said Caylie. "I don't feel much of anything right now. The baby hasn't been very active lately. But they say that's normal when it gets this big. We might be dealing with an eight-pounder."

"Dude, that's phat!"

"That's not a fat baby, Allison. It's bigger than my others—they were only seven pounds—but it's still within reason."

Allison laughed. "I didn't mean fat as in big and chubby. I meant *phat*! P-H-A-T. Like, it's a good thing. Like cool, or awesome. And you're one hot mama!"

"God, I'm old," said Caylie with a sigh. "Which reminds me, I had better call my son, Frankie, just in case I do go into labor. Do you think it would totally traumatize a fourteen-year-old boy to be in the delivery room?"

Allison screwed up her face. "Definitely."

* * *

The Oakland airport was small and easy to navigate. Jenny quickly made her way to the rental car transfer station and was soon loading her bag into a cherry red, Chevy Blazer. Allison, Caylie's assistant, had left a message for her to meet them at the John Muir Medical Center in Walnut Creek, rather than at Caylie's house in Dublin. She assured Jenny that Caylie wasn't yet in active labor. "Get here as soon as you can, but like, don't rush and get into an accident or anything," said the young woman.

"O-kay," Jenny said as she pulled her cell phone away from her ear. She pushed the OFF button and stored the phone in her back pocket. Once she reached her car, slot E-13, she programmed the hospital's address into the navigation system, pulled out of the parking area, and waited for the system to tell her which way to go.

"In half of a mile, turn left and onto Interstate Eight-Eighty," said the computerized, female voice.

Jenny frowned and looked at the digital lines of the map illuminated on the four-color screen. With a feeling of disbelief and confusion, she shook her head upon seeing the series of white, yellow and blue lines—a meaningless spider web of routes and labels. She couldn't help but laugh.

The voice coming from the device sounded just like her mother.

Just

like

me.

From my glass-top table, inside my home in my Heaven, I continued watching the afternoon unfold. I held my Irish Twins in the palms of my hands. Molly sat across from me. My parents were on either side. We all watched as Jenny took hold of her gold watch with one hand, and tightened her grip on the steering wheel with the other. She willed the navigation lady to speak to her again.

"Turn left," the system directed.

Jenny obeyed. "It's uncanny! Thanks, Annie," she said with a chuckle. And as she pressed the accelerator and merged onto the freeway, she whispered a prayer. "Mom, I know you're with me. Please keep watch over Caylie, and let me make it to her side in time."

I whispered in response, and my parents and sister echoed my words. "Yes, my darling. I am with you. I am with both of you. Keep your focus. Keep your faith."

Traffic was heavy on the freeway; however, it moved at a quick pace. Jenny thought it was similar to rush hour in San Diego. My daughter had always marveled at how Californians managed to maintain sixty miles-per-hour speeds in bumper-to-bumper traffic.

"Proceed on Interstate Eight-eighty."

Jenny was well on her way from the Oakland Airport to Walnut Creek when ahead and to the right, she spied a bright blue sign for an AM-PM Mini Mart looming beyond the freeway embankment. Severely parched, she took the next off-ramp, believing a quick stop for a bottle of water would only set her back five minutes or so.

As she veered right, the navigation system beeped three times, and the woman's voice that sounded like me told her to turn left at the next light.

"I know what I'm doing, Annie," she said. "This will only take a second."

"Make a U-turn," commanded the system.

"Quiet!" said Jenny, speaking to the computer as if it were one of her daughters. She pulled into the parking lot. Putting the car in Park, she grabbed her purse, locked the door by remote and stashed the key in her front pocket. It was chillier than it had been in San Diego and she shivered slightly before stepping into the harsh lights of the convenience store. When she pushed open the door, an electronic doorbell rang and she was greeted by the smell of overcooked corndogs and cigar smoke. The young man behind the counter, busy ringing up the purchase of another customer, did not look up. She made her way to the back of the store, momentarily catching a glimpse of her purple shirt and bouncing red curls in the round, surveillance mirror hanging in the back corner. Once she reached the wall of refrigerators, she saw a row of large, glass bottles of Calistoga water. Checking to make sure the bottle had a lemon on the label, she grabbed it and brought it to the register.

"You want a bag?" asked the indifferent clerk. He glanced at her only briefly, not looking her in the face.

"No thanks," she said.

The clerk handed her change, and she took the bottle. She pushed open the door, and again heard the doorbell ring.

The early evening air was filled with the sound of cars racing past on the freeway. She smelled diesel. As Jenny reached into her pocket to retrieve the car key, she heard heavy footsteps approach her. She turned to the left and her head was suddenly yanked back. It felt like someone had put a wire around her neck. As she gasped for air, the Calistoga bottle slipped from her hand and shattered on the concrete. Glass and carbonated water exploded like a firework. She bent at the waist, fighting the pull, and whatever it was that had seized her neck, pulled her forcefully away from the direction of her car.

Jenny dropped her purse, and with both hands, she reached up and grabbed the thin, coiling weapon. She lowered her head, and pulled it over her face, past her lips, and over her nose and forehead. It tore through her hair—causing lightening bolts to crash through her brain. She felt the crackle of hair follicles being torn from her skull.

Freed, she fell to the sidewalk amidst the spilled contents of her purse, the glass shards and bubbling water.

Spilled bubbles. In a flash, Jenny pictured her little sister, Caylie, with straight blonde bangs and a toothless grin, rubbing Five and Dime bubbles into her extended forearm. She heard her sister call her name in panic: *"Jeeeeennn-nnnneeeeeey?"*

Jenny reached for her purse and put her hand to her pounding heart, feeling for her golden watch. It was gone.

"Oh my God!" she cried as she searched for the perpetrator, who was nowhere in sight. "What was that?"

Inside the store, the clerk ran to the door, opened it, and the doorbell sounded. "Are you okay?" he called. "Did you see him?"

Jenny put her hand on her neck where a red streak had formed. Her eyes were wild. "See who? I don't know what happened."

"Those mother-fuckers," said the clerk. "It was that gold chain, wasn't it?"

That gold chain. Yes. That and her mother's watch—her grandmother's watch. It was *her* watch, to one-day pass on to one of her daughters. Jenny closed her eyes and mourned. "My watch," she whispered. It was just over an inch in diameter and made of solid gold. A tiny cabin—a home—was etched into the cover protecting the face of roman numerals in a circle of time—I to XII. The watch didn't work. It was broken when she received it on Caylie's wedding day, and she'd always meant to have it repaired. But suddenly, it was too late.

Still splayed on the ground, Jenny looked up at the clerk and nodded, feeling guilty. It was as though she'd just admitted to doing something wrong.

"I should have told you to be careful wearing something like that around here," he said. "I keep telling the owner we need to get security cameras outside."

"It was special," said Jenny, breathlessly. She stood up and brushed off her jeans. There was a bleeding abrasion on the palm of her hand. She held it close to her face, examining it, and flicked away a small piece of glass. Her eyes filled with tears. "It was my mother's watch."

"Do you want me to call the cops? I will, but I don't know if they'll do anything about it. That thing's gonna get pawned faster than you can say methamphetamines."

"What?" she asked. "I don't know—"

"You should check out the pawnshops down in San Leandro in a few days. I know someone who found his shit down there."

"I don't live here," said Jenny. "I'm just here because—" She stopped, closed her eyes and took a deep breath. She thought of Caylie. She had to get to Caylie.

Her temples pounded. Her head felt like it was in a vise. She knew she'd made a mistake she couldn't take back. "I can't believe he tore it right off my neck! My God, why did I wear it? It was the most special gift I've ever received. No one could even begin to understand—"

"Sorry," said the clerk. "It wasn't your fault."

She shook her head. "Yes, it was."

He pointed to his neck. "That doesn't look good, *mija.* You might want to go to the hospital."

Jenny didn't feel the pain of her bruised neck. It had happened so quickly, she was still confused. Regardless, she felt the warmth of this young man's kindness and concern. She studied him for a moment, taking in his black, Oakland Raiders cap sitting sideways on his head and the silver gauges in his ears. They were like thimbles, distorting his earlobes—like something she had seen in Kenya when on safari with Caylie. His jeans were oversized and hung well below his waistline.

She knew it was the style, but she didn't get it.

"Actually," she said, "I'm on my way to a hospital right now. My sister's having a baby."

"*¡Felicidades!*" he said. "Let me get you another bottle of Calistoga. It's on me, okay? I'm really sorry about your mother's watch. I hope she doesn't get mad at you."

Once again, Jenny brushed her hands over the front and back of her jeans. Tiny glass shards tinkled to the ground. "She's dead," said my daughter, checking her hands for additional cuts. "And she never got mad at me for anything."

* * *

Dr. Wolfe felt it was best to admit Caylie and monitor her overnight. He mentioned something about "inducing," and told Caylie to think about it. Allison didn't want to leave her alone in her hospital room, but Caylie insisted she go. "If you really want to help me, you can run down to Dublin and stay with my kids. Their dad is still in Africa—Tanzania, I think—and won't be back for another week. This baby wasn't supposed to make an early appearance."

The room in the birthing center was lovely, peaceful. There was a private bathroom and a window offering a partial view of Mt. Diablo. Caylie pressed her cheek to the glass, and the nuggets of her turquoise necklace clicked against it. The window was airtight, yet through it, she could hear the hospital breathe. People were born and people died in this building every day, she thought. And in the meantime, they worked, they lived, they loved.

At that moment, Caylie wondered how life could seem both very short and very long at the same time.

She was going to do her best to love this baby. She wrapped her arms around her stomach. It was hard and solid and silent. The nurse, who initially showed her the room and pointed out the features as though it were a hotel suite, would soon be back. She'd advise her to change into the thin, polka-dotted hospital gown. Monitors would be strapped around her and the churning sound of her baby's heartbeat would fill the room. Since she arrived at the hospital, there had been no additional labor pains, no further discharge. The baby hadn't moved or kicked in days. "Are you sure you're ready to come out into this world?" she asked her unborn child.

The mountain loomed majestically in the distance. Diablo, named with the Devil in mind, was a landmark hard to miss. It wasn't because the mountain was very tall, only 3,849 feet in elevation. And it wasn't because it was part of a dramatic or prolific mountain range. Diablo rose solo from California's Central Valley and the terrain surrounding San Francisco Bay. The rock at the top was known, in geological circles, to be older than the rock at the base. An anomaly, this was the exact opposite of the way it was supposed to be. It was like the mountain had been turned completely upside down.

It was like an afterthought of nature—seemingly out-of-place.

Caylie felt the same way about her presence in the birthing room. She was an expectant, advanced-aged mother, without a father there to support her. Her world had been turned upside down again and again. Was her life the exact opposite of what it was supposed to be?

Or was it exactly the way it should be?

She looked at her watch and wondered if Jenny had landed in Oakland. Would her Irish Twin—her other half—be there in time?

* * *

In a car alone, driving, it was always the worst. It was when Jenny's grief welled-up. Tearful emotions could be brought on by a song on the radio, a smell in the air, a sight on the side of the road. Or it could be nothing in particular that brought on her sadness over my passing. But losing the golden watch was like losing me all over again. Death, especially one that was as unexpected as mine, afforded too many possibilities for unfinished business.

I felt the same when my mother, my sister and my child were gone.

Their deaths caused feelings of regret, helplessness and, of course, loss. Loss was, perhaps, one of life's biggest obstacles. And now she had lost the one tangible piece of me she held most dear.

"Merge onto highway twenty-four and proceed east," said the navigation system in my voice.

"Proceed," she said. "It's all we can do."

Jenny put her hand on her heart, feeling a hole where the non-ticking watch had once been. The person who stole it—who tore it from her neck—would never understand its value. How could the world have changed so much? From a place where her grandmother and her mother were able to keep the heirloom safe, to a place with people who felt entitled to take things and pawn them for the price of a fix? It just didn't make sense.

"Why does God let things like this happen?"

The teakettle on the stove behind my sister, my parents and me, let out a high-pitched whistle. Steam burst through it and surrounded all of us. "God doesn't let things like this happen," said my mother. "We do."

The Bay Area air had grown foggy and Jenny switched on her windshield wipers. She pushed the radio button, and melodic piano notes filled the car. The sound faded as she drove through a long tunnel, and when she emerged into the early evening light on the other side, the music resumed and the sky was clear and bright. Tall eucalyptus trees flanked the highway, and in the ribbon of sky before her, she saw the half moon was rising early. The D-shape meant it was waxing. I had taught her about the waning, C-shaped moon, like Christ dying on the cross. Jenny wondered what the "D" meant.

"Dumb!' she spat. "Dumb, stupid, idiot!" She banged her hands on the steering wheel. "Goddamn it!"

Molly rose and made her way to the screeching teakettle. She removed it from the stove and it let out a small chirp before silencing. "This will be your last cup of tea for some time," she said as she filled my cup to the rim.

Jenny's navigation system beeped. *"Ahead, merge onto highway six-eighty."*

My daughter second-guessed her decision to leave the convenience store without filing a police report. She didn't know how long it would have taken, and she was eager to get away from there and to get to Caylie. It just didn't feel like the right thing to do. The watch was gone, her mother was dead, and Caylie was alive and well and waiting for her arrival.

"In half of a mile, exit right. Then turn right."

A pang of fear hit her as she imagined confessing to her father that she lost the watch. Did he even know she had it? She wondered if he had noticed it hanging around her neck at my funeral.

No, he hadn't. I didn't tell Michael about the day I gave Jenny my mother's watch. He wouldn't have understood.

I studied my father, seated to my left. He bowed his head and stared into his tea. I believed it was possible that fathers and daughters could have special, meaningful moments between them, but I hadn't had that experience during my life. Nor had Jenny and Michael found that path. The main thing that Jenny had been given by her father was the feeling of resentment. She felt he resented her for being born, and she, in return, resented him for teaching her the meaning of conditional love. It was one reason why nothing ever seemed quite good enough to her.

She had such a difficult time forgiving him. It was her cross to bear—her challenge to overcome. Jenny had finally learned that life would always be riddled with disappointments and the consequences of choice.

My father looked up. "Daughter," he said, placing his right hand upon my cheek, "we forgive others when we forgive ourselves."

"Now turn right."

Jenny switched on her blinker, turned the wheel and came to a stop at a traffic light. The piano solo on the radio ended. *"We'll have more on our tribute to Johann Sebastian Bach and the chapter from the Notebook for Anna Magdalina after this message from our sponsor."* She unscrewed the cap on the Calistoga bottle and took a long swallow. The bubbles tickled her throat.

"Is forgiveness a conscious choice or an emotional state?" asked the radio announcer in a low tenor. Jenny frowned and looked at the radio dial. *"Bear with each other and forgive whatever grievances*

you may have against one another. Forgive as the Lord forgave you. A quote from Colossians 3:13. . . ."

Jenny took another swallow and returned the cap to the bottle. The light changed to green, and she eased the red Blazer forward. She pushed the search button on the radio. Coming toward her on the opposite side of the street, was a semi truck with an icy bottle of Miller Genuine Draft painted on the side. She let out a short, flustered breath, thinking there was no escape from the constant reminders of her parents and her childhood. Miller beer was her dad's drink of choice. She couldn't help but picture him—sprinkling salt in his frosted mug, a foam mustache momentarily forming on his upper lip. She visualized his wide, expressive forehead and the deep furrow between his brows. And his wind-burned cheeks and baby-blue eyes, bloodshot from a day spent working outdoors in the punishing Midwestern weather. She heard his stern voice, scolding her, calling her ungrateful. And then she remembered his laugh—how he once laughed so hard at something he saw on television, that he nearly fell backward in his upholstered, swivel chair. He had beautiful teeth, a nice head of hair, long legs. In spite of a tendency toward bigotry, he was intelligent, well-read. He told a good story.

She had always heard how good-looking and charming he was—a real catch during World War II. She knew her mother, I, was his biggest fan. And she realized how hard I had tried to assist their relationship by always including his love in my letters, and by calling him to the extension every time she telephoned. Now that Jenny was a mother herself, she realized the emotion and toil involved in raising children. Was there anyone who believed raising children was as romantic and wonderful as making them? It must have been truly difficult for him to carry out the day-to-day, blue collar routine of supporting a family with all those palms outstretched and all those mouths to feed—especially the two that came unexpectedly and rather late in his life—the Irish Twins.

It was too bad he'd grown so disappointed with his life. Children don't ask to be born. And many parents don't understand the magnitude and never-ending nature of their role. She thought of Caylie's decision to raise this new baby without a father. Was it better, she wondered, to raise a child without a father than with one who was only equipped to hand off his damage?

She thought of her husband, Don, at home, lovingly making macaroni and cheese and hot dogs for the girls. She knew she married the man who was right for her—just as I had married the man who was right for me.

Her sister didn't have the same kind of luck.

Jenny glanced in the rear view mirror and caught a glimpse of her blue eye—her father's eye. Michael remained in Atlanta with Darlene, and would probably stay there for the rest of his days. His health was failing but Jenny knew it wasn't too late to make peace with her father. After Caylie's baby was born, she would to return to Atlanta to spend some time with him.

She vowed to find a way to forgive him.

"Continue one mile. Your destination will be on the right."

In my Heaven, my mother and father reached for my hands, and the hands of my Irish Twin, Molly. Together we recited the words of Luke: *"Do not judge, and you will not be judged. Do not condemn, and you will not be condemned. Forgive and you will be forgiven."*

We released our hands and turned toward the large windows offering an unobstructed view of the lake. Light bounced off the waves and flashed throughout the room like twinkling stars—like signals.

"Are you finished with your tea, dear?" asked my mother. "It's almost time."

CHAPTER 20

"I'm looking for the old lady having a baby," said Jenny as she pushed open a heavy door and stepped into the hospital room. She heard the sound of the baby's heartbeat churning through the monitor before she saw her sister.

"Over here," called Caylie from the bed. "Thank God you're here!"

Jenny set down her purse and her water bottle, and went to Caylie's bedside. She leaned over and kissed her on the cheek. "Gosh, you look so pretty!"

"Yeah, right!" scoffed Caylie. She brushed blonde follicles away from her face. "You always say that to me. I'm sure I'm anything but pretty right now."

"No, really, *dada yangu*. You do look beautiful. You've always been the most beautiful girl I've ever known," said Jenny. "How's the pain? Are you having regular contractions yet?"

"Not really," said Caylie. "They're coming, but they don't feel like contractions. They just feel like menstrual cramps."

"Well, duh! That's what labor feels like. You can't remember from twelve years ago?"

Caylie smiled and then she gasped. "Oh my God, Jenny. What happened to your neck?"

Jenny reached for her scar, the red reminder etched into her skin that had replaced her precious watch. "Is it really bad?"

"Come here. Bend down."

Jenny leaned over and Caylie raised her hand to her sister's neck.

An I-V tube traveled with her. "What do they have you on?"

"Petocin," said Caylie absently. "Jenny, it looks like a laceration. What happened?"

Jenny straightened and shook her head. Her eyes filled with tears. "I still don't believe it's gone."

"What's gone?"

"My watch. Mom's watch."

"Someone ripped it off your neck?"

Jenny sighed and nodded. "Wait, how did you know it was ripped from my neck? Can you tell? Did I say that?"

"Oh Jenny! I don't believe it. I mean, *you're* not going to believe this but I had a dream I was wearing that watch on a chain around my neck—just the way you wore it—and I was riding on the El train going to the Oak Park station by our old house. I was holding onto the pole when the doors opened, and the next thing I knew, some kid ripped the necklace right from my neck and ran off the train!"

"You're kidding."

"No, I'm not. It was a pretty traumatizing dream—like one of those when you wake up and for a second you don't know whether or not it was real? It was like someone stole Mom."

"I know the feeling. Why didn't you tell me?"

"I don't know, Jen. I forgot about it, I guess. And I didn't want to upset you."

"That's crazy," said Jenny. "That's almost exactly what happened. But I wasn't on the El, obviously. I was walking to my rental car with a freaking bottle of Calistoga. I never even saw the guy before the chain was ripping through my hair."

"I'm so sorry. I know how much it meant to you."

Jenny ran her fingers through her hair. "I feel so stupid for losing it."

"You didn't lose it. It was stolen. And it's not your fault."

"Yeah, but it was the only thing of hers' that I had."

Caylie grasped her sister's forearm. "That's not true," she said. "Mom gave you everything, Jenny. She gave you your life. And no one can take away the memories you have of her—or the memory you have of her giving the watch to you."

Jenny sighed and sat on the bed. "I wish she were here."

"She is," said Caylie. "Mom's always with us. Haven't you learned that yet? It's the way I was able to get through most of my life after she moved to Mitten Lake. Not that I plan to do the same thing she did, but—" Suddenly she closed her eyes and winced. A low pain came to a quick crescendo. Jenny squeezed her hand as Caylie puffed out four short breaths and then opened her eyes. "Not a bad one. But I don't think this petocin drip is doing anything. And I'm starving. I've had nothing but ice chips and popsicles since I got here. The doctor said if it doesn't come by nine, he'll take me off for the night and then come back in the morning and break my water. He said I'm close enough to term and at my age, it's better to bring this baby home." She pointed across the room. "That's a foldout bed over there. And the bathroom is stocked with fragrant soaps. I'm telling you, Sissy, it's the Cielo Grande Hotel of hospitals."

Jenny looked around, and nodded her head in approval. "I wonder who designed the landscaping."

* * *

I took my mother's outstretched hand and we moved through the wall of windows and across the expanse of lawn toward the long, narrow pier reaching out to the waters of Mitten Lake. Behind us, my father and my sister stood on the deck and waved. We passed the plot of rich soil where I first saw my father toiling with a small spade in his hand, digging holes and planting bulbs. As we drifted by, one-by-one, white, trumpet-shaped lilies shot up. Their sweet fragrance permeated the air.

I filled myself with their beauty. They tasted of hope and of life. "Michael brought me lilies just like those every Easter Sunday."

* * *

Before first light, Jenny awoke, wondering where she was. Within moments, the smell of the room and the hum of the monitoring equipment reminded her she was with Caylie. The baby had not yet come. At nine o'clock on the previous night, as directed by Dr. Wolfe, the nurse had come in, checked her, and turned off the Petocin drip. Caylie immediately ordered her sister to go to the nearest Subway deli and get her a turkey club, a carton of milk and a chocolate chip cookie, which she proceeded to scarf down as quickly as a person who hadn't had a meal in a week.

The scar on Jenny's neck stung. She was afraid it might leave a mark.

Caylie insisted it would clear up, because a permanent scar would be colossally unfair. One of the nurses recommended she use an ointment to help heal the wound, and promised to bring her a sample. Jenny secretly wished there were ointments available for every type of wound.

"Jambo, dada yangu," said Caylie.

"You're awake!" Jenny rolled to her side and twisted her long legs out of the foldout bed. Her bare feet hit the cold, tile floor.

"Yep. I thought I'd wake up today and have a baby."

"I talked to Allison last night. She stayed with the boys and will bring them to school today. She says Frankie has the hots for her."

Caylie laughed. "Yeah, I know. I spoke with her. And I don't doubt that about Frankie. He thinks she's 'the bomb.' "

Jenny stood up and stretched. "You doing okay? Can I get you anything?"

"Tea?"

Jenny pressed her index finger to her sister's nose. "Sure," she said. "Let me get dressed and I'll be right back. Hot? Four sugars?"

"Hold the sugar," said Caylie. "But definitely make it hot."

* * *

Mitten Lake spanned before my mother and me. The waves were as blue as the Caribbean Sea and I could see clear to the smooth, sandy bottom. Schools of minnows scurried by, and a pure white seagull, like a dove, soared above us. "It was a beautiful place to live," said my mother.

I nodded. "And to die."

"Anne, would you say you had any regrets?"

"I had a lovely life, Mother. And I did my best."

"That's all God asks of us, and all we ask of ourselves."

"I will say I was disappointed that I never got to see Ireland."

Mother put her hand to her mouth and a smile formed beneath it. "Neither did I."

* * *

Dr. Wolfe burst into the room with what felt to Caylie like too much energy. "Good morning," he boomed. "Are we ready to get this show on the road? I'm going to go ahead and break the water, and I predict this baby will be here no later than three o'clock. Any more labor pains?"

"Not really."

"Okay. We'll put you back on the drip. Go ahead and slide forward for me, please."

The day shift nurse, a bleached blonde wearing pink scrubs, walked into the room and glanced at Jenny's unmade bed. She curled her lip in distaste, probably lamenting the extra chore. "Did your husband spend the night?"

"Start her back on petocin, please," said the doctor. "We want to move this along."

Caylie turned her head and watched as the nurse connected the tube to the I-V needle that had remained in her arm. She spied her nametag and smiled. "Your name is Molly?"

"That's what they call me," said the nurse. "Good golly, Miss Molly."

"I had an aunt named Molly," said Caylie. "Unfortunately, I never knew her."

"Sorry to hear that." The nurse squeezed the I-V bag and pushed aside the pole on which it hung. "Let me get these monitors going again, too. You know, I never knew my aunts either. My mom had three sisters who either died before I was born or when I was too young to know them. I came along pretty late in life."

"Tell me about it," said Caylie. "I've got three sisters, too. One of them, my Irish Twin, is here. That's her bed over there. I don't have a husband."

"Me neither," said the nurse.

Dr. Wolfe stood up and removed his Latex gloves. "Okay, we're all set here. By the way, Caylie, I think I saw that Irish Twin of yours in the cafeteria. Tall redhead who looks just like you?"

"That would be Jenny."

"She was with two other women who looked a lot like you, too."

"Really?"

There was a soft tap on the door and both the nurse and the doctor turned their heads. Caylie pushed herself back in the bed and leaned over, trying to see who was walking into the room. "Oh my God! I don't believe it! What are you doing here? How did you— "

"Jenny called us before she left San Diego," said Marie. "I was with Darlene and Dad in Atlanta for Mother's Day weekend. We hopped on a redeye and here we are."

Darlene stepped past the nurse and checked the label on the I-V bag. "Neither one of us thought we'd get here in time, but it looks like that kid is taking its sweet time after all." She smiled, leaned over and kissed Caylie on the forehead. "You look beautiful, Kiddo."

Caylie looked at the kind faces of her three sisters and beamed. "I can't believe you're all here. Thank you, Jenny."

"Of course," she said. "We *all* wanted to be here for you."

The door opened again and a man walked into the room. "Hey remember me?"

"Ronnie!" they all shouted.

"What? I'm still a part of this family."

"I honestly don't believe this," cried Caylie. "You never want to come to anything!"

"That's not true," he said. "You guys just never call me."

Jenny threw an elbow into his chest. "Clearly not true, brother."

"Okay, so Jen-Jen called me last night," he said. "So, tell me. Is it a boy, or what?"

* * *

From the edge of the dock, I stood perched, watching all five of my beautiful children as they stood around a hospital bed—the same way they stood around my bed on the day I left them.

Marie... Darlene...Ronnie... Jenny... Caylie.

I felt my mother's hand on my naked shoulder. "Are you ready?" she asked.

"Thy will be done, on earth as it is in heaven."

She tapped me, and I felt a little off balance. "Don't push," I said.

"Anne," she whispered. "Here. I have something for you." And into my hands, she placed a wrapped bundle—a baby.

I looked into the baby's eyes and saw myself.

We became one.

Then, head first, I dove into the water.

* * *

"Will one of you help me?" asked Caylie. "I have to get up and go to the bathroom again."

"I've got you," said Darlene. She took Caylie's arm and gently eased her from the bed.

Caylie lowered her feet to the floor, stood up and all at once, a downward *whoosh* traveled through her. "Holy shit!" she cried. "I think this baby's ready!" She reached for a panel mounted on the bedrail and pushed a red button. Then she locked eyes with Darlene.

"It's coming. The baby's coming right now."

Jenny, Marie and Ronnie reached out to their sister and helped her back into the bed. Nurse Molly sauntered into the room. "Someone pressed the panic button," she said. "Is there a problem?"

"The baby's coming," said Jenny.

"Like, right now," said Caylie, and she puffed out her breath.

"Okay, okay," said the nurse. "Hold on a second and let me check."

"It's coming! I've got to push it out!" cried Caylie.

"DON'T PUSH!" scolded the nurse.

A second nurse entered the room. "Call Dr. Wolfe," directed Darlene. "STAT!"

"Don't say STAT," said Nurse Molly with her head between Caylie's knees. "He doesn't like that."

"She's a freaking doctor," cried Caylie. "She can say STAT! For God's sake, say STAT! This baby is coming."

"Yes, it's coming," said Molly. She gestured to the other nurse, spinning her index finger then turned back to Caylie. "Just don't push until he gets here."

Caylie let out a series of short breaths and Jenny clutched her hand. "I can't guarantee that's going to happen."

"DON'T PUSH!" Nurse Molly repeated. "You can control this."

Caylie gritted her teeth. "Darlene, make sure somebody catches this baby because neither of us wants to wait."

"I haven't delivered a baby since med school," said Darlene. "I doubt the hospital would care for—"

"Shut up! Shut up!" screamed Caylie. Jenny squeezed her sister's hand and they shared a blue-eyed gaze. Just then, Dr. Wolfe burst into the room with his arms outstretched. The second nurse held out a green gown and he forced his hands through the sleeves. "Are you ready all ready?" he asked. Darlene stepped back and the second nurse moved behind him, tied shut his gown and then handed him gloves. A small puff of powder emerged from each as he snapped them in place.

"We're crowning," said Nurse Molly. She stood up and Dr. Wolfe took her place between Caylie's knees. Caylie was perched on her elbows and he looked her in the face. "Hi, Caylie. I told you this baby would be here before three." He looked at his watch. "Oh! Earlier than that. Ready?"

"God, yes!" she cried. Without any effort—with more of an exhale than a push—the baby's head emerged.

"Whoa!" said Dr. Wolfe. "Good job. He looked up and noticed Jenny. "You must be the Irish Twin."

Jenny smiled. "That's right."

"Never mind," hollered Caylie, who let out three more breaths. "Does my baby have red hair? I need to . . . I need to . . . push this baby out of me."

"Okay, okay," said Dr. Wolfe.

Jenny looked around Caylie's bent leg. "Black hair, Caylie. A head full of black hair."

"Would you like to do this Caylie?" asked the doctor.

"Yes, all ready!"

"Okay, then sit up," he directed, "and give me your hands."

"He's going to let you deliver it yourself," said Darlene. "Can you handle that?"

"Yes!" cried Caylie.

Jenny and Darlene put their hands on her back and helped Caylie sit up. Ronnie and Marie, as well as the two nurses, stood at the foot of the bed and watched as Dr. Wolfe guided Caylie's hands until she found the torso of her child. She slid her hands up the slippery skin to the tiny armpits. It was as if she had already picked up this baby a dozen times. And with an easy motion, she pulled the child out of her womb, into the world, and toward her eager eyes. And then she smiled.

"It's a girl," she said.

Caylie held up the child and turned her head. "Oh my God, Jenny, I have a daughter."

"You did it!' cried Jenny.

Darlene smoothed Caylie's hair. "A girl!"

"Oh Caylie, she's perfect!" said Marie.

"Ten fingers. Ten toes," said Ronnie.

Caylie laid the baby against her chest and released a long, slow breath of relief.

Darlene and Marie accompanied the nurses as they cleaned and assessed their newest niece. They dressed her in tiny, white leggings and a tiny white shirt, and put a pink knit cap on her head, then wrapped her in a pastel receiving blanket.

"She is beautiful," said Marie. "Clear skin, no stork bites, a fine-shaped head full of rich black hair." She picked up the bundle and handed her to Jenny. Jenny cradled her and kissed her forehead, then handed her to Caylie.

"Jennifer Anne," said Caylie. "I'm going to name her Jennifer Anne—for you and for Mom. And I want you to be her Godmother, of course."

"Oh Caylie," cried Jenny. "Thank you. That's a wonderful gift." She stroked her sister's hair and then leaned over and kissed little Jennifer's forehead. As she did, the baby's eyes popped open.

"Holy cow," gasped Caylie. "Her eyes are green."

"They are?"

"Yes," said Caylie. "Look! They are strikingly green. All my boys had blue eyes when they were born. Even Zachary and Adam, who both ended up with brown eyes."

Jenny leaned over her sister to get a closer look. She took a deep breath. Her sister was right. The baby's eyes were green. "Caylie," she said. "This baby looks just like Mom."

"Really? You think so?"

"Absolutely. You guys," she said gesturing to her siblings. "Don't you think she looks just like Mom?"

"She does," said Caylie. She stuck out her index finger and Jennifer's tiny fingers curled around it in a tight grip. "You're right."

Jenny smiled. "Have you ever seen such a tiny infant resemble someone so closely?"

"She looks like me," said Darlene.

Marie pinched Darlene's shoulder. "Brat! She definitely has a lot of Mom in her."

Jenny put her hand on the baby's head and looked into the eyes of her Irish Twin. "A lot of Mom," she said, "and she has a little bit of God in her as well."

Acknowledgements

The first person I need to thank for the reality of this book is Ric Bollinger, who continues to believe in me and always makes me feel good about my work. The first person I need to thank for the story; however, is my mother, Kay. It was her voice that ultimately inspired and shaped the telling of Irish Twins.

Here's what's true: My mom died while waterskiing at the age of 80. She was from Melrose, Mass. And she was, indeed, a war bride who followed her handsome sailor/husband to Chicago. I knew very little about her life in Melrose and I never knew her sister (and by the way, they were not Irish Twins), so I decided to make up the story of their lives. If any of it is actually true, it's either coincidence, good guesswork, or—perhaps—she channeled the material through me.

I will never stop missing her and pray she'll one day greet me with a hot cup of tea.

Thanks to Mike Cozzens and Anne Beaver. Thanks to Jeanine Ertel, Debra VanOrt, Mary Beth Urbanek, Christine Cozzens, Debbie Hendryk, Karen Gardner, Robin Meloy Goldsby, Bisi Adjapon, Corra McFeydon and Emily Liebert.

Thanks to Camille and Willow Cozzens for putting up with an emotional mama.

Thanks to everyone at McKenna Publishing Group, especially Leslie Parker.

Finally, unlike my mother, I am an Irish Twin and it is with great love and respect that I thank my sister, Gayle, for sharing her life with me.

www.ingramcontent.com/pod-product-compliance
Lightning Source LLC
LaVergne TN
LVHW091046080826
845145LV00002B/646

* 9 7 8 1 9 3 2 1 7 2 3 6 2 *